NIGHT

GUERNICA WORLD EDITIONS 94

Night Comes Down

Richard Aronowitz

GUERNICA
World
EDITIONS

TORONTO—CHICAGO—BUFFALO—LANCASTER (U.K.)
2025

Copyright © 2025, Richard Aronowitz & Guernica Editions Inc.
All rights reserved. The use of any part of this publication,
reproduced, transmitted in any form or by any means, electronic,
mechanical, photocopying, recording or otherwise stored
in a retrieval system, without the prior consent of the publisher
is an infringement of the copyright law.

Guernica Editions Founder: Antonio D'Alfonso

Michael Mirolla, general editor
Scott Walker, editor
Cover design: Allen Jomoc, Jr.
Interior design: Jill Ronsley, suneditwrite.com

Guernica Editions Inc.
1241 Marble Rock Rd., Gananoque (ON), Canada K7G 2V4
2250 Military Road, Tonawanda, N.Y. 14150-6000 U.S.A.
www.guernicaeditions.com

Distributors:
Independent Publishers Group (IPG)
600 North Pulaski Road, Chicago IL 60624
University of Toronto Press Distribution (UTP)
5201 Dufferin Street, Toronto (ON), Canada M3H 5T8

First edition.
Printed in Canada.

Legal Deposit—Third Quarter
Library of Congress Catalog Card Number: 2024947446
Library and Archives Canada Cataloguing in Publication
Title: Night comes down / Richard Aronowitz.
Names: Aronowitz, Richard, 1970- author.
Series: Guernica world editions (Series) ; 94.
Description: Series statement: Guernica world editions ; 94
Identifiers: Canadiana (print) 20240473957 | Canadiana (ebook) 2024047838X | ISBN 9781771839785 (softcover) | ISBN 9781771839792 (EPUB)
Subjects: LCGFT: Historical fiction. | LCGFT: Novels.
Classification: LCC PR6101.R66 N54 2025 | DDC 823/.92—dc23

> Forget six counties overhung with smoke,
> Forget the snorting steam and piston stroke,
> Forget the spreading of the hideous town;
> Think rather of the pack horse on the down ...
> —William Morris, *Earthly Paradise*

> Nature, it is well known, always supplies its own antidote, and if it is natural for men to feel superior to women it is also natural for women to feed them with henbane when this superiority is carried past a joke.
> —Rebecca West, *Black Lamb and Grey Falcon: A Journey Through Yugoslavia*

For Henry, my beloved son

PART ONE:

ASH AND OAK

Chapter One

Much Purlock, Herefordshire, 1841

So little is chance, and so much in our lives is governed by things we only catch out of the corners of our eyes. I cannot prove it, but I know it is true. Call it an intuition, a sixth sense, whatever you like, but chance is as rare as hens' teeth. Things happen for a reason, because of some pattern of actions or events that is set off perhaps miles and years from where you are now. The echoes of these events come at you in ripples and waves, soundlessly, without you even knowing.

It is like that in the valleys around Much Purlock. You think you are immune from the outside world, impervious to its intrusions, and nothing can reach you there. But it can and, once it has come, it is very hard to get rid of again. The world brings with it dangers you cannot see until it is too late. What happened to the navvies' foreman Mr Sansom—a Gloucester man, almost one of us—just shows you how true that is. He might not have been a good man, but he did not deserve to die when and how he did.

They cut a branch line through the next valley over from ours five years ago now. The blasting of the gunpowder, the steam hammer breaking up the rock that forms the bed of the valley, and the shouts of the Irishmen as they worked were a profound shock to the nature there. They were met with a stunned, reverberating silence. I did not like that silence. It did something to me.

The top-hatted gentlemen from the railway company board were calling it 'progress' at the town hall meeting they had convened before their men began blasting out the bed of the line. I and many others had quite another name for it: unwanted intrusion. While the men from the railway board tried to win us over with their slippery words, we shouted back that they could keep their bloody progress, that we did not want them to ruin our land just to line the silk pockets of their suits. The men and women, girls and boys from the newly formed Herefordshire branch of the Anti-Railway League who were in the audience that heaving, hot night told them in no uncertain terms that we did not want things to change, that we wanted things to stay the way they had been around there for hundreds, thousands of years; but they did not listen. The mayors and the men of business in the towns further down the proposed route of the line had other ideas. I blamed the shock to nature on them.

First it was the rooks. They started to fall stone-dead from the trees once the blasting had begun. I thought at first it was the shock of the cacophony the railway workers brought with them that had the birds perishing where they perched. I believed the harsh waves of sound from this so-called advancement of the modern world had driven the life spirits out of them. There is nothing subtle about gunpowder. It stamps man's presence on nature with all the fire of the devil's own forge. But it was not the assault of noise and reverberation that was killing the rooks.

I was out walking up Channers Lane one fine morning when the navvies had begun their blasting that summer. It was still too early for them to have started their infernal work and the whole valley, the entire world, seemed to be at peace. The spire of Blackthorn church rose up pink in the sunrise against the green of the trees in the distance. There was no sound except my footsteps dragging on the unmetalled lane. Suddenly, a dark bird dropped from almost directly above onto the lane in front of me. I turned it over with my black boot and it was blacker still, and a large thing: a rook. Where I was expecting to see a hard, shiny beak I saw only scaliness and mould.

Night Comes Down

On my journeys up and down Channers Lane and through the fields and woods, either to the manor or to the mill, over the weeks that followed I saw more of the birds: glassy-eyed, mouldy-beaked and dead before they had fallen from the sky or the trees. This was no mass death from shock or accident; this was the result of some insidious disease spreading through the local rook population. I blamed the navvies for bringing the disease with them from the outside world. Perhaps they had stirred up something, some malignancy in the soil, in the very rock of the valley that had lain dormant since ancient times, since even before the Romans or Celts were here.

Right from the beginning, I wanted to do something to stop the navvies, to stop their masters, and halt the building of the branch line. But the railways were so new, and the Anti-Railway League had little experience of mounting a successful campaign of resistance against them. Our branch members, a dozen or so in all, of varying ages and not all men, were good at talking but not much else. We met fortnightly at Jacob's Inn, where the far side of the town gives way to open countryside. I suggested having printed a mass-produced pamphlet or card protesting at the railway and handing it out on market days in Much Purlock, but I was told we had no money for such an enterprise. I could not turn to my father for the funds; because he is a man of science, I suspected he saw only merit in the building of the railway. We had never discussed the matter. Since Mother died, he usually ate in silence as we faced each other across the table at supper. Besides, he was always so busy with his patients.

I knew the Anti-Railway League would ultimately not be able to stop what was coming, for the work had already begun and could not now be undone; but there were still others who were not part of the League who felt like me about the railway, if for very different reasons than mine. I had seen them at the village hall meeting, standing up querulous and questioning. Perhaps if I could only talk to them, we could win the support of our local Member of Parliament or go up to London by stagecoach and protest outside the Houses of Parliament. But a young woman like me could not simply go knocking on the doors of men and women much older than her to try to form an attachment and an alliance with them. Much Purlock is not a small place, and although I had lived there all my life, my father and mother had protected me as their only child when I was young and not everyone there knew me well. I spent much of my childhood walking in the woods, either with my parents or alone. Even as a child I felt as if I was a guardian of the woods and fields who had to defend nature from attack.

Having been to school until I was fifteen, I had an ear for understanding how language could be used in argument. I wrote a letter to the editor of the local newspaper, *The Golden Valley Courier & Argus*, laying out my concerns. I wrote it in my neatest hand, and I took a long time to phrase it as forcefully and carefully as possible, but it was never published. The editor of the *Courier & Argus*, I can only suspect, hoped the coming of the railway to this part of Herefordshire would increase the population and, therefore, his paper's circulation. There is always self-interest at the heart of every interest, be it railway, newspaper, classroom, or love affair.

Not long after my mother died, in the depths of his grief my father decided that he could no longer bear to have grown women who were not his wife under our roof, as they would remind him at every moment of what he had lost. He dismissed our housekeeper of seven years, and our new cook (who made the most delicious stews I had ever tasted), and told me, his head bowed down towards the dullened surface of the dining table, that we would have to take the domestic duties upon ourselves from then on. I was only ten years old, and when I was not at school, he expected me to clean the house and wash our clothes and bedsheets, to rake out the fire and sweep the hearth, while he prepared our breakfast, lunch, and evening meal. My heart sank still lower than it already was. I felt even then like an indentured servant.

Once I left school, it is true I did not have much else to occupy me. With all my years of domestic training, I was expected to marry eventually and have children rather than go out and earn a living.

But I had begun running errands for the owner of the mill on the river Leadon that winds its way slowly along the bottom of our valley; those errands were my way out, my excuse to be in the nature that I so loved rather than being chained to the kitchen sink or to the laundry all day long. Quite how my father expected me to meet a prospective husband like that I do not know. I was not even sure that I wanted to find one.

* * *

I was still out walking the woods at seventeen. Entranced by the mighty oak trees, the ash trees with their broad leaves, the coppery chestnuts, and the great beeches, I thought my heart would break to imagine this place of tranquillity and beauty threatened by change, by crowds of incomers, by the trampling of unwanted feet. I was too late to do anything at all. I felt powerless, bereft of ideas or hope, when the branch line was approved by an Act of Parliament, farmers' fields were acquired by force, and woods that had stood since before the Romans were felled not for the timber but for the land: a corridor of devastation.

Then an iron rod used to drive the gunpowder deep into a borehole in the valley's rock detonated the charge too soon and shot at lightning speed into the head of the foreman, Mr Sansom. It caught him just below the brow and he died instantly. I took that as some kind of sign, as an omen, when I read about it. I was not happy that Mr Sansom had died, for as I have said he was a Gloucester man, almost one of us, and he was a father of three young children who gave his life for the railway, leaving his poor wife to do the best she could on her own.

I knew his death would change little with the progress of the railway, but still it represented a small victory, a brief pause, in this new battle between man and nature. We cannot assert our will over nature, for it will destroy us: that is the lesson his accident seemed to be telling us. It is a lesson for our age of steam and steel. I fear it is a lesson no-one will heed.

Those dead rooks were *us*. We might think that they, being of nature, were harbingers of the collapse of the natural order through the interference of man, but the rooks were only incidental casualties of a skirmish in a hundred-year war that we will not win. The steam engine and all of its uses will be the end of nature, the death of us. Mark my words.

CHAPTER TWO

County Sligo, autumn 1840

Endless, singing rain on the tin roof of the shack that is our shelter while we work and relentless mud in the trenches that we are digging. Binn Ghulbain blocks the horizon to the east: a green wall of mountain made of limestone and mudstone that weighs down our world. With all this rain the pasture is emerald green, but the farm only has forty head of cattle left. We cannot eat the grass ourselves. We can only eat the cattle that eat the grass or take the milk from the heifers when they are in calf.

It has not always been like this. A decade ago, we had three hundred head of cattle, and our pasture and fields of wheat and barley seemed to stretch almost to the sea. But our father had been careless with his money, not gambling or spending it on drink or women but investing it unwisely in Dublin. Of the two men, his stockbroker was the less wise and cost our father three hundred acres and a failed court case against the man who had lost him half his farm. Niall will inherit what is left of the land and I will have to make my own way. For now, we dig side by side, two brothers bonded by blood and rain-soaked soil.

'Sean, it's getting too deep again. We'll have to bail out the water before we can carry on.'

'It's up to my ankles. These boots are sodden through,' I reply. And they are: heavy leather made heavier by the water; boots sinking in the mud as if they want to drag me down into the earth. Niall always knows what to do, and I always have the physical strength to carry it out. Even as a boy, I was powerful: built for digging and lifting and hard outdoor work. When I was not doing physical things, I was reading and reading up in my room or, if the weather allowed, out under a tree somewhere or on top of the haystack; Gaelic poetry and lyric and stories, mostly, exercising the muscle of my mind.

We scoop out countless buckets of water from the trench, using the wooden pails from the house, but it seems to fill up just as quickly as we can empty it.

'It's no good, Sean. We'll have to wait until the rain has stopped.'

Our boots leave slicks of mud on the flagstone path up to the house. In the kitchen, Ma is cutting up ox tongue and oxtail for tonight's stew. Our new copper kettle shines red-gold on its skillet over the fire. There is nothing dainty about Ma: she is big-boned and tall for a woman, the skin on her face and hands reddened by years of the weather. She chops the flesh and bones skilfully and quickly, just like the butcher in Sligo. In this house we do it ourselves. We do everything ourselves—the milking, the birthing, the ploughing, the harvesting, the mowing, the butchering, the building—with only two farmhands and the team of horses. Ten years ago, we had seven farmhands and I used to watch them as they worked, aiming my bow and arrow at the tall thistles in the margins of the fields.

'Sit down, won't you,' Ma says. 'The water's coming to a boil; I'll make us a pot of tea. Da's sleeping in the back.'

'Is he bad again?' Niall asks.

'He's trembling and stumbling over his words just as he was a fortnight ago. People mustn't see him like this.'

'Has Da tried to tell you what he feels when he has these attacks?' I ask.

'He finds it hard to get his words out; I mean to find the right ones to say what it is he thinks is making him like this.'

'Perhaps a palsy?' Niall asks. 'Or some degeneration of the

nerves? I have seen something like it in one or two of the heifers when they are very old.'

'Whatever is affecting him, each attack is slightly worse than the last,' Ma says. 'I'll send for Doctor Linehan if Da doesn't improve.'

The kettle's shrill whistling interrupts us and Ma fills the pot. The wind gusts the rain against the windows, pummelling and scouring the house. There will be no more digging today.

* * *

The water in the trench is up to our knees but the rain has stopped. When an incessant sound suddenly ceases, you realise just how profound the silence is. Here, you can almost hear the static of the stars in the sky. Only the lowing of the cattle breaks that stillness, and the heave and splash of the pails as we empty the rainwater from the trench out across the field.

You cannot build a wall without a secure footing and this long trench and the one at right-angles to it at the corner of the field will make the foot of our limestone wall three feet deep. The wall itself will be five feet high and take us, and the farmhands in their spare moments, a month to build. We do not use mortar; we lay the stones so that they lock together and settle into themselves. The sudden sun is on our backs as we work, a latecomer in this season of leaf fall and decay. The cut grass is darkening and hardly growing now. Piles of large stones are heaped by the side of the trench at intervals, and Niall, Joseph the farmhand and I work side by side, lifting and laying the stones so that they fit just right. When the year turns, we will put sheep in here for the first time in years. A rare laying out of money in these straitened times. For now, Niall has not consulted Da.

'By the look of things, there's more coming our way from the east,' Joseph says.

A great, metal-grey bulkhead of cloud fills the sky above Binn Ghulbain, whose face and green slopes sit in darkness while the sun still shines on us over here, as if the farm and the mountain are on two different continents. We work as swiftly and as carefully as we can, emptying the last water from the trench and then putting the first two layers of stones into place along a ten-foot section of the wall's footing.

'Let's stop for our food but not take too long,' Niall says just after midday.

We sit on the grassy bank near the trench, each of us immersed in his own thoughts. We have cloth-wrapped hunks of bread and slabs of cheese for our lunch. I can feel the sun on my back even through this thick jacket, but there is a sea chill in the air coming in from the Atlantic half an hour's hard ride from here.

'We need to finish these walls before winter gets its teeth into the farm,' Niall says, leaning towards me and putting his calloused hand on my arm. He has always had a clear vision of what order things on the farm need to be done in. The rhythm of the life here is in his blood, and in mine, but he is the more meticulous. My hands hurt from all the bailing and all the laying of stones. It is just the beginning: we have four hundred feet of wall to build.

We start each morning at sunrise, with mist still clinging to the fields and the trees, a net that catches the sunshine and is washed away with the rain. Our walk with Ma every Sunday morning to church and back home again afterwards occupies the only daylight hours in which we do no work. Our labour on the farm is a religion, and building the wall has become our communion. The cattle and the horses are God's creatures to which we have devoted our lives, and they theirs to us. Our farm does not exist to make money; we work only to keep it alive. What would we be without it?

*　*　*

Early November and the wall is almost done, the limestone gleaming white in the morning light. Our backs are bent as if beyond repair from all the lifting and laying of stones.

Da is confined to bed. Speaking seems impossible for him now. He raises his head up from the pillows and smiles when we enter the room, but there is that trembling on his lips and a stammering *uh-uh-uh* when he tries to get his words out. It is pitiful to see him like this. Ma has called Dr Linehan out twice already, and he has taken Da's pulse, felt his brow and listened to his chest, and all seems to be in order. Da just looks up at him, silent and blinking. Dr Linehan has talked to us quietly in the kitchen, out of Da's earshot, of a stroke or a palsy, but nothing is certain yet.

Chapter Three

Much Purlock, 1841

'Grace Matthews,' a child's voice said. 'Are you Miss Grace?' I turned to see who it was addressing me, a boy's voice I did not recognise. Evening sunlight was slanting between the trunks of the trees, creating diverting patterns on the leaves and the decaying matter on the forest floor. I did not see the child at first. When I turned round, he seemed to be slipping between the trees like a wood sprite; he would be there one second and then gone the next in the half-light.

'Who's there?' I asked. I had stopped under an oak tree whose massive trunk was veined with riven bark and worn with the scouring of the wind of five centuries.

'I'm Jack,' he said, emerging from the gloom. He looked to be about nine or ten years old, and he was a slight thing dressed in loose-fitting clothes.

'What are you doing out here on your own at this hour?'

'My mother sent me to find you,' he said. 'She has heard that you know about the old ways and needs your help.'

'I only know a little about nature,' I replied. 'And how nature can help man.'

'Please come with me,' he said. 'Please come.'

'I'll come, but if your mother is ill, she should ask for a doctor.'

'It's not that,' the boy answered, retreating into the gloom again.

'Our hens wouldn't lay, and this morning she found them laid out dead in a circle in the chicken coop.'

'Perhaps it was the lightning that did it. There was a storm in the night.'

'I don't know,' the boy said. 'My mother just asked me to find you.'

'I'll come, but don't know how I can help.'

We walked slowly out of the wood because the black-haired boy stopped often, as children do, to look at things. He lived with his mother and his father, who was away for work, on the Marshfield Road in a rundown cottage. Mrs Jenks could not have been more than thirty-five years old, yet she was already almost toothless, her face collapsed in on itself like an abandoned sett. She had the exhausted look of someone who had raised a large number of children almost single-handedly. The boy, Jack, was one of the eldest of five, and all them swarmed around her as she spoke.

'Grateful that you came,' she said. Her burr was very strong. 'I knew your father when we was children. He went away from the village for a long time. I never went anywhere much.'

'He studied the Natural Sciences at Cambridge,' I replied. 'He's the doctor here now, as you know.'

'I know he's a man of learnin',' she said. 'I've heard you have an interest in the old ways, in nature. The children have seen you about.'

'We must always remember that we're a part of nature and need it. There's not much more to it than that.'

'I needed those hens,' she said. 'They gave me eggs and, when they'd stopped layin', something for the pot.'

'I'm sorry for your loss. Would you like to show me where they are?'

She took me through her ramshackle house to the garden; pots, pans, and jars covered all surfaces of her greasy kitchen, and furniture was spread higgledy-piggledy in what might be called a parlour at the back of the cottage. The garden sloped up towards the wood, but any lawn was beset with bare patches and the few fruit trees—pear, apple and cherry, to look at them—were mildewed.

Milkweed and dandelions crept through the broken flagstones

of the path and the garden was surprisingly long. At its far end, sheltered by a large ash tree, was the chicken coop. There were perhaps a dozen red hens there, all lying on their backs or their sides with their stiff legs out in front of them like frozen twigs. Mrs Jenks said that she had not touched them or moved them, so shocked was she by what she saw when she came to collect the eggs that morning. They were more or less lying in a circle.

'I don't know what has done this,' I said. 'I have heard of coops of chickens being killed by lightning. That is the most likely cause.'

'I thought we had been cursed,' she said. 'I thought the Devil himself had got in there.'

'Come now, Mrs Jenks. Those are just old wives' tales. We live in the modern world.'

I went closer, up to the fence, and peered in at the hens, looking for evidence of a lightning strike: scorched feathers, a mark on the ground. What I saw struck fear into me: looking closely, I could see that their beaks were brittle with a dark mould that emerged from beneath the feathers at their bases. I said nothing to Mrs Jenks.

***

The next morning the detonations in the valley were louder than they had ever been. The thunder rolled off the sides of the hills and the thick woods did little to absorb or deaden the shattering echoes. I have no science but could see that the blasting of the railway line and the deaths of the birds could not be directly connected, that an unnamed disease was at play, yet a fear of the railway had lodged in my throat, in my heart, and I could not shake myself free of it.

I walked through the woods, over the brow of the hill and down the other side. I stopped where the trees thinned out and gave ground to grass and rock. Down the valley a hundred or so yards away from me, men were swinging pickaxes and sledgehammers. I saw them move before the sounds of their striking at the bedrock of the valley floor reached me.

One in particular caught my eye. He was darker-haired than

the rest of them, and thicker-set, with great muscled shoulders and upper arms. He looked to be no older than twenty-two or twenty-three. He was beating the rock with unusual vigour; it was as if something possessed him. I did not know exactly what it was, but I felt something stir inside me. He looked almost like a wild animal cornered by the world, corralled by man.

I slipped away into the trees again, leaving the men to their work. I knew that they knew no better: it was their masters who were intent on ruining things, destroying the mystery and magic of this part of Herefordshire in the name of progress. These men were simply the expression, the embodiment, of that idea.

I knew nothing about men, apart from my father, but the image of that powerful man followed me through the woods. I did not like what he represented, but I liked the look of him. It was not a romantic thing, not then—I did not know what romance was, in any real sense—but he looked like the kind of man who would have the strength to protect you and not hurt you.

Over the days and weeks that followed, my memory of the man, the impression that I had of him, became entangled with my horror of the dead birds, and I could not unpick one thing from the other. They were both invading our lives because of the railway: if the birds' deaths were not caused by the blasting, they were still no accident of timing, I had little doubt. Their black corpses were harbingers of an evil that would come to this untouched valley from the line being driven through the next valley over from ours foot by foot, yard by yard, mile by mile.

Chapter Four

County Sligo, New Year 1841

In the end, Da slipped away in his sleep. It is hard to say whether he suffered because he could not tell us. Certainly, if he did, it was in silence. There were rarely so many glasses of stout drained in the Harp at Mullaghmore as on the night of his wake, and there was not a dry eye in the house. Father O'Conlon took the service and led the eulogy and the singing in the Harp. No-one mentioned Dublin or the loss of half the farm.

Ma, dressed in black from head to foot, moves around the house as if all its contents, all our possessions, the accoutrements of our lives, have been moved without her knowing. She seems unsure of herself, her surroundings, for the first time that I have known. Perhaps she was like this when she was newly married, finding her way around Rose Farm Cottage after Da had carried her over the threshold.

Niall has been harder hit than me. Perhaps it is not just our losing Da, but the realisation that the continuance of the farm rests on his shoulders now. A four-hundred-year lineage of McClennans at Rose Farm will end with him if he does not put things right. Centuries of history is quite a weight to carry. Niall left school at thirteen to work on the farm, but I stayed on studying for as long as I could. I have both brawn and brain. I have my books, my reading, before I go out like a light after all the hard work the day brings.

Brawn serves me well on the farm, but the horizons are narrow here, caught as we are between Binn Ghulbain and the ocean. I want other views, other landscapes. I have never gone further than ten miles east of the mountain.

The great green weight of Binn Ghulbain has been on my shoulders since Da's death. His grey eyes were always wise despite his folly, and I miss his advice and his willingness to listen. He never made you feel as if he did not have time, however busy life was on the farm. Ma has so withdrawn into herself, and Niall has so much to do that I have no-one. A man of nineteen needs to be able to stand on his own two feet.

Things are worse than suspected: Dublin was not the end of it. Da left unpaid debts with the land agent and with his lawyer. My sadness at his passing is mixed with an anger that I cannot shake. The sheep will have to wait if we are to feed the cattle and ourselves. It is a bitter legacy to have left his sons.

Every morning when we wake, the sky still dark as ink, a white margin of light just lifting itself off the land to the east of Binn Ghulbain, an iron-hard frost has covered the fields in the night and tried to work its way into Rose Farm Cottage. We have to scrape the ice off the inside of the windowpanes to see out.

Ma stokes the fire at dawn or rebuilds it if it has burnt too low in the night. Until it has taken hold, red flames becoming yellower and paler like the dawn itself, even the kitchen is too cold to stand still in without a woollen coat. This old house is showing its age, letting in the weather around its seams. It has become a part of the landscape, of our land. Like the McClennans, it has been here for almost four hundred years. Its slow settling has exposed cracks in the masonry here and there, gaps in the window frames, that let in this cold.

Ma goes out only to feed the cattle and the horses. Otherwise, she stays inside, wrapped in layers of wool and sheepskin. Our breath plumes in the air inside, and outside it seems to hang there momentarily as ice crystals before being blown away by the wind. There has been talk of the Atlantic beginning to freeze over nearest the shoreline, but I have not ridden out that way for weeks, not since Da's wake. The cattle are huddled in the barn, licking the walls in search of salt in the stone and restless to get out onto pasture again. Until this lock of frost and ice is undone, they will have to stay inside, eating the hay and the silage that we cut last August. Only the horses are still out in daylight, running together to keep off the cold, but blanketed in their stables during the iron grip of the night.

As the month of January passes, the cold only endures. The farm has gone into hibernation and for once there is little work to be done. Lately, Niall and I have spoken only rarely about anything other than the necessities of getting through each day, but with this pause something else has changed.

'Sean, the money is almost gone,' he says. 'We need to find other ways to keep the farm alive.'

'It is that bad?'

'It is doubtless worse than I know. Some of Da's creditors have still not come forward, out of respect for us and because of how recent his passing is. But they will, you can be sure of that.'

'What can I do?' I ask. There is something unspoken hanging in the air between us.

'You need to find paid labour away from the farm,' he replies.

'I would not know how to begin looking.'

'I will help you; I will always help you,' he replies. 'I heard talk when I went to Dublin last that men are going to England to work on the railways. They give you a roof over your head and feed you, as well as paying you a wage. It will be hard work, you can bet on that, but it might be an adventure, at least for a while until things improve here.'

'How will you manage? It will be just you and Joseph.'

'I will find a way; I have to. Ma will help as much as she can, I have no doubt.'

'I do want to see something of the world, but this is a sad reason to leave. Can you see no other way, Niall?'

'We can sell off some more fields if the neighbours will buy them or we can tighten our belts and hope that things get better, but your feeding yourself and earning money for a while will help. It won't be forever, Sean.'

'I need to think about it for a day or two,' I reply. 'It will be very hard to leave Ma and you and the farm behind.'

'I know it will, Sean, but you will be helping us so much by saving money you can bring back home with you one day. I was told that the foremen pay promptly and well.'

* * *

Two days of thinking, of turning the decision over and over in my mind like a well-worn penny, and I am still no nearer to knowing what to do.

It is as dark as pitch when I walk to the cow barn. The candle flame in the lamp flutters, but the breeze is not strong enough to blow it out behind its glass. The smell of straw, manure, sweet hay and silage hits you when you pull open the heavy barn doors. This stone shed, built by my grandfather's men in the late 1700s, is very large, and the forty head of cattle each have yards of space. They stand or lie chewing the cud and are surprised by the flickering light at this hour. Their dark eyes are haunted by—what exactly? The ghosts perhaps of the wolves or bears that hunted their ancestors in ages past. For the most part they are placid creatures, but a look of fear is never far from their eyes. The lamplight dances on the wall of the barn nearest the door, but it is too weak to reach far into this darkness. Only the gleaming of the cows' eyes tells me where they are, their bodies black against the blackness.

Cattle run towards food and away from danger. What would they do if they were me? I can make no picture in my mind of England or of the work that I might do there. With a farm, you know exactly what each field is for: where the horses run, where the cattle feed, where the crops grow, where roots and weeds need to be tilled out of the soil. No other work is so anchored to the land. If I leave Rose Farm, I will be set adrift. I have never seen these railways: where do they take you in such a hurry? Will I ever come home again?

I climb into the hayloft and lie awake for hours in the cold dark, cocooned in sweet hay, the candle having long since burned itself out. The cattle below breathe deeply in their slumber. As first light comes through the boards, words that I cannot stop forming in my mind have reached my lips: 'I will go.' I do not want to say them, but I have little choice.

Chapter Five

The Irish Sea, 1841

The ship. The rickety, stinking ship. It tosses and bucks like a harpooned whale on the rough waters. The Irish Sea is churned grey by a fierce gale in the crossing, and we are all as sick as dogs. The stench of vomit is in the air and there is bile and fear in my throat. I can taste nothing else.

Three hours out of Belfast and nine hours more to go before we are due to dock in Liverpool. The hundred and twenty of us are bound for farms, factories, and railways across England and beyond. There has been no food handed out yet, and not one of us would be able to stomach it even if we were given some. Cramped together in the lamplit dark below deck, we rock back and forth like cargo in the hold, vessels spilling liquid. We drink ladles and ladles of water from the barrels to quench this thirst. It is as hot as hell in here, even though it is only March.

I did not see anything of Belfast, only the paved roads on the way into the city and the docks. The carter drew up and dropped me and three other men from County Sligo off at the quayside, then turned around and left us. The journey to Belfast from Sligo took us the whole of yesterday afternoon and evening. We stopped for the night at a sad wayside inn before travelling on all of this morning. Shipwrights were building a great schooner in one of the drydocks; iron rivets were being hammered into place, echoes bouncing off the stone buildings of the port, and carpenters were cutting huge timbers with long-toothed two-man saws. Their work went on all afternoon while we waited to set sail. Men embarked from across Ireland, and it was nearly midnight before we left the docks and were towed out into Belfast Lough, from there going under sail out into the Irish Sea.

It is three o'clock in the morning and the candles in the lanterns are burning low. It will not be light until after six. We would be up and milking the cows and giving them their winter feed by then, them lowing and calling for their calves and for their food, hot urgent breath pluming in the cold morning air. Niall will be doing all the work alone this morning, and I do not know who I am sorrier for: him or me. The boat creaks and groans in the sickening swell and there is another round of vomiting before the men quieten down again. The buckets are brimming and threatening to spill.

For the love of God, what am I facing? I know nothing of where I am going, and I do not know why I have come. We must save the farm; we must save it. If I have to make the sacrifice of going away from all I know, then that is what I will do until the time comes for me to go back home again one day. I have not even brought any of my books with me. What am I going to do without my reading in the quiet of the night?

The lanterns swing from the low beams, scattering their weak light over bent heads and huddled bodies. We are too close for comfort and do not even know each other's names. The black-haired man behind me is breathing down my neck. It is by no means mother's milk. I try to rest with my head in my hands and my knees pulled up to support them, but the sea is too rough to sleep even without this discomfort. My stomach lurches with every roll of the ship.

First light filters through the sea-soaked portholes and onto our upturned, ashen faces like a benediction. With it comes the first sight of land when the heave and swell of the waves permits, at least for those men sitting along the starboard side of this deck. Those nearest the portholes on that side have been murmuring and

Night Comes Down

pointing and passing the news back to us in the midship. We, in turn, have broken out into friendly chatter as the sun's rays reach us and the news of the sighting of land gives us hope of getting off this festering vessel. We should be in Liverpool in a few hours.

There are suddenly angry voices raised somewhere in the stern. It is hard to tell what the argument is about, but it seems to have something to do with one of the buckets being spilled. There is the flicker of arms and legs hitting and kicking out far down the deck, then whatever argument it was fades into silence again.

I can feel the ship slowing, and there are running feet and voices overhead. I try to push my way to the side so I can see out of a porthole, but there are simply too many men around me to get through. The ship has slowed almost to a stop, and it seems to be drifting sideways. At last, I catch a glimpse of a dockside and a thick rope thrown snaking outwards towards a pier. There are legs clad in trousers and booted feet gathered on the dockside and then there is a great judder and thud as the boat slides into the side of the pier. I can almost hear a collective sigh of relief from the men around me.

It seems like an age before the hatches are opened above us and we climb stiff-legged up the wooden stairs that lead on each side to the main deck and to sunshine. It is a beautiful day in Liverpool, the morning sky shining with a clear spring light and the sky the burnished blue that is good for seeding crops under. A shrill whistle sounds from somewhere and we are told to make our way to one of the gangplanks positioned near the bow and stern of the main deck. Even here there is a short delay while we form two jostling queues to leave the ship down the bending gangplanks and set foot on land again.

We seem to have arrived at the centre of the world. The size of the buildings in this port is something to behold; it is all so massive and new-looking. I am so tired after the night that I want to sit down somewhere but there is nowhere at all to sit, and we are left standing on the quayside in groups of ten or twenty, waiting for further instructions that do not come. We are given some bread and weak beer from jugs set on a row of trestle tables near a brown-bricked building about a hundred yards from the quayside. We all devour the bread but drink the beer with more reticence, our stomachs remembering the awful sickness of last night.

A man in a grey waistcoat and overcoat walks up and down past the tables, looking at us through round spectacles that glint in the morning light and make it hard to see into his eyes. He is looking at us like a farmer looks at livestock at the weekly cattle auctions in Sligo. A farmer wants to know only what he can get out of a cow, milk or meat, or how far the horse will take him or how long it will pull the plough. The man seems to have some authority about him; he walks straight-backed and with his clay pipe rammed into his mouth, but no-one knows who he is. He looks no more than half a decade older than me.

'You there,' he says suddenly in an English accent, pointing at one of the men in the group standing next to us. 'Come over here, will you?'

'Me, sir?' The man with blond hair, who is obviously around a decade older than the Englishman, seems unsure whether he is the one being pointed at.

'Yes, you. Where're you from?

'County Tipperary, sir. The name's O'Donnell.'

'Well, come over here, O'Donnell.' The Englishman's glasses flash in the light. The older man walks over to him, and the Englishman leads him away by the elbow for some thirty or forty yards, back towards the ship we have only just left and well out of earshot. They speak to each other for a few minutes; rather, the younger man seems to be doing most of the talking. He gestures towards us now and then and looks over at us. O'Donnell from Tipperary comes back on his own after a while, the Englishman having gone off somewhere behind the brown-bricked building in front of which many of us are still standing, waiting to see what is going to happen. Some men have gone off to the latrines and come back again; others are taking their time.

'Mr Jones might look young, but he's our gangmaster,' O'Donnell says to my group and the cluster of men standing next to us. 'He's made me what he called the hagman because I'm older than you lot.' He gives a short, weary-sounding laugh. 'We're going to be working on the railways somewhere down on the Welsh borders.'

'How're we going to get there?' one of the men nearest me asks.

'Well, not with the railway, that's for sure! It goes from here to Manchester but doesn't exist yet where we're going,' O'Donnell replies in his lilting, deep voice. 'Mr Jones says we'll be going by stagecoach that covers the route. It's only thirty of us who're going there, the rest are bound for elsewhere.'

'What did he say about our wages?' another man asks.

'We'll get the going rate, which is twenty-five pence per day, payable weekly each Friday. It's backbreaking work, but we'll get used to it, he says.'

'Most of us here are young and fit enough for such heavy work,' a stocky lad in front of me with an Ulster accent says, 'but I'm not so sure about you.' The men around us all laugh slightly nervously.

'Well, I'll be the brains and you can be the brawns then,' O'Donnell says. 'But I bet I can lift a load as heavy as any of you.'

'We'll have to see about that,' the young lad says.

'Oh, you will, you will,' O'Donnell replies, and laughs.

The thirty of us bound for the Welsh Marches spend our first night in England at a decrepit inn near the docks, five to a room. The proprietor does not seem to have changed the bedsheets since the last lot were in here. The bedclothes smell of stale sweat, and it is not just coming from my fellow men in this large room, snoring and whimpering with nightmares on their flea-bitten mattresses in the dark.

I wish more than anything that I was lying in my soft bed in Rose Farm Cottage, under the same roof as Ma and Niall and my memories of Da, however painful they may be. But I need to be a man now, even though I feel no more than a child alone in the wide-open world.

Chapter Six

Hereford, 1841

It is beautiful country, this. It reminds me of home in the lushness of its pasture and the denseness of its woods. We are all aching and exhausted from the discomfort of our journey here by stagecoach. We left Liverpool only two days ago, but it seems like weeks.

O'Donnell the hagman will be our work master day-to-day and he seems to be a decent enough man. He has the gift for talking that all southerners seem to have. He also commands some respect in the men, being a decade or so older than most of us. We have been billeted in what seem to us to be dosshouses in Hereford, a city I had never heard of before arriving here. The cathedral's tower stands gleaming in this spring light, but there is not much else about this town that I have seen so far to recommend it. It is like a Sligo without the familiar faces or the charm.

The longer I am away from home, the more Niall and Ma are on my mind. I cannot seem to shake myself out of these thoughts of Rose Farm. Four days of not forking the silage out for the cattle, of not taking fresh water to the horses, of not milking the cows and of not turning over their bedding in the barn: the rhythms of our life on the farm are who I am, who I was. Who am I here in this foreign city, in this landscape whose every dip and hidden valley, whose every stream and copse I do not know?

Night Comes Down

Tomorrow we are leaving for the valley where we will be working on the line. O'Donnell says that it will take us at least a year's work to build the line between the part of Herefordshire where we will be working and the city of Gloucester before we move on to building another section of the railway elsewhere in the country. The hours will be long and the work hard, but the pay will be regular, and we will be given food and lodging on top of that. I am not afraid of the physical labour, but it will be strange to live surrounded by all these men day and night.

I am sure there are lice in this bed. The blanket itches terribly, and I am top to tail with a red-haired man from Donegal called Seamus, who cannot be any older than me. He does not take his boots off to sleep. O'Donnell has promised us a bunkbed each to ourselves when we get to where we will be working. Sharing a room with other men is something I could never get used to; sharing a bed is something else entirely. His boots keep knocking against my shoulder. I cannot wait to get out of here.

I must have drifted off for a few hours, as sunlight is streaming through the uncurtained windows. It cannot be long after dawn: the birds are still singing their first songs. Seamus and the other men (there are eight of us in this room) are all snoring away, dreaming no doubt of home. They are surely too young to have wives or betrotheds back home in Ireland to dream of. I would like to get to know a girl, to fall in love with her, but that does not seem to be my fate for now.

Breakfast is a cup of milk—less creamy than ours at home, so the pastures must be drying out a little here now—and hunks of rye bread spread with unsalted butter; then we are off by open cart towards the west of the county. The sun is sheltering behind high cloud, but breaking through here and there, sending light and warmth onto our upturned faces. The roads are rough, and our convoy of carts bounces along over the ruts and the channels in their surface that rainwater has left behind.

Many of these men are from farming families: you can tell by the way they look at the land as we travel through it, their eyes seeming to light up when we pass herds of cattle newly released onto their pasture or fields full of neat green rows of winter wheat. For all of us from across Ireland, from farms and smallholdings and villages miles from anywhere, our salvation will be that we will be working in the open air, not stuck in factories or foundries in some blackened town somewhere.

The cart ahead of ours has damaged a wheel in the ruts, and we have stopped while the drivers replace the broken spoke with a spare. They talk in a broad dialect that I find hard to understand, and all six of the carters are wearing the same broad-rimmed brown felt hats pulled down low over their brows to protect them from the sun and the rain alike. They belong to a company based in Hereford and seem to know these roads well, despite the accident.

We are standing at the side of this country road talking in small groups, some men smoking clay pipes and others drinking from flagons of beer.

'Where're you from?' a dark-haired, thickset Ulster man asks me. He blows pungent smoke from his pipe up into the air and then takes another puff, the stem of the pipe clamped between his teeth.

'County Sligo,' I reply. 'A farm in the shadow of a mountain called Binn Ghulbain. Have you ever been out that way?'

'I'd never been ten miles out of Belfast before this,' he replies, gesturing around us.

'That's the same for me: I'd only seen County Sligo until I came over here.'

'I imagine we'll get used to it,' he says with a resigned laugh.

'We don't have much choice, do we? At least we're seeing something of the world.'

We are on our way again at almost midday, westwards towards the Welsh border. We pass the occasional hamlet and village, but this is a county of farmland and untamed nature. The clouds have cleared, and the pale March sun is high in the sky. The birds are still singing in the trees: I have missed their voices since I left the farm.

I am sitting with my back to where we are going, and O'Donnell the hagman is in the cart behind ours. He looks more serious with every passing mile: I can only imagine that the work ahead for all of us is weighing on him, and the not knowing what we will find when we get there. These thoughts are no doubt preoccupying all of us, and the men around me are barely speaking.

A silent rook has been following us for some miles. It flies from tree to tree as we travel at the plodding pace of these tired horses, waiting for us to catch up with it before flying further off again. I was told a story as a small boy by great-uncle Daragh in which a coal-black and cunning rook led a traveller to his fate along a high and winding cliff road where the cliff had recently fallen away. There is something disquieting about this bird. It is watching us, not letting us out of its sight.

It is early afternoon, and we have stopped at an inn for some refreshment for the horses and the men. The rook is sitting high up in an elm tree at the back of the inn's garden where it gives way to a copse. It is calling now, suddenly, in its harsh, croaking voice and it does not seem to want to stop. I do not know if its call is a greeting or a warning. I hurry on inside with the other men for some bread and cheese and ale. When we come outside again to start on our journey, the bird has gone.

Chapter Seven

Much Purlock, 1841

That July, my father went to a conference on medical matters in London, leaving me in charge of the house. His patients from the town and the farmlands beyond it had to go without his counsel for one week. In my early childhood when he had to travel by stagecoach all the way to London, the journey took him two and a half days each way. This time, he took the stagecoach to Gloucester on the Ross Road and changed at Gloucester for a steam train to London, switching trains at Swindon. The whole journey took him under eight hours, and my father's need to travel by the swiftest means possible eclipsed any care that he might have had for the earth.

The house was very quiet with my father away and without his patients coming in to see him in his consulting room. I swept and cleaned and ran my errands, and in my spare moments, as it was still light until after nine o'clock, I walked the woods and fields, coming back home to eat a late supper alone. My resentment at my father grew the more I scrubbed at his underclothes, the more I thought about the journey he had made, the longer he was away. Our branch of the Anti-Railway League disbanded without telling itself it had; those other angry voices at the town hall meeting had grown reticent as they saw the first signs of coming prosperity in the town: once-rundown houses being done up, people we did not recognise looking about our streets with eager eyes. The landscape of Herefordshire that I loved so much would have to be my ally, but I was not foolish enough to think I could stave off the change that the iron roads would bring. I would have to protect what I loved most, the world that I had grown up in, the only one I had known, with whatever powers lay at my disposal. Nature itself would be my guide.

I had some reading in the herbalist's arts as a child from old books in my father's library—a later edition of *The boke of secretes of Albertus Magnus of the vertues of herbes, stones, and certayne beasts* and Kenelm Digby's *Rare and unheard-of medicines, menstruums and alkahests*—and I had been seduced by their language: obscure and mysterious words that hinted at obscure and mysterious worlds in nature and beyond. I had read somewhere in another book in my father's library that Albertus Magnus had been a thirteenth-century friar, bishop, and saint who was a *doctor universalis* and had studied everything from the cosmos to the ant, the laws of nature to the laws of man. He knew how to harness the power of nature, to use it for good and for ill, for curse and for cure.

But what was I to do with this reading, this book learning, this knowledge? Queen Victoria was on the throne, and I had been told at school about the empire she was building. Even to a girl of only seventeen it seemed we were living in an age where alchemy, mystery, spells, curses, potions had no meaning anymore. My arms, my armour, were rather a way of looking at the world: still seeing the wonder in it, despite the factories, the coal-black smokestacks, the stagnating canals that I knew lay not many miles beyond my woods and fields. You do not have to see something to know it exists. I was trying to see the world not blinkered by the perspective of humanity. What is magic if not the reaching for something that is beyond our grasp?

My father owned those books, but I do not think he had ever read them. His doctor's logic would have held them to be only laughable curios, exotic curiosities, an extinct panacea for people who had lived at a time when the magical was still possible. I wanted to prove something to myself and to teach him a lesson for treating me like a servant, for having let my mother die, for travelling by train to London. I wanted to show him that the old ways, the use of native plants, the herbalist's art—not just the medicine he practised—still had a place in our world.

I had been too long without my mother, without her guiding feminine touch in our household, and I thought I would not be in the least bit jealous if my father decided to marry again. If nothing else, his new wife might relieve me of some of my endless chores. I decided to concoct a love potion and slip it into his wine: perhaps my infusion would ignite a spark of amorous infatuation with one of his needy widowed patients. A widower doctor of some means would make a very good match in our pastoral land of promise.

I went out looking for plants that would leave no scent and impart no taste. Crushed berries always colour water, and seeds are hard to grind by hand so they cannot be seen in suspension. I was after fleshy things whose clear juices would go undetected: fungi, mushrooms, the things growing in our countryside that people in times long since passed would have used in their medicines.

I went into the trees to look for them: deep in the woods where the sunlight slants sideways between the cathedral pillars of beech, oak, ash and elm. These mushrooms grow in the shadows, in the half-dark, but I had read that their juices are light, astringent and almost tasteless. I had also learned from my father's library that they could do strange things to the senses: make people see things, hear things that were not really there. Some said their juices had magical properties but would not cause you any physical harm. I would be an apothecary of sorts, a healer, a doctor just like my father, but using the medicines that I could find out in nature.

I gathered a basket of those little mushrooms with thin stems and delicate, light-brown caps and pressed them in our white enamel colander with a large wooden spoon over a glass beaker; but the juices that they gave off were disappointingly meagre: perhaps only a thimbleful. I then resolved to dry them in the small alcove behind our kitchen range, well out of sight, and use them at a later date in a stew for my father once I had seen what effect the thimbleful of liquid might have on him.

He came home in a fanfare of dust raised by the cart's wheels, the lanes dried out by the unending sunshine that summer, and he was gleeful with the news from London.

'My speech seems to have been a great success,' he said, his dark whiskers seeming to expand as he smiled. 'The Society is going to adopt my recommendations on hygiene and the rigours of hand-washing with Castile soap before handling patients.'

'I have made you a pot of tea,' I said.

He would not drink his tea with a drop of milk: it had to be limpidly clear, and strong. He sipped from his cup slowly, blowing down on its surface now and then. He was obviously tired after his long journey by rail and road, and suddenly deep in thought.

'It's very restorative,' he said. 'It has an aftertaste that I do not recall having on my palette before.'

'I added some dandelion leaves from the garden to the pot,' I said, lying. 'They're good for the circulation, Herefordshire folk say.'

'Those are just old wives' tales; there's no science in that belief,' he replied with dogma in his voice. He never let me have thoughts of my own, he always wanted to tell me that I was wrong, that I was not looking at things properly, that is: his way.

'There's not everything that can be explained by science,' I said.

'Come on now, look at it objectively. You're a clever girl, it's just that your mind hasn't been honed yet by the rigours of academic learning. I'm only interested in things that you can prove. What proof is there in this folklore of yours? What proof is there that dandelions are good for you? They're best left to the rabbits, I'd say.'

'There's belief, if not proof,' I replied, sourness creeping into my voice now. 'I believe that nature is there to guide us, if only we would listen.'

My father carried on sipping his tea and said nothing more, retreating into his thoughts as he was wont to do. I prepared the evening meal, chopping vegetables from the garden and bringing the pans to the boil on the stove. I felt myself echoing the movements around the kitchen that I had seen my dear mother perform many times when I was a child and one of our cooks had been given the night off from her duties or was sick, tucked up in bed somewhere.

It had been seven years since she died from a cancer of the breast for which my father and his medical friends in Gloucester and London could do nothing. It had eaten her from the inside out and then, after emerging through the skin, from the outside in, and her pain had been unendurable. My father buried himself in his books, as if there, if he only looked hard enough, her cure would be found. I think it was then that my real disgust at my father began. He shied away from her diseased flesh, from our sickening household, and retreated into the womb of his study. He called himself a doctor, he spoke at medical conferences on diverse diseases and their cures, yet could do nothing for my mother.

After supper he went into his study to begin writing up his notes from the conference. There was no obvious sign that the infusion of the juices of the mushrooms in my father's tea had any effect on him. I cleared the dishes and then sat reading on the bench in the garden for a while. I read until it was too dark to see the letters on the page in front of me, as the Herefordshire moon had not yet risen sufficiently high in the star-filled sky to light the page. When I went back inside, my father was sitting at the kitchen table, clutching at his head.

'I'm seeing demons,' he said. He looked very frightened and somehow ashamed of his own words at the same time. There was that pressing and pummelling at his temples again. 'They're talking to me, and I can't hear what they're saying.'

'Your journey has perhaps overtaken you, father. The speed of the rails has somehow confused your mind. It must just be mental and physical depletion.'

He looked at me with a glazed expression, a sheen of sweat on his face. 'Beelzebub the cloven-hoofed one is calling me,' he said, and collapsed from his chair onto the floor.

Chapter Eight

Hereford Insane Asylum, 1849

The walls of this building are as thick as a castle's ramparts, draining the sound from the outside world. I crave contact with nature, with grass and trees, but for twenty-three hours each day I am locked in with only brick and barred windows for my eyes to feast upon. It is a barren meal, a meagre diet. It is my harshest punishment. Occasionally, a finch or a sparrow comes to rest on the ledge outside the window. Those moments are like a benediction from God.

The women mutter and shout all day long on the wards. Sometimes, there are screams in the padded and padlocked rooms at the ends of the corridors. When the women come out of those rooms after weeks or months, they look numbed somehow, with glazed, faraway expressions in their eyes. Those are the patients who have been treated with sedatives when talk and human touch alone has failed to quell their mania.

I am only allowed out for walks in the asylum grounds with an escort, and it is always one of the strongest orderlies. The trees in the parkland are not as ancient as those in our woods: they have not yet grown to maturity and must have been planted not long before the asylum was opened in 1802. Before that, there was no asylum and the insane mixed with the sane in Herefordshire or were burnt at the stake as witches. It is strange that so many women are deemed by men to be mad. Most of them here seem sad to me, defeated or sick, but not insane.

Take it from me that whatever they may say, if they think we are ill, we are not here to be cured. It is nothing more than a gaol staffed not by prison warders but by alienists, nurses, and orderlies. I can still only think of escape, of getting out of here. I want to find Sean again, my peaceful, dark-haired, blue-eyed Sean: I meant something to him once. But I am getting ahead of myself before what happened has even really begun.

Over the last four years, I have noticed that many of us have synchronised our menstrual cycles. Our 'monthlies' follow the lunar calendar. Are we not all lunatics after all? We have to improvise with ripped-up pieces of cloth, nightgowns and old bedsheets from the laundry. The bovine male orderlies, chewing the cud of their silence on our walks, provide us with nothing. In the wintertime, we burn the bloodied rags in the stove that heats the day room. This burning of our blood is an incantation, a warding-off of the evil that the asylum and all those that work here represent.

Is my father laughing quietly to himself at his victory, sitting all alone in that empty house of his, staring as he does into the fire with those unblinking eyes? He had no right to do this to me, to have me locked away like this. They pretend to be kind, to want to cure us, but I am not mad and there is no cure to be had. It is the world and its people like him who are the mad ones. Physician, heal thyself, I say; physician, heal thyself. The canvas straitjackets sit in a locked cabinet at the end of this ward, just to remind us of what they did in the old days, and what they could still do to us if we go too far.

There are rumours that some of the older women here—Maud, Phyllis, Annie, and others—were given that treatment when they were first here: done up in those jackets, hugging themselves behind, not even able to scratch an itch, when they were at their most ill. And look at what good it has done them! Years and years of sitting, of rocking back and forth, of stewing in their own juices, staring out of these windows waiting for their hour's release each day. And still just as unwell as on the day they arrived.

I will say it again until they listen: I am here against my will. I was ripped away from Much Purlock and all that I knew. I have become an orphan from Mother Earth; I am no longer her thriving child. Plants grow pale and weak when deprived of sunlight and I have grown enfeebled, lost my will to life, by being taken away from my fields and trees. Their imprint remains on me, in me, but I have not seen them since the day I was sent away to this place where hope has its end. But I will never abandon the hope that I will get out of here one day.

Chapter Nine

Herefordshire, 1841

There are rooks in the trees here, more than we ever see back home. Great-uncle Daragh's story has always made me think of them as an ill omen, for no good reason other than that is what stories can do to you. Their dark gleam and strutting gait bring the devil to mind.

It is a beautiful valley where we will begin our work on the railway. Tomorrow, we start digging out the bed of the track up towards Much Purlock, where the branch line begins. The men are all eager to get going and the foreman Mr Sansom is here to oversee this stage of our work. He is lean and strong, with a serious but honest look about him. His dark sideburns meet at his chin, but he has no moustache, and he has a black head of hair beneath his hat.

O'Donnell the hagman seems less sure of himself with Mr Sansom around. Gone is the confidence he had gone about with since the gangmaster Mr Jones left us in Hereford to visit another team of navvies out towards Birmingham. Mr Jones will be back with our gang in a week or two. In the meantime, it is Mr Sansom who will be in charge, and O'Donnell from County Tipperary walks around with shoulders hunched and head down as if he has lost a fight.

The huts they have built for us at the edge of this wood each sleep four men in bunk beds arranged in pairs. The huts are poorly built and draughty and when the weather gets colder in the autumn, we will no doubt have to keep the stoves going at all hours to have enough warmth to get us through the night. I have swapped a fine stone farmhouse surrounded by land that I love for a rickety shack in an unfamiliar place. And for what? To save a bagful of coins and Niall from having to feed me for a couple of years? It is hard not to feel sorry for myself, but I must stay strong. I will be no good for anything if I do not give this labour and my time everything I have.

All these young men with no mothers or wives to care for them. Who is going to stop them from taking to drink or falling into bad ways while they are so far from home? I have only ever drunk communion wine, the blood of our Lord Jesus Christ, and I have never been with a woman. This silver crucifix on its chain is a testament to that. I dream sometimes of falling in love, of a beautiful brown-haired girl with blue eyes, but I know no-one like her. How will I be after months of hard labour, of being forced to share even my nights with these roughshod men, with no time or space to myself?

Beer or wine might just be a salve, a salvation, to me. There must be public houses around here where men go to drink. If the regulars will have them, there is no doubt that some of these men, these ill-formed Irish navvies, will look for somewhere to drink on a hot summer's night after a long day of hard labour.

I have the misfortune of sharing a hut with O'Donnell from Tipperary. He seemed to be a decent enough man when I first set eyes on him at the docks in Liverpool: he had an amusing turn of phrase and held his own in an unfamiliar situation, but he is full of himself. He will be a tiresome bunkmate and he sleeps in the one directly below mine.

'May I remind you that it was me,' he said on the first morning here, before we had even had our breakfast, 'who Mr Jones made hagman back in Liverpool, so I'll run things my way when he and unsmiling Mr Sansom aren't around.'

'What're you talking like that about Mr Sansom for? He seems to be someone worth listening to,' I reply. 'You're as new to this labour as I am.'

'You're wrong there,' he says in his southern lilt. 'See, I worked on the last of the canals back home. That's why Mr Jones chose me as hagman.'

'Canals and railways aren't the same thing. Quite the opposite.'

'They're both about getting people and things from one place to another,' he says.

* * *

We dig in teams of six for three hours at a time. The grating of iron shovels on earth and stone makes a rhythm that never seems to stop so long as there is daylight. Bending to shovel for hours each day is back-breaking work, and it is made harder by this spring weather: March has only got warmer as it nears its end. The leaves on the trees in the woods on both sides of this valley are turning brittle, even though they are only newly emerged, and the grass is drying out and losing its lushness. I have never known a spring like this. I wonder if it is raining back in Sligo. The pastures are always emerald green on the farm at this time of year and the cattle are out day and night, fattening up on the grass.

The sweat from my brow is running into my eyes and I have to stop every ten feet or so to wipe it away with a handkerchief that Ma gave me. She embroidered it with my initials just before I came here.

'Ever seen a steam engine?' a wiry lad from Belfast called Adam asks me as we are digging side by side.

'No. Don't think any of us have. I saw a picture of one in the *Sligo Champion* a year or two back.'

'Suppose we won't be seeing one neither,' he replies. 'Just digging out the bed of the track and laying it, then off somewhere else before it's even run over the rails.'

'O'Donnell said they make a fearful racket and that they're faster than any galloping horse.'

'He's full of horse manure, that's what he is,' Adam replies. 'He's probably never even been within a hundred miles of one.'

Night Comes Down

About a hundred yards from where we are now, right where the line will run up towards Much Purlock, there is an outcrop of rock that needs to be blasted away. That will mean drilling and boreholes and gunpowder: the men are all agog as Mr Sansom tells us that he will oversee this dangerous work in April. Only O'Donnell does not seem to be the least bit impressed, as if he has seen it all before. There will be more blasting, judging by the outcrops of rock at the far end of the valley away from Much Purlock.

This tiredness is not just from the relentless labour: I wake every morning exhausted to my bones after a broken night's sleep on the thin horsehair mattress of the bunkbed and O'Donnell's nightlong snoring immediately below me. I never slept in the same room as Niall even when we were small boys. Oh, for a room of my own to sleep in! It will be a long time before I have that again.

The spring sun is still beating down and we have taken shade under a beech tree at the edge of the wood on the eastern side of the valley to drink from our flasks and eat our lunch. There is that rasping, raucous voice again: I look up and a rook is sitting high up in the tree above our heads. Perhaps it has its eye on our lunch or wants to warn us of something?

'What's wrong, black-feathers?' Adam asks it, chuckling as he does so. It coughs up its call again and flaps off to sit on another branch a few trees further away.

'There're lots of them around. I don't care much for them. On our farm I was always worried that they'd try to take the new-born lambs, when we still had sheep. A while ago now, mind.'

'He's a fine fellow though, isn't he? Shiny feathers and bright black eyes.'

'Perhaps he wants some of this bread and cheese?' I say. 'He's not having any of mine.'

Our shift is over, and we have the afternoon to recover before it all begins again tomorrow morning. I have not visited Much Purlock yet and I want to see what the town is like. For the next year it will be the nearest place to me with people in it who are not my fellow navvies. I wonder how they will see us: as rough-and-ready labourers with nothing to offer them except the railway, or as men who might be worth getting to know despite being outsiders. I bet they have not seen many Irishmen around here before.

The walk takes me up through the woods, mostly beech trees with some oak and ash, and over the top of the hill to the next valley, where the line will eventually run through a deep cutting. No-one else is about and there is almost complete silence here, with no wind to stir the trees and only the occasional birdsong from high up in the canopy, where the sunlight filters through a thousand branches. As I am edging down from the high slope of the wood and the trees begin to thin out, I can see the small town lying below me along the floor of the valley. The houses and buildings are all made of a pale limestone with slate-tiled roofs. This looks like a closed-in sort of place, surrounded as it is by this steep-sided valley.

'Afternoon,' a voice from nowhere suddenly says. I turn around but, at first, I see no-one. 'Afternoon, mister,' it says again. It is a boy's voice, before it has quite broken.

'Who's there?' I ask. There is no answer. 'Hello,' I call again. Slowly, a thin boy of about ten years old emerges from the shadow at the edge of the wood and comes out into the sunlight.

'Mister,' he says, 'what's your name?'

'Sean McClennan from County Sligo. What's yours?'

'Jack,' the thin boy replies. 'Jack Jenks from, well, right here.' He does not seem at all awkward or shy, as some boys his age can be.

'Well, pleased to meet you, Jack. I'm on my way to look at your little town.'

'You've got a very strange accent,' he says. 'Never 'eard the like.'

'Ah, that'll be the Irishman in me: everyone where I come from speaks just like me. They'd say your accent was strange.'

'It's just 'ow we speak in Herefordshire.'

'Well, I'll be on my way then,' I say, and am about to start my walk down the side of the valley towards the first houses of the town when he runs up beside me and grabs my right arm with his surprisingly strong hand. 'Is something wrong?' I ask, taken aback by this sudden, unwanted closeness.

'Mister,' he says, 'my Ma says never to talk to outsiders, but I've liked talking to you.'

'Why, thank you, young Master Jenks,' I reply, gently trying to pull my arm away without hurting his feelings.

His next words are wise beyond his years: 'This place has always been far from the world, so don't be sad if people aren't as friendly as you'd like 'em to be.' He lets go of my arm and looks fleetingly back into the trees, as if at someone or something I cannot see. 'I have to go,' he says, then darts off back to the edge of the wood and disappears into the gloom again.

Chapter Ten

The outcrop of rock must be blasted away today. It is blocking our path up towards Much Purlock, and we need to start digging out that section of the line. Some thirty of us have been given the morning off while the blasting takes place, and we have gathered to watch as Mr Sansom works with a team of six men, led by O'Donnell, drilling boreholes into the bloodred rock. Each borehole has had to be drilled to a depth of three feet, and the men began that work yesterday morning shortly after dawn. The rock is the size of a small country cottage, and it will take great quantities of gunpowder to blow it up in stages, from the outside in. The drilling has gone on today again for two hours; they are now three-quarters of the way round the rock. They should be ready to lay the gunpower and the fuses by mid-afternoon.

O'Donnell struts around as if he is Mr Sansom, but all of us know he is not even the foreman's pale ghost. He may have been something in the digging of canals back in Ireland, but here on stony English soil he is often careless and nearly always arrogant. I asked our gangmaster Mr Jones when he last visited us if I could move huts: he listened patiently to me but said that would cause difficulties with the others because they would see it as him choosing favourites. It seems that no-one wants to share huts, let alone bunkbeds, with O'Donnell. Last night, as we were trying to get to sleep, he was telling us three, his hut-mates, a long story about a girl back in Tipperary. As he told it, she was the prettiest girl in the whole of the county and he courted her and kissed her and she would have married him, but his work took him away from her.

Us younger men listened to him half asleep and wholly unsure of whether to believe a word he was saying. I still felt a stab of jealousy as I have never kissed a girl.

I saw a very lovely brown-haired girl in the marketplace yesterday, just like the girl I have seen in my dreams. It was as if she had become real right there and then, but I cannot imagine how I could ever get to talk to her. We may be on the same patch of soil here, but we are in two different worlds. I am still sore at seeing her; it just reminded me of my loneliness, of my stupid inexperience with the female sex. All this muscle and sinew, this animal flesh and bone, and all I have are these callow men, this hard mattress, for my bedfellows.

The rock has blunted the long drill bits, but the boreholes are ready. All the men, the workers and the watchers, unpack bread and cheese and fruit—meat pies bought from the market in Much Purlock if they are lucky—and sit in the sunshine on the grass near the bed of the line, or under the shade of the trees at the edge of the wood, and eat their midday meal at almost two o'clock. With the sun shining down and the mood bright after the hard work, with more hard work to come, it feels like a saint's day picnic. If only all these days could be filled with this sunshine and this sitting in the long grass. The work is so hard and endless: my hands are calloused and blistered and my back throbs at night. I miss Ma and Niall and the farm, and it keeps me from the sleep that is my time for forgetting.

O'Donnell's is the loudest voice, his southerner's brogue eclipsing the birdsong even from half a field away. He has an opinion on everything and is a master of nothing. Mr Sansom is up on his feet and O'Donnell is following him back to the rock. The five other men working on the detonation follow the foreman and the hagman around the giant boulder: whenever Mr Sansom speaks, they look at him square in the face; but whenever O'Donnell talks, they look down at their feet or over at us as we sit in the grass or under the trees.

It is time to ram home the gunpowder and set the fuses. Two large metal boxes are pulled on a handcart over to the rock and the men open them almost as if they expect to see snakes inside. All the smokers here have been told not to bring their clay pipes with them today, for fear that they might set off the gunpowder. This is already the third time now in the six weeks that we have been here that the detonation team led by Mr Sansom has blasted away an outcrop of rock. Both times it has gone off without incident and the way has been cleared for the line at the far end of the valley and out over the flat land that runs towards the border with Gloucestershire. The atmosphere will become more and more tense until the blasting has taken place safely. We are all told to retreat into the trees and watch from the edge of the wood until the all-clear signal is given.

Each of the six men working the detonation has an iron ramrod that he uses to push in and tamp down the plugs of gunpowder deep into the holes in the rock. The dull clinking of iron against rock lasts for about an hour as Mr Sansom hands his men a wad of gunpowder for each of the fifty or more holes. Once they have rammed in the gunpowder, the men feed a long fuse into each hole, and the ends of the fuses snake over the grass for thirty or forty feet to the spot where they lie bunched together and Mr Sansom will light them. It takes a fine, dry day such as this for the fuses to light and burn properly and for the gunpowder not to get damp before the blast is set.

O'Donnell seems to be slower than the other men, checking each of the holes that he has filled and then going back again to them as if he is slightly unsure that he has done things right. After he has filled his last hole, he goes over to talk to Mr Sansom and to swig with both hands from a large flagon of water. A question from Mr Sansom that I cannot hear from this distance makes O'Donnell look around and shake his head. He goes back to an area of long grass on one side of the giant boulder to search for something but cannot seem to find what he is looking for. Eventually he gives up and walks off towards the trees on the other side of the valley.

'The rooks are back again,' Adam, the lad from Belfast, says and points over to the trees behind O'Donnell. 'Must be curious about what's going on.'

'Let's eat up and not leave them a crumb,' I say. 'They bring no good with them.'

'I can't really see that they do much harm either,' Seamus from Donegal says.

'Have you ever seen what they do to a field of crops? On our farm in County Sligo, they were canny enough to learn not to fear our scarecrows. We had a real battle to keep them off our wheat and barley.'

'Some people say they have something magical about them,' Adam says. 'Like an omen or a warning or something.'

As we are talking, Mr Sansom blows his whistle and the five men retreat to a spot near to where O'Donnell is standing, deep in the trees on the other side. Mr Sansom bends down to one of the boxes and pulls out his fire steel and flint. He crouches over the fuse, striking flint against steel over and over, sparks showering his hands as he tries to get his tinder to catch. After a minute or two, there is the lick of flames in the tinder and then the thick cord of twined fuses is alight. At first it burns brightly but slowly in the brilliant sunshine, then its flaming tip seems to speed up as it eats away at itself on its journey towards the rock.

Mr Sansom runs to a dip in the open ground about forty yards from the outcrop, and the men around me throw themselves to the ground. I drop down, too, with the fuse burning away about ten feet from the rock now. All the birdsong seems to have stopped and there is only the sound of the breeze in the trees above us. Mr Sansom is still standing, but ducked down, watching to see that everything happens as it should.

There is an almighty series of bangs that seem to go on for minutes but only last seconds. Holding our hands over our ears does not ever stop the terrible ringing afterwards.

Shards of rock fly out from the shattering blast, but we are safe lying flat on the ground at this distance in the trees. The echoes of the explosion reverberate again and again around the valley and up through the woods.

Then there is a silence so deep that the whole of nature seems to be in shock. When I raise my head again, I cannot see the rock at all: the cloud of red dust has obscured it completely. Slowly, the dust settles on the sunlit grass and earth, and what is left emerges: the outcrop has been cut down to about half its height, jagged and fractured and broken.

The men over on the other side start to get to their feet. Those around me raise themselves up on their elbows and knees and then stand, too, stiffly at first after lying under the trees on the cold ground. Where is Mr Sansom? He is not standing in the dip in the ground where he was before the blast, and he is not over with his detonation team. O'Donnell has come out from the trees now and the other men are not far behind him. Suddenly he turns as white as a sheet and raises his hands to his face in horror as he reaches the dip.

I run over towards him as the detonation men gather behind him: Mr Sansom is lying on his back in the grassy hollow, with a thickening pool of blood behind his head. My heart is pounding, and there is a nausea rising in my throat. I bend down to look at Mr Sansom more closely and to take his wrist in my hand to feel for a pulse. His skin is still warm but he has got no heartbeat, and now I can see why: there is a neat round hole punched in his face just below his right eye. I try to lift his head up so that I can put my ear to his mouth to listen for a breath, but it seems stuck to the ground somehow.

O'Donnell turns around to vomit in the grass, and one of the men is hunched over, shoulders shaking as he sobs into his blackened hands. I try to lift Mr Sansom's head again and have to pull it up as if I am removing a stake from the ground. Behind his head, protruding from the thickest part of his hair now slick with blood and brain, is an iron ramrod. His bright blue eyes are still open and seem to be looking at me. I wipe my hands on the grass and cannot stop myself from vomiting over and over until there is nothing left.

* * *

Night Comes Down

Mr Jones the gangmaster is white with fury, shouting right into O'Donnell's face. He has ridden down from Shropshire by pony and trap and looks as if he has not slept. He has come to bury Mr Sansom, who is in his coffin at the undertaker's in Much Purlock, and to oversee the writing of a report into the accident for his masters, the Hereford, Purlock and Gloucester Railway Company. 'And you left the ramrod in a borehole and couldn't remember where you'd put it, you Irish donkey?' he asks the white-faced hagman for the third or fourth time.

'M-Mr Sansom asked me where it was and I-I thought I'd dropped it in the grass,' O'Donnell stammers, quite abandoned by his usual bravado.

'And you didn't think to check the bloody holes you'd worked on?'

'There was no time: Mr Sansom was waiting to light the fuses and asked me to hurry up.'

'Didn't he tell you to give him your bloody ramrod like the other men did, so that they were all accounted for?' The young Englishman looks as if he is about to explode. His face has turned from white to crimson.

'Yes, b-but I thought I'd dropped it somewhere. What were the chances of it shooting out and hitting him like that?'

'Next to none, but it did, and now you've got his blood on your hands. He was a far better man than you are. Now get out of my sight, you buffoon,' Mr Jones says and stalks off to the hut that is reserved for him and him alone.

The mood in the camp is the worst it has been, and we are sitting on our bunkbeds still numbed with shock two evenings after Mr Sansom's death. The sound of the detonations is still ringing in my ears. The night is too cold to be outside without our labours to warm us, but we would all much rather be away from one another and have time to ourselves. Only O'Donnell is nowhere to be seen. He has, no doubt, gone off into Much Purlock against orders to lick his wounds at the likelihood of having his hagman title taken away from him, at the very least, rather than to cry with remorse and guilt over what he has done.

Chapter Eleven

Much Purlock, 1841

My father's bout of weakness and confusion only lasted a matter of hours, but he was very subdued for days afterwards and he seemed to doubt what he was seeing. A cloud of distraction and bewilderment hung over him and he cancelled all but the most urgent appointments with his patients. For a man who was usually so clear in his thinking, so firm in his views, it was strange to see him so bewildered. My herbalist's art had done that to him, and it gave me a feeling of power where I usually felt none. It was as if I was fighting the injustices of the world not only for myself and for nature, but for my dear mother as well.

The dried mushrooms were secreted away in their niche behind the stove, and I left them there while I decided how else I might use them. I must admit that I felt little guilt for what I had done because I knew that the juices of the mushrooms would do my father no physical harm while teaching him a lesson.

The dead birds were back again, or perhaps they had never really gone away, their falling from the sky, from the trees, just happening when and where I was not there to see them. There were two dead rooks out on the lane when I woke one morning in early August. I went out and prodded them with my booted feet. Their eyes were vacant holes and their beaks had mouldered down to sickening stubs. No-one else seemed to pay them the least attention. There were three more at intervals on my way down from our house to the mill where I had some casual work that morning.

My father always insisted that there was no need for me to earn money, but I wanted to have sixpences and shillings in my pocket that I had gleaned through my own labours. I did not want to run to him for every ribbon and lace that I needed.

'Miss Matthews,' the foreman said when I first entered the mill, 'how are you on this fine summer's morning?' He had a pleasant, open face, spoiled by upper teeth like a rabbit's that pushed his top lip out.

'I greeted the sun with a smile when I woke at six o'clock,' I replied with a fitting smile, 'but my enjoyment of the beautiful day was undone by the sight of some dead birds on the way here.'

'Dead birds?' he asked, sounding doubtful. 'I haven't noticed any.'

'They're up Channers Lane and on the path here through the wood, all eaten away and rotten.'

Just then there was the sound of an explosion from the next valley, dampened by the distance and the thick stone walls of the mill. The navvies were back after a few days of deceptive silence. I thought of blasted rock speeding like lightning into the trees, of the animals in the woods fleeing in alarm and of the bark on the trees nearest the line being flayed by the blast. Violence against nature! Oh, the arrogance of mankind, thinking that it can tame nature and that nature will not fight back. It will, it always will. Leave a house to ruin for long enough and a tree will grow up through its foundations. Cut the earth, cut the rock, and one day plant life will cover over all trace of us.

The foreman was a kind man, and he let me come and go as I pleased, just so long as I delivered the packages that he needed taken to householders and enterprises in Much Purlock and beyond. There were small sacks of cornmeal and flour to pull by handcart through the village; oatmeal to take to the Star Inn. I was strong and lean, not depleted by all this sitting then, and the work did not trouble me. It allowed me to be outdoors, and I liked the sound that the coins made in my pocket. The work also gave me a reason to be out in the village and the surrounding land, listening and looking. Listening for talk of the branch line, now that the Anti-Railway League had ceased its vigilance, and looking for signs of the railway's destruction of the world I loved. Tearing, guttural groans as the rock split asunder in the next valley were hard to ignore, but most of the people who had been my neighbours all my life seemed to have become so used to the sound of explosives that they no longer heard them. There had been no further public meeting at the town hall for months, and the members of our local branch of the League had given up all hope of having the Act of Parliament annulled. People were becoming complacent, accepting of the intrusion of the railway into their age-old lives. With their complacency my anger and resolve only grew. I was young and idealistic, but I did not know how to focus my anger, where and how to fight.

All my reading on the herbalist's art and on the old ways had, though, given me the boon of knowing one thing at least: that I could harness the power of nature for my own ends. I had to find a way to use it, but I did not know how to begin. I only had my father's books, and they were of little use. They were all theory and philosophy and alchemy and told me nothing about how to apply my talents practically, how to use my gift for finding and identifying plants. Magic potions belong only to folklore, but I would find a way to make a modern-day version of them. I had no-one else to teach me, I would just have to learn by trying and doing.

* * *

I crept out from the edge of the woods again early one August morning, long before I was due down at the mill. A great team of bare-chested men were hammering at the rock and cutting down any vegetation that stood in their way. At the heart of the group was the man I had seen before, towering above the others, dark-haired and clean-shaven, his skin tanned from all the outdoor labour. I thought that I was well hidden by branches and foliage, but as I was turning to slip back into the trees again, he looked up. Just for the briefest of moments, he saw me.

Chapter Twelve

Hereford Insane Asylum, 1849

I did not kill my father. I did not kill my father, for he is still alive. That is reason enough to say again that they have locked me up with no justification. What exactly is my crime? The administration of poison? Those plants were not poisonous, at least not to the body. Why does my father not tell them that I did him no physical harm, no lasting damage? He is the good doctor, after all.

We are withering away in this place without sunlight like plants that cannot take root properly and do not thrive. We are a failing crop of madwomen: that is what they call us here beneath their breath, even while pretending to want to cure us. I will not be cured by the screams and cries of my ward-mates or by the bars on these windows. What cure do I need but my freedom?

Mr Osney has taken to holding my arm when we are out on our daily patrol of the grounds. It is ordinarily not in order for orderlies like Mr Osney to make such audacious overtures. He says that they do not want me to try to escape the grounds again like I did two winters ago. That time, they had to search the streets until they found me, admiring a majestic ash tree in Aylestone Park. I say that he likes to be close to me, right by my side, but I do not speak this out loud. I suppose my looks have not faded, even at twenty-five. We have no mirrors to see ourselves in for me to know, as they fear we would break them and use the shards to hurt ourselves or each other.

I have written another letter to my father, in which I have laid out the facts yet again. That I meant only to teach him a lesson but do him no physical harm; that my mother's death was the beginning of the end of everything for me; that the coming of the railway to our part of the world was the beginning of the end of the natural world that I so loved; that nature had become a kind of surrogate mother to me. I told him that my anger at his not being able to save my mother was really my anger at having lost her so young, that my hatred of his using the railway to get to London was my hatred of the railway itself. I have sent him perhaps thirty letters, but he has only replied once: to the very first one, when he wrote that he was severing all contact with me because my letter had re-awoken painful memories of the mental turmoil he had suffered because of my actions. He wrote that he still loved me as a daughter but could never forgive me.

Catherine Orr hanged herself by her bedsheets in the dark hours of the night. On this ward of sixty women, I did not know her well, but she seemed a gentle type. My impression was that she rarely spoke, and I certainly never heard her scream or cry out. She did it from a beam in the latrine when we were all asleep in our bunkbeds. The falling stool might have woken some of us but, if it did, we were too cold to leave our meagre sheets, and she was not discovered until after dawn when it was too late to do anything for her. Her dead body hanging there and the pool of liquid beneath it caused a panic to break out in here, like a fox in a chicken coop. It only abated when two orderlies came in to cut her down and carry her out by the hands and feet like a half-filled sack of potatoes. We are all grieving, but as much for ourselves as for her.

Catherine Orr's is the third suicide since I have been here. They certainly do not make it easy for us with all the knives being locked away, there being no mirrors, no glasses to drink from, only tin mugs. All we have are our bedsheets and those mean a slow, asphyxiating death while we swing from a beam or from a rafter. That is not something you can do on impulse, with the flick of a wrist. It requires planning, courage, overcoming your animal urge to stay alive.

Chapter Thirteen

Herefordshire, 1841

High summer and the larks are singing in the grass. The weather has been so hot that the stream through the wood where we fetch our water is not much more than a trickle; it is threatening to run dry if this weather does not break soon. The huts are now too hot at night, and some of us have taken to sleeping out under the trees.

Since Mr Sansom's accident, O'Donnell has skulked around, sullen and silent. It has surprised us all that Mr Jones did not send him straight back to Ireland, but it seems that O'Donnell's experience on the canals of our native soil has made him useful, in Mr Jones's eyes only, for what will come towards the end of our work on this line: the deep cutting to the north-west of Gloucester that we have to carve through a limestone hill there. I am trying to avoid speaking to O'Donnell, which is not so easy when he sleeps below me, and I need to climb up to my bunk using his as a foothold.

I have received no letter from home since I arrived here: it feels as if I have disappeared from the world somehow. I dream of Ma and Niall and Rose Farm, but I have no time to think of it in my waking hours. There is no room for daydreams when all around me the earth is being broken open and tonnes of soil are being moved by men and horses, when rocks are being blown apart and tonnes of ballast poured into what was once virgin meadow. Places such as Much Purlock will not be so isolated from the world for long.

I wonder when the railway will come to County Sligo, what it will bring with it and what it will take away.

We are working up towards the head of the valley now, about a mile outside the town. The locals generally keep their distance, but children come to gawp at what we are doing here now and then. What child does not like the sound of gunpowder going off with a bang? We have to tell them time and again not to come out of the woods on detonation days. Still, they creep as near as they dare before we shoo them away again.

Sometimes Mr Jones himself has to tell the younger children to clear off if he is around, or the new foreman Mr Menzies blows his whistle at them, and they scatter back into the woods like headless chickens. Mr Menzies is as unlike Mr Sansom as it is possible to get: while Mr Sansom was almost one of us and had no airs and graces about him, Mr Menzies keeps himself apart and thinks more of himself than he does of us. He and O'Donnell cannot stand each other because they are too alike, and it is only because of Mr Jones the gangmaster that O'Donnell is still here.

Yesterday I saw that beautiful girl who I have seen before in the marketplace. She was standing like some earth angel in the last of the trees on the edge of the wood, but when I looked up again, she had gone. I wish I could see her here every day: she would put some fire into the work of my arms, the flexing of my muscles as I bend and dig, bend and dig, hacking away with this shovel and pick at earth and stone.

'Look out,' Adam calls out suddenly. 'He's lost control of his horses. They're coming our way!' I look round, and the carter is slumped over his reins. Before we know it, his cart has slewed sideways and tipped over, its load of ballast emptying itself out in a cloud of white dust about twenty yards from where we are standing. The two bay shire horses somehow keep their feet between the twisted shafts and seem untroubled by the mishap behind them, but the carter is unconscious.

'Hey, fella,' I shout, running over to him as he sprawls on the ground beside his upturned cart, his sweating horses stamping their

Night Comes Down

hooves only inches from his face and the mound of ballast slipping behind him. I pull him away and lay him on his side. His eyes have rolled back in his head and his hair is matted with sweat. He is as pale as a ghost.

Still he is not stirring. I run to fetch the flagon of water from under the tree where I left it and then straight back to the man again, uncork the water and douse his face with it. His eyes roll back to where they should be but see nothing: the dousing seems to have had little effect. I slap him hard on one cheek and then on the other; he murmurs and slowly comes to.

'Wha—?' he says. 'Where am I? Who are you?' He sounds as if he is from my part of the world.

'You've been delivering ballast out near Much Purlock. Do you remember?' I reply.

'Any idea why you passed out back there?' Adam chips in.

'I was feeling very hot and light-headed. I don't think I've drunk enough water today. Could be that.'

'How d'you feel now?'

'Dazed like I've woken up suddenly from a deep sleep.'

'Where are you from?' I ask.

'County Sligo, not far from the town of that name. You won't have heard of the little place.'

'I grew up on a farm just west of Binn Ghulbain, so I just might have.'

'Well, I never!' he exclaims, smiling for the first time. He is sitting up now and he has much more colour in his cheeks after a long drink of water from my flask.

He stands up slightly unsteadily and turns to his team of horses. 'Well, they seem to have come out of this unscathed,' he says, patting and stroking the flank of the horse nearest him, which has bowed its great head down towards him. 'Can you fellas help me right this cart? The foreman is not going to be any too pleased about where his ballast has ended up.'

'Come over here and help us, Joe,' Adam calls over to Joseph from County Kerry. Righting the cart is like trying to roll over a granite boulder, but with Joseph's help and some cursing, swearing, and sweating we finally get it up onto its wheels again. 'You haven't told us your name,' I say, 'and where exactly are you from?'

'My name's Fintan Donaghy,' he says. 'I'm from Collooney. Ever heard of it?'

'Ever heard of it? Of course I have!' I reply, laughing. 'My cousins live on a farm just outside the town. It's a nice spot.'

The carter takes the horses' reins and leads them over to the shade of the beech trees at the edge of the wood. They are pulling the empty cart behind them and buck in their bridles, perhaps surprised at the sudden lightness of the load. He ties them to the trunk of a sapling and gives them their nosebags before heading back over to us. He seems to be steady enough on his feet now: as he says, it must have been the heat of the day and not having had enough water to drink.

'Could I have one more drink from your flask before I head off?' he asks. 'Isn't there somewhere I can water the horses and fill up my bottle? This is my first time here.'

I like listening to his voice; it reminds me so much of home. 'Sure, just leave me a little,' I reply. 'There's a stream where the horses can drink over the other side of that outcrop of rock down at the far end of the valley, but there's not much to it now. You can fill up your bottle there as well. It's good clean water, what's left of it.'

'So, what's your name?' he asks, wiping the water from his chin. 'And who are your cousins?'

'My name's Sean McClennan,' I say, reaching out to shake his hand and to take back my flask from him, 'and my cousins out your way are the Hanrahans. Have you ever come across them?'

'The Hanrahans with the farm out at Laragan? I used to know John a little: we were at Sunday school together in Collooney, but we've lost touch over the years.'

'My God, it's a small world,' I reply. 'And you haven't had any news of my family at Rose Farm in the shadow of Binn Ghulbain by any small miracle?'

'You're a McClennan?' he asks. 'No, I don't think I've ever come across your family, but it's not as near to Collooney as Laragan is. But I'm sure you heard there was a big landslide on Binn Ghulbain a couple of months back?'

'What? No. How bad was it?'

'Pretty bad, I think. A section of the western face came down after a heavy rainfall. I heard there was a lot of rock debris to clear away on the land just below the mountain. It took some weeks to put things right. Thank God no-one was killed.'.

'I hope that our farm was left unscathed. I've had no news from home since I came over here.'

'I heard about the rockfall when I was still in Liverpool. I've had no letter myself since then.'

After the carter has led his horses away to the stream, the cart bouncing behind them over the uneven ground, I walk back to Adam and the other men who have been charged by Mr Menzies with moving the spilled ballast to the section of the newly levelled bed of the line that it is destined for. While we work with our shovels and barrows, I cannot get Binn Ghulbain and the farm out of my mind. Have Ma and Niall sent me a letter that has not reached me? Have my letters ever made it to Rose Farm? It is very hard to put my body and mind to this endless labour when there is so much uncertainty and only silence from home.

I have a mind to tell Mr Menzies and Mr Jones that I want to leave and go back to Ireland, but I signed a contract to work as a navvy for two years and I do not know whether they would even let me go or how I would get back home. What would I go back to Sligo with, in any case? My tail between my legs and a purse full of half-crowns and shillings and sixpences? Niall would not be happy to see me again so soon. I would be just one more mouth to feed on a farm with not enough food even for the mouths of man and cattle that are already there.

Chapter Fourteen

Much Purlock, 1841

Summer did not want to give way to autumn that year. It clung to the ground and to the air and we lived under clear blue skies that did not darken completely until late into the night. After the harvest, my father's consulting room grew quieter as the villagers and the farm workers from the surrounding land took a few days' holiday to visit relatives in other parts of the country or were busy with domestic chores after the demands of harvest time. My father told me that he needed to work on a medical paper and that he would use the lull in his work to go back to the library in the British Museum in London.

'I should be home again in a week,' he said. 'I'm taking the steam train again from Gloucester to Swindon and then onwards to London.'

I could feel the heat coming into my cheeks. 'Father, the railway's a filthy scar running through the countryside. Look at all the destruction it has wrought on nature already.'

'Nonsense, Grace, it's nothing of the sort,' he replied. 'And you can't stop progress, there's simply no denying it. Before too long I'll be able to take the train right here in Much Purlock to Gloucester and change there for the London train. Won't that be quite something? No more days on rutted roads in unsprung carriages!'

'I would have rutted roads any day than belching smoke and deafening tonnes of steel.'

'You haven't been to Gloucester yet and seen them standing there gleaming at the long, curving platform.'

'No, and I have absolutely no intention of doing so, Father.'

He seemed to have recovered his spirits completely: there were no obvious lasting effects of the mushroom essence in his tea, either physical or mental. The mushrooms had dried out now behind the kitchen range, ready for grinding into a fine powder. If my father had not learned his lesson the first time, he would have to be taught another one when he came home from London again. I knew I had no power to protest or to effect change on the level of the Government or the Queen, even more so now that the Anti-Railway League had lost its way and the locals who had tried to protest at the building of the branch line had got nowhere. All I could do was to resist, assert my will locally, right there in Much Purlock, and my father was the very closest person, the most local, to me. His having been unable to save my mother, his having used me as his housekeeper, cook and maid only made him the greater target for my wrath.

My errands for the mill kept me busy for part of each day that long week of silence in the house. There were no more dead rooks on the path. The corpses of the other birds had long since been taken by other corvids or by foxes and stoats, devourers of the dead and the decayed. I could not be sure if the disease that had killed them was gone or would be back again. With work on the line in the next valley over at full pace, I could not believe it would stay away for long. I had read in one of my father's books that anthrax spores could be released by the ploughing of the soil, and something ancient had been stirred up; some essence, some balance had been disturbed, and it was the birds that were suffering.

The first small signs of autumn were creeping into the woods. Supple green leaves were turning brittle, and hints of yellow, brown, and red were beginning to show themselves. The air was cooler in the early morning and mist clung to the bottoms of the valleys until the sun's power melted it away. I walked up through the woods and over to the next valley again. The men had moved some two hundred yards since I had last watched them work. Now they kept their vests and jackets on despite the exertions of their labour. A great boulder of red Herefordshire sandstone, some twenty-five feet tall, stood right in the way of the line at the foot of the valley. Some of the men were boring holes into the boulder with long-bitted handdrills while others were hammering metal stakes into it by fractions of an inch with each sledgehammer blow. They worked bent into the boulder, ringed around it while other men were clearing the path where the rails would be laid still further down the valley from this immense piece of rock. Young though they were, the men already looked exhausted, and it was still only early. All that enormous labour and for what—to get from one place to another more quickly than the pace of hoof or foot allowed? I just did not understand why the convenience of man should be to the detriment of nature.

I hid myself in the shadow cast by the trunk and canopy of an oak tree that I visited from time to time on the edge of the wood. It had the initials *G* and *S* on either side of a love heart incised into its bark, and I liked to think that the *G* was me. I might have been the only person who had ever seen those letters apart from the boy or girl who had carved them into the trunk years ago. Who was it, what lover lost or found, that had cut them into that tree? So much of our past is unwritten and answers to such questions can never now be retrieved. I asked myself whether I would ever meet a man and what his name might be if I did. It would be too much to hope that it would begin with an *S*. What was he doing at the very moment that I was standing by that tree?

The bear-like navvy who I had seen before did not seem to be among the workers on the line that day. I think I felt disappointed not to see him again and wondered what had become of him. There were perhaps twenty men there and they all looked so young, even to my younger eyes: the oldest could not have been more than twenty-five. Only the foreman in his worn bowler hat and waistcoat, his stocky brown pony tethered to a tree, looked older. He flicked a long metal rule against his trouser leg, and it was hard to tell whether it was an impatient or a threatening thing. He stood smoking his pipe and giving orders that I could not hear, while the others all worked without rest for the hour that I hid under that oak tree watching them.

The men stopped their drilling and hammering after an hour or so. The foreman bent down to a metal box that was lying on the grass near his pony and took out what looked like short brown sticks, which he handed to each of the navvies in turn. They turned back to the giant red boulder one after the other and carefully pushed the sticks into the deep holes that they had bored into the rock. They then affixed very long lengths of twine that the foreman had given them to each stick in its hole, all the way round the boulder so far as I could tell from that angle and distance, and trailed the free ends of the lengths of twine to meet at the side of the rock nearest the foreman. He tied all the ends together and added another very long length of twine, which he pulled back towards the tree under which his pony was standing. I heard a very faint 'Now!' and all the men ran at full pelt down the bed of the line to where the other group of men was standing some three or four hundred yards away. Once they had reached the other men, there was a flash of fire in the foreman's cupped hands, and he jumped on his pony and rode off as fast as it would carry him away down the line. I watched as the fire crept up the first length of the long fuse, for that is what it was, and then I turned and ran.

I did not get far before I found myself knocked off my feet by a blast that I felt before I heard it. I was in a hollow in the wood, one of the pits where they mined for limestone in Roman times, and landed face-first in a patch of brambles and long grass. I lay there winded as the shattering thunder of the explosion reached me, followed by another blast and yet another. Then a silence so deep that it seemed as if the air had been sucked out of the sky. I did not feel any pain, apart from the stinging of the scratches from the thorns on my face and hands; there were no muscular or skeletal aches in my legs or back or body. Once I had got my breath back, I pushed myself up and walked back to my oak tree on the lip of the wood where it meets the open valley. I could not seem to stop my legs from shaking and my ears were ringing terribly.

A line of navvies with pickaxes and shovels were making their way up from the bottom of the valley to where the great boulder had stood only minutes before. It had not gone completely, but more than two-thirds of its height had been blown away and shards and lumps of red rock lay all around. The men set to work on the remains of the boulder, swinging their tools of iron and steel as if slaughtering a giant cowed animal.

I turned and began my walk back home. I think now that I was in shock. My ears were still ringing, and every sound was muffled as if it had snowed heavily. I could not accept that a majestic piece of Herefordshire rock that had stood there for millions of years was now no more than rubble. They were clearing the way to nothing less than our own destruction. The ringing in my ears was like my anger singing to me. Why could no-one else see what was happening?

'You look like you've seen a ghost,' the foreman said that afternoon when I arrived at the mill. 'And what have you done to your pretty face?'

'I tripped and fell while I was out walking in the woods. I wasn't looking where I was going and caught my foot on a stone that was sticking up out of the path. I fell right into a bramble patch.'

'You should go and wash your face in the spring,' he said, smiling at me with his buck teeth. 'You don't want an infection setting in.'

As friendly as he was, I did not want to have to explain myself to him. Being a man of gear wheels, cogs, pistons and pumps, he doubtless thought that the railway was a good thing. He would see only the mechanical advancement, the money, the influx of people, not the loss to nature and our way of life. While the lay citizens of Much Purlock were more wary of change than he—raising their voices at meetings, gathering in small groups on street corners to protest, and writing finely penned letters to the newspapers—they soon seemed to assimilate and accommodate to whatever change it was and then curb their tongues and do nothing. I was not one of those people.

I had a long list of errands to run, and I already felt exhausted by the events of that morning. The afternoon sun accompanied me as I pulled the handcart around the village. I dropped a heavy bag of oatmeal off at the Queen's Head: the landlord, a patient of my father's, was tending to his small flower garden out front, as it was not yet opening time.

'Miss Matthews,' he said, his goitered throat bobbing up and down with merriment, 'have you been kissing thistles?'

'No, Mr Farr,' I replied, lifting the bag off the cart without him making any offer to help, 'because I am not foolish. I tripped and fell into some brambles.'

'Well, mind how you go with that handcart, won't you?' he said.

'I certainly will, Mr Farr. A good day to you now.' I did not hope that he had a good day; I hoped that his goiter burst and that the bag of oatmeal split as he carried it to his storeroom at the back of the inn. There was still a ringing in my ears from the explosion and I could not get the shattered rock out of my mind. It had made my view of my fellow citizens of Much Purlock far less than benign. How could they have allowed that desecration to happen? I wondered about getting away from there, perhaps going into service as a maid or cook somewhere in another county altogether. After all, I had had plenty of experience of domestic arrangements since my poor mother's death.

There was a familiar low, dark shape on the footpath as I made my way home in the twilight that evening. A dead rook was lying prone on its back, its vacant eyes staring up at heaven. I turned it over with my boot, but I could see no obvious sign of injury. Only its black beak had mouldered down to a stub, evidence of the disease that had killed it, stopping it from eating in its last days or weeks. I suspected that the sickness had not gone completely but had remained out of sight that summer, the birds falling silently, secretly in the woods or into undergrowth where it was hard to spot them, but that encounter left me again with a profound sense of foreboding and disquiet.

My father was due to return from London in a day or two. The way I saw it, it would not be quite the homecoming he was expecting.

Chapter Fifteen

Dried mushrooms are hard to grind into a fine powder. The cluster I had picked was about the size of two large, clenched fists, and the mushrooms had been turning from flesh to bone behind the range for many weeks. My father had an apothecary's pestle and mortar in his study, and I spent part of one morning bending over it at our kitchen table, grinding and grinding two or three desiccated mushrooms at a time until they had turned into a brown powder that looked like snuff. I took out any remaining hardened knots of matter with the sieve.

While other men of his age might take their tobacco in a pipe, my father still took snuff from the back of his hand. He was how I imagined a country squire from a hundred years ago might have been. He kept his black lacquered snuff jar in his study, within easy reach of his Sheraton armchair. Every evening after supper he retreated into the study, sat with a glass of ruby port and sniffed snuff loudly and forcefully from the back of his hand into first one nostril then the other. He called it his 'pep'.

I was interested to see what effect an admixture of snuff and powdered mushroom would have on him. Albertus Magnus had made no mention of the subject in his mysterious text, and none of the other tracts that I could find on plants of the forest and the field in my father's library made any reference to what might happen to a man if he ingested those slender mushrooms. They were held by Herefordshire folk to cause hallucinations, visions, strange phenomena of the mind, but the herbalist must learn by doing, by experimenting, by testing admixtures and concoctions herself. That is the only way to understand what plants can do, to find the appropriate dosage, the correct medicine, the right cure. I simply had to wait and see.

By midday I had ground up enough mushrooms to fill a teacup. I put half of the powder in my turned applewood box that I kept up in my bedroom under the bed and the other half I mixed thoroughly with my father's snuff. Although his snuff jar was slightly fuller, I knew that he would not notice; he would only be happy that he had more of it than he remembered. My father enjoyed his creature comforts, that was for sure. He was never one not to ask for a second helping of something, another glass of wine.

There was a September storm on the day he came home. He had been gone nearer to ten days than a week. Rain pummelled the lanes and the stubble fields and the woods, and I went out in it, the sharp drops stinging life into my upturned face and my hands. It was exhilarating, and I was soaked through when I got back home.

The pony and trap drew up at five o'clock as it was already getting dark, the sky streaked with flames of orange and red over the church to the west. My father's black boots clicked on the cobblestones of the yard outside our house as he stepped down from the trap. I saw him from the drawing-room window in his charcoal coat and black top hat: he made me think of the devil himself on his dark horse. He rapped on the door with the tip of his cane.

'Grace are you in?' he said. 'Open up so that the man can bring in my travelling case.'

I slid back the bolt on the door and my father came over the threshold, hat in hand. He smelled of soot and smoke as I took his coat from him.

'Hello, Father,' I said. 'You have the smell of the locomotive on you. It's somewhat acrid, I must say.'

'I see that you have lost none of your charm while I've been away,' he replied, laughing his irritated laugh, and stifling no doubt a sharper reply.

'My charm is inborn, dear Father, after all I am your daughter.'

The man brought in my father's case and kept his eyes to the ground the whole while, although I noticed the merest hint of a smile playing on his thin lips as he listened to us talk. The thinness of his lips was only matched by his long, lean body and beanpole legs. 'There you are, Sir,' he said in his thick Herefordshire burr. 'I wish you a pleasant evening.' He had his crumpled cloth cap in his hand and my father gave him a shilling by way of a tip. As he went out the door, he gave me a sly wink without my father seeing and put the cap back on his head. Then he was gone on the trap, with a few quick flicks of the loosely held reins on the pony's flanks, his lantern swinging with the movement of the trap over the rutted lane in the thick and starless darkness.

My father retired to his bedroom to unpack his case and then to his study to get his papers in order while I prepared our supper. Each time he went to London—a teeming, tumultuous city that I could only imagine from his descriptions and from reports in the newspapers to which he subscribed—he came back full of renewed mental and physical vigour and energy. It was as if he had grown younger somehow. It served only to make me angrier with him. It always made me think back to the cold morning of my poor mother's burial in St. Andrew's churchyard and the awfulness of that day. My father with his head bowed by the open grave, saying no words of comfort to me, laying no soothing arm around my shoulders, weeping silently, sorry only for himself.

In near silence we ate the beef brisket and dumplings I had prepared, the scraping of our knives and forks on the bone China plates and my father's careful chewing of his food the only sounds in the stillness of our house.

'You're looking rather pensive this evening, Grace,' he said, breaking the silence as he poured himself a glass of Bordeaux wine from the decanter. 'And what happened to your face? Did you run through a thorny thicket?'

'I tripped and fell into a bramble patch while I was on a walk in the woods. It wasn't anything much.'

'You need to be more careful, Grace: I'm often telling you that. How were things while I was away?'

'I went about my chores and kept myself to myself, as I always do,' I replied. 'There was a great deal of work being done on the railway line, and I went over and watched the men going about their labour for a while.'

'Still haunting the woods out that way, are you, Grace?'

'How can you fight an enemy that you don't know or recognise?' I asked.

'There are no enemies in any of this, only progress that would have been unimaginable a few years ago,' he replied. 'It took me just under six hours to get from Gloucester to London this time. Can you believe that?'

'It won't feel like progress of any kind in the future, believe me,' I said. 'When people look back at our time, they'll feel that we turned our back on nature and all that was good for us. They won't thank us for it, I'm telling you.'

'We've only gone as fast on land as a horse can carry us or as fast as we can run on our own two legs since we were first on this earth,' he said. 'Now think about what these engineers have done for mankind. It's a miracle.' He helped himself to two more dumplings from the pot at the centre of the table and dabbed at his lips with his napkin.

'Miracles are not always what they seem,' I replied. 'As you'd be the first to point out, there are quacks out there in every marketplace who talk of miracles when they sell elixirs made only of honey and hot air.'

'I agree, but the railway really *is* a miracle of technology. It'll be the greatest achievement of our lifetime.'

'I suppose that we'll have to wait and see,' I said. I could tell that there would be no way of changing his mind. My herbalist's art would have to work its magic if he was ever going to see things differently, to understand the error of his ways.

We went back to our silent scraping of the plates, and I then cleared the dishes and washed them with the stiff brush in the pail of water in the kitchen. I was so used to doing all that work after seven years that I did it automatically, without even thinking about

Night Comes Down

it. My father yawned, poured himself a glass of port and retreated into his study. I heard him reading some of his medical notes out loud to himself through the half-closed door: they seemed to concern the letting of blood from a patient to cure a fever. I did not yet hear the sound that I was hoping for.

The brilliant white moon had risen above the wood, which was cast in pitch-black shadow by the hill above it and by the brightness of the moonlight. The gale had blown the clouds away and left a cold, clear sky behind it. An owl was sending out its echoing cry across the valley, out hunting for voles or mice in the moonlight.

I went down to the well at the bottom of the garden to fetch some fresh water for the night. The moonlight reflected on the still surface deep down where the water found its level. When I winched up the first bucketful, the halfmoon itself shone like a broken, brilliant stone in the water. When I bent down closer, there was my dark face lit by the moonshine, distorted and fragmented by the movement of the water in the bucket on its wound rope.

A heavy wooden pail in each hand, water spilling over their brims onto the backs of my hands, I walked down the path to the back door trying not to lose too much of the water. The owl was still out there somewhere in the dark, flying on its soundless wings. Its hooting haunted the night air.

My father was sitting in the more comfortable of the two armchairs in the sitting-room when I went back inside. He was just staring into space and smiling slightly, as if at a joke that he had just heard.

'Father, would you like some cheese or some fruit? We've the first of the blackberries that I picked.'

He did not answer me but just sat there staring on blankly and smiling.

'Father, can you not hear me?'

There was no response. I went up to him and waved my hand in front of his eyes, but he did not blink. There was just that gently amused staring out into space. It was then that I noticed a dusting of brown powder where his bushy grey moustache gave way to sallow skin and, looking more closely, I saw a shadow beneath each of his nostrils. He must have taken his pep when I was out at the well. Despite the coolness of the night, there was a fine sheen of sweat where the flesh of his neck met the collar of his shirt.

    I left him in his chair and took my candle up to bed. He had the ebbing fire in the hearth to keep him warm and I had no heat at all: the bedroom was ice cold and I crept beneath the sheets, pulling the counterpane up over my head. I clenched my jaw to stop my teeth from chattering and waited for the heat from my body to warm the bed.

    Once my body had given out enough of its heat, I no longer felt as if I was trapped in a frozen cocoon of sheets and my muscles began to relax, to lose their rigid resistance to the cold. My thoughts drifted off into the universe, out into the ether, then plunged back down to earth again, to my woods and my valleys, homing in as if through a telescope on those strong men around that great rock. The bare-chested navvy who had been absent that morning, the one who had had the look in his eyes of a wild animal trapped by man, excited me in ways that I could not put into words.

Chapter Sixteen

The armchair was empty when I went downstairs the next morning. One of the thick woollen blankets we kept folded on the dresser had been left where my father had dropped it on the floor by his chair, but he was nowhere to be seen. The house was silent, and the fire had not been rebuilt.

I looked out of the dining room window onto the lane beyond the yard in front of the house and saw a dishevelled rook hopping past, its feathers covered in a film of dirt as if it had just taken a dust bath. I looked more closely, and its beak was a stub, perhaps half the length it should be. It had obviously not been able to eat for some time or to preen itself. I did not want to let it suffer, and I ran in my nightdress to fetch the spade from the back garden. When I went around to the front of the house, the rook was still on the lane about thirty yards away as it dips down towards Cutler's Bottom. I chased the rook to put it out of its misery, but it ran into thick undergrowth at the side of the lane, and I could not reach it. I heard the trotting of a horse coming towards me, so walked as quickly as I could back to the house with the spade in one hand and my nightdress held up above the mud with the other. The disease was obviously still among the corvid population and if you were unlucky enough to see the diseased birds, it was hard to ignore.

Father was in his armchair when I got back to the house. For the briefest of moments, my mind could not separate out the escape of the black rook from the reappearance of my father. It was as if a magic trick had been conjured before my eyes and in a puff of smoke and with a clash of cymbals unseen hands had turned the diseased bird into the slightly corpulent, bewhiskered man sitting before me in his black flannel pyjamas. A quiet smile was still playing on his lips, and he was looking with his beady eyes out of the sitting-room window at something that did not seem to be there.

'Father, where have you been?'

'It felt as if I had gone right to heaven last night,' he said. 'It was not like me at all: I had a celestial experience, and I can't say that it was unpleasurable.'

'What do you mean? What kind of experience exactly?' I needed to understand more precisely what my herbalist's arts had conjured.

'I can't really put it into words. I was sitting in this chair after supper and suddenly my vision took on a palette of colours and a brilliance that I've never experienced before. And sounds came at me as if down a long tunnel. It really was most strange.'

'I've told you before: the railway's no good for you. It does something to the brain. All that speed; the nervous system can't possibly keep up.'

'It had nothing to do with the railway or my journey. It felt almost like a divine experience, something God-given. I can hardly believe I'm saying that. I still feel this strange sense of elevation, exultation.' He sat there, his black-clad legs stretched out in front of him and that beatific smile on his face.

I wanted to slap some sense into him, I wanted to laugh out loud. 'Well, I'll leave you to the divine while I go and lay out some breakfast,' I said. 'You must be hungry after your celestial journey.'

Of course, I knew full well what had caused his experience, but he seemed to have made no connection between his snuff and his overstimulated senses. It gave me a feeling of power to know something about him that he himself was completely unaware of. I realised I could cook, darn, clean, fetch water, listen to his hypothesising and self-congratulation, and I could work at the mill, do all the little chores that occupied my days and diminished me somehow; but I could also control something through those mushrooms: his emotions and his moods. He might be the man of the house and the good doctor to the people of Much Purlock, but I had a power no-one else knew about. Secrets themselves are very potent things; they conjure their own magic.

Over the course of the day, he went from apparent bliss to a state of moroseness and silence. In the mid-afternoon he said that he was going out for some fresh air, and he did not come back until it was getting dark. The blackbirds and thrushes were returning to their roosts in the trees in our garden and a pipistrelle bat was out hunting for gnats and flies in the half-light above the orchard.

'I believe I've been afflicted by a cerebral malignancy of some kind,' he said over our supper of boiled potatoes and a roasted half-chicken. 'There's no other explanation for these extraordinary visions—think of the devil I heard talking to me that other time!—and my sudden changes of mood.'

'You're the learned physician, Father, but I'm sure there must be other, less alarming explanations.'

'I can't think of any at all,' he replied, and went back to his silent chewing. He looked as if he had seen a ghost.

While he was upstairs in his bedroom changing into his nightgown, I went into his study and carefully poured the adulterated contents of his snuff jar into a small cloth bag that I kept tucked behind some spice jars up on one of the shelves in the kitchen. If he ever discovered the bag and asked me about it, I would simply tell him that it was old nutmeg or ground pepper long past its prime. His supply of fresh snuff was in a paper-wrapped packet near the jar, and I filled the jar to the same level with the pure snuff. I had to limit the frequency with which my father took his pep of snuff and ground mushroom powder so he did not make the connection between his snorting of the pep and his episodes. He was a man of science, after all.

* * *

The days were becoming cooler but there was still no frost first thing in the morning, and the sunshine stayed with us right through September. The grain and fruit harvests had been plentiful and the Wednesday market in Much Purlock was busy with stallholders from the surrounding farms and smallholdings, their tables piled high with fresh produce. I used to go to the market with my mother, holding her hand tight when I was a small girl and then walking beside her more confidently, arm in arm, when I was older. She was always my protector and my greatest friend. She doted on me like mothers of only children often do, while my father was busy with his patients or away at conferences. I loved her like I have loved no-one else.

For all his published medical papers and his speeches at conferences, my father could not save her; he could not even find a way to soothe her unbearable pain. For that, and for his treating me like a scold and a housemaid, and for his use of the railway, I had no choice but to punish him. I had to punish him while keeping my mother's life's work—him and me and our household—and her memory alive.

I took her wicker basket to the market with me. When I held its worn wooden handle, I could feel her warm hand right there in the sunshine. It gave me great comfort to feel her near me. Sometimes when I went about the tasks that I used to watch her perform or I went to the places that she used to go—the well, the market, the woods, the Star Inn—I felt almost as if I was occupying the very same spaces in which she had moved and breathed, as if I was her living ghost somehow. It was a strange feeling, but not an unpleasant one. I know that she loved my father, but she would have understood. She would have really understood.

On the last Wednesday in September the weather changed. A cold front came in from the east and the morning sky was lead grey. The swallows were lining up along the rooftops and on the weathervane of the church, readying themselves for their long journey south. They would not be back again until the summer. When I saw the last of the swallows gathering to leave our corner of the world, I knew winter was not far away. The earth would soon go into its time of sleep; ice and snow would cover the ground, and the trees would stand against the grey-white skies like blackened skeletons.

But that Wednesday morning, autumn was still on its way to us and the good folk of Much Purlock were out on the lanes, going about their work or heading for the market to buy food or to greet their neighbours. I clung close to the shade of hedges and walls and, when I got to the market, I spoke to the stallholders only to tell them what I wanted from their careful displays of fruits and vegetables, cakes and bread and salted butter. When I saw the foreman from the mill, I greeted him with a smile and a few friendly words to match his own, as he was always kind to me.

I went between the stalls with mother's basket now heavy with fresh food. All those faces I had known from my earliest years, patients of my father's, friends of my mother's, neighbours near and far: they had all become estranged to me somehow. There were new divisions between them, too, perhaps not on the surface of things but deep down. The building of the railway, the coming of the outside world into our closed-in valleys, had caused differences of opinion, fractures that were buried deep but were there in all of us and would be very hard to heal.

There was laughter as a group of half a dozen men came out of the Star Inn. On market days it opened early and stayed open late to serve the stallholders and their customers, who came from far beyond the town to buy their food at the market. The men had stopped beneath the inn's sign of a single, eight-pointed star against a dark sky. They had lilting, musical accents that I had not heard before and they were wearing rough smocks and coarse trousers over heavy boots. It was hard not to stare a little at those strangers to our town: outsiders from faraway places were not such a common sight in those days.

The men were all young and strong-looking and among them was the one I had seen before, the ox-like giant of a man who looked as if he had been captured and brought to our world from some wilder place. I had thought about him often since I first saw him, particularly when I was up in bed on those cold, cold nights. He intrigued me, he excited me for reasons that I found hard to understand at seventeen and find hard to explain even now. He looked threatening and safe at the same time, both wild and gentle, bestial and noble. I wanted to follow him, to be able to look at him again, to find out where he lived.

The men left the inn and made their way from the marketplace out through the town towards the woods. I followed them at a careful distance, keeping to the shadows. They talked merrily, jostling each other, and laughing, and I caught the odd word of their singsong brogue. They did not turn around even once, and I must have followed them for more than half an hour that morning under the cold grey sky. When they went into the wood, I walked behind them down the long track that leads towards the next valley, moving from the shade of one tree trunk to the next to make sure that they did not see me.

They made an abrupt turn to the left down an overgrown path near the Roman pits I had never followed before in all my years of walking through the woods. It led steeply down through a dense stand of beech trees and some chestnuts to an area of level ground about a hundred yards from the section of railway line they were working on. There were perhaps fifteen small wooden huts lined up in a row, poorly built and leaning towards one another as if they were in quiet conversation, stovepipes jutting out at uneven heights from their roofs. The men sat down on some chairs that were set out beside the smoking embers of a fire, and gradually more men joined them from the huts. One or two of the men were drinking from what looked like stoneware jugs of beer. It seemed that Wednesday must be their day of rest.

The powerful, dark-haired Irishman appeared to be at the very heart of the group. He turned suddenly and looked right at me, his bright blue eyes staring almost through me, and I slipped behind the trunk of a beech tree as quickly as I could. I did not know if he had seen me in my dark coat and black stockings in that dark wood, or if I wanted him to have seen me, to have noticed me standing there, but my heart was pounding beneath my ribs, and I found it hard to catch my breath. I turned and retraced my steps as fast as I could up the path and made my way back home again.

My father was in his consulting room with a patient when I got back to the house. I put my ear to the door and heard his gloomy voice as he counselled the unseen man, who also spoke in quiet, melancholic tones with a strong Gloucestershire accent. Perhaps the good doctor was delivering some sombre medical diagnosis, or they were discussing the affairs of men: some failed business venture, perhaps, or debts owed to the bank, or a foolish bet lost on the Saturday races at Ledbury. I could not hear their exact words through the thick oak door, but their tone was serious and downcast.

When the patient and the learned doctor came out of the consulting room, I was sweeping the kitchen floor with the stiff besom. I looked up and was surprised to see that the patient was none other than Doctor Gillespie from Gloucester, an occasional visitor throughout my earlier childhood: it seemed as if the patient was, in fact, the doctor and the doctor the patient.

'Hello, Grace,' Doctor Gillespie said. I had not recognised his muffled voice through the door. 'My, how you've grown, dear girl. And the very image of your mother. How many years can it have been?'

'I'm not quite sure, Doctor Gillespie,' I replied. 'You certainly visited us not so long before she died when I was ten. I'm seventeen now.' He did not flinch at all when I mentioned my mother's death. He was yet another of the learned circle who had been unable to do anything for her.

'Your father asked me to pay him a visit as he has some concerns about his health. I think he'll be just fine, but you'll need to keep a close eye on him for any other strange turns, my dear girl.' My father simply stood there, his arms hanging down by his sides and a blank expression on his face. He looked like a puppet that had had the stuffing plucked out of it by some mischievous child.

'Rest assured that I will, Doctor Gillespie,' I replied. 'I'll be sure to keep a very close eye on him.'

Chapter Seventeen

The weather became colder and greyer with October's arrival. The detonations on the railway line were louder and more frequent than they had been before as the navvies reached a large outcrop of earth and rock below Simeon's Pitch and they had to blast the lot away to lay the line. The explosions came every three or four hours then during daylight for four days in a row. I can still hear that desecration of our landscape even now. When I ventured back into the woods at the end of that week of terror against nature, I found saplings on the edge of the woods ripped apart and the bark of even the most ancient and majestic of trees nearest the bed of the line flayed by the flying rock and stones. There where the great outcrop of rock below Simeon's Pitch had been, was now a clean, straight cutting through the land.

My father was still speaking of the march of mechanical progress in his brighter moments. On the occasional evening, I switched the unadulterated contents of his snuff jar for the admixture of ground mushroom and brown snuff in its bag high up on the kitchen shelf. Having taken his pep, he sat late into the night in an apparent state of ecstasy in his armchair in front of a dying fire only to sink into a deep depression the next day. Whenever I overheard him with patients in his consulting room—between my errands for the mill, my work in the house or in the garden, and my walks through the woods—his tone was always melancholic. Sometimes there was no-one for him to see in his consulting room, and he spent long hours alone instead, reading sections of his medical textbooks out loud to himself, trying to find a diagnosis for the affliction of colourful and disturbing visions, of highs and lows of mood that he seemed to be suffering.

Despite the cold, I walked up through the woods and sat watching the navvies from high above their camp soon after dawn or at dusk every few days. I always went to the same beech tree well off the path and sat in the shadow that it cast, watching the comings and goings of the men, the pattern of their lives away from their work on the railway line. Why did I not despise them? Why did I choose to watch them as they ate their breakfast around the campfire or shaved their beards while stooping over buckets of water, the slivers of mirror that they held up to their faces catching the morning light? I think because even at seventeen I was wise enough to separate the worker from the work. I knew who deserved my anger at the destruction of nature and the intrusion into our world: the Members of Parliament in London, the men of business, the railway companies, the gang-masters, the thoughtless passengers who would use the line. These navvies were just trying to survive in a world that they barely knew.

There he was again, that ox-like man. He was a head taller than the other men, but he looked younger than I had thought when I saw him working on the line that first time and then later when I had followed him along the path through the wood. To look at him now down there in the camp, he could not have been much older than twenty. The other men seemed to move around him with respect, but also with a certain admiration; it was as if he was the centre of things, somehow.

I often saw the men only quite briefly when I watched their camp, as they left for work on the railway line soon after sunrise and only spent a short time outside around the fire in the evenings before retreating into their huts. As their work on the line progressed over the autumn, it took them into the open land of the valley, and I could not watch them at their labour so closely from the safety of the trees at the edge of the woods.

My errands for the mill and my chores in the house kept me busy for most of the week. The days became shorter, and the nights grew ever longer and darker. My father sat silently in his armchair in the evenings, staring into the fire, or he spent long hours reading in his study as if he was searching for an answer to some fundamental mystery that only he had access to. Of course, I could have cast some light into that mystery, but I let him labour away in the obscurity of not knowing. For someone who prided himself in his medical learning, it must have been especially hard for him that he could not diagnose himself. I see that now, I see that now, but I feel less guilty than I should.

I was the apothecary and he the patient taking in his doctored snuff. I switched the powders perhaps three times each month, and his highs and lows of mood punctuated our lives every ten days or so. The lows became lower as the weeks and months went by and he sat expectantly in his armchair each evening, as if hoping for another visitation from the visions and the euphoria that he had described. When the entrancement came, it was always followed the next day by a slowness and a lethargy, as if my father were walking through cooling molasses. He seemed to be spiralling into a despondency that never really left him. I cannot say that I felt any guilt then: I saw what I was doing to him only as a form of retribution. I did not consider for a moment what my father would do if he found out.

* * *

Jack, the son of the chicken-keeper, came looking for me again in mid-November. He seemed to have grown an inch taller since I had last seen him.

'Ma's hens' eggs 've gone from brown to white. She thinks it's a curse of some kind,' he told me. 'She's asking if you'd come and 'ave a look at the birds.'

'I'm not sure who'd curse the laying of hens' eggs,' I replied. 'I'll come, though.'

'Thank you, Miss Grace,' he said. 'Ma will be much obliged to you.'

I followed him down to Brook Cottage, which was even more rundown than before. Mrs Jenks looked somewhat dishevelled herself when we got there.

'I've been cleaning out the chicken coop and run,' she told me, brushing her long loose hair back behind her ears. 'This new clutch of hens are scared of something. Perhaps another fox has been coming around at night.'

'What makes you think they're scared, Mrs Jenks?'

'I've just got 'em from a farmer over Ross way and they're laying *white* eggs. I've never seen the like. It must be shock, or it's the devil playing his usual tricks.'

'Might I go and have a look at these new hens, Mrs Jenks?'

'You know where the run is, Miss Grace. Please go and have a look and tell me what might be wrong with 'em.'

I walked up the sloping garden towards the large run that lay in the shade of the wood. There were eight or nine hens there and they all looked healthy enough, with no hint of the disease that I had seen in the others. They were scratching in the earth for worms or grain and clucking contentedly. Their plumage was solid white or cream, and it was as if they were the pale ghosts of the red and brown hens that Mrs Jenks had lost earlier in the year. I knew straightaway why they only laid white eggs.

'Mrs Jenks, it's not magic or the devil that's doing this. These hens are a different breed to the others you had. Didn't the farmer tell you that their eggs would be white?'

'No, he said nothing about the hens layin' white eggs. Only ever seen 'em in swans and ducks and hedgerow birds before,' she replied. 'The children won't eat 'em white.'

'I wouldn't have thought their taste would be any different at all. Haven't you tried one yet?'

'I only got the birds a day or so ago,' she said. 'They took some settling. I sent the children to collect the eggs this morning and they came back as white as those sheets on the washing line. I thought it was a curse.'

'Don't you worry, it's no such thing. It's just nature,' I replied. 'They're the eggs that these hens are supposed to lay. Perhaps the children will grow to like them.'

Mrs Jenks was an uncommonly innocent creature, and I could not bring myself to look down on her for her lack of book-learning or her naivety. But she reminded me that my fellow men in Much Purlock were the more easily persuadable because of their lack of education and their uncorrupted simplicity. They would not hesitate to use the railway as soon as they had the chance. I despaired of them, I really did. My campaign against the coming of the railway, against the breaking-in of the outside world, was never one that I could win. I would have to continue to fight my battles much closer to home.

Chapter Eighteen

Hereford Insane Asylum, 1849

We have been rebelling against the orderlies by refusing to help to clean the ward. There are piles of our dirty clothes and bedsheets along the corridors and the unemptied commodes in the dormitories are really starting to stink. If they will not make the place orderly themselves, as their name suggests they should, we do not want to do it for them any longer. They mostly treat us with disdain, and worse. Only Mr Osney is kind to me, although I suspect he has his reasons.

It is a beautiful, sunlit September. The sky through these barred windows has been an unbroken blue for more than two weeks now and there is still warmth in the air. Today will be the breaking point: our uncleared ordure will stir the orderlies into action, there is no doubt about it. The air is thick with the stench, but we will not back down now. If we are patients, then we are not also domestics. They will be in here with their mops and clanking buckets and cloths before the afternoon is out. We will line the benches and watch them as they work and take delight in it. Their faces will be as sour as this air.

I have written another letter to my father, and Mr Osney has given it to the Warden to send out. Recently, I have begun to wonder if my letters ever leave this building, or whether they are kept in a pile on a desk somewhere or locked away in a drawer or simply thrown away. That would be one explanation for why he has only replied once, to my very first letter. I understand now that my treatment of him was cruel, as I have been told it was over and over again ever since I have been here, a cruelty born of my mental sickness, but I do not feel it warranted this never-ending silence from him.

Here they are, the clanking orderlies, come to make the wards shipshape and spick and span again. They do not deign, they do not dare, to look at us as they file past. They walk straight by with their mops and brooms raised up like useless weapons in the arms of toy soldiers. These wooden benches are hard and have no cushions, but we enjoy watching the men as they begin their work in their brown smocks and trousers. Where is our madness when we can take such delight in these small victories?

'They're even weaker-minded than they say we are,' Lizzie says, 'because they think they'll grind us down in the end.' She laughs and points as one of them further down the corridor bends forward to move his tin bucket and exposes the pale top of his buttocks between his trousers and his rough smock. 'But they won't, looking at that.' She laughs again. 'And we'll win as we don't have nothing to lose.'

'I suppose they could cut our food rations or the hour we spend outside each day,' I reply.

'They can try,' she says, 'but there'll be all hell to pay. The women in here won't stand for it.'

'I hope you're right. I couldn't bear it if we weren't allowed out of here at least once a day. It's what keeps me going.'

'Watch out left,' she says, and laughs her over-eager laugh again. The chamber pots and buckets have been emptied down the sluice by the men, the latrines mopped and scrubbed, and two of the women orderlies have bundled up the piles of washing and are taking them past us to the laundry. One of them, broad Mrs Swain, frowns and tuts at us as she walks past our bench. She has a distracting purple wart on the tip of her nose, and it makes me think of a miniature radish, perhaps one crafted for the doll's house of some fortunate child. Her scowl could darken the summer sky.

'Good afternoon, Mrs Swain,' I say as politely as I can muster.

'Not much good about it, girl,' she replies with a sneer. 'You lot in here have seen to that.'

She stalks off, her arms laden with our dirty bedsheets, blouses, and underskirts, muttering and casting backward glances at us. She has never had a kind word to say to any of us. It is almost as if she despises us for being here, sees us as beneath her, as not worth the effort of getting to know even a little as human beings.

I have only just realised that today is the seventh anniversary of my being here. Seven long years of my life wasted away in this god-forsaken place at the mercy of people like her. Seven long years far from the woods and the valleys that I love. Seven long years with no news at all of Sean. I have only my father to blame, while he blames only me. I will get out of here if it is the last thing I do.

Chapter Nineteen

Herefordshire, 1841

The gunpowder packed into the rock goes off with a shattering blast and two-thirds of the boulder disappears in front of our eyes, or at least it has gone when the plume of dust has settled. We are up the valley away from the outcrop at such a distance that this time we have not been told by Mr Menzies to lie flat in the woods until the detonation has happened. My ears still ring like buggery, and I walk around for a few minutes afterwards as if I have been hit over the head by a cosh.

Every time there is a detonation now, I think of Mr Sansom and what happened to him. O'Donnell talks as though he is not to blame for the accident, but we all know the truth. I have asked Mr Jones again if I can move hut, but he still says no.

Through the local drinkers at the Star Inn some of the men have heard about Mary, a widow with two young children to feed. They come back from hers with cocky smiles on their faces and lighter purses, boasting about the delights of lying in the warm embrace of a woman still of child-bearing age, while we lie cramped and cold in our bunkbeds. I am lonely but could never do that.

I have no answer to why I have never even kissed a girl. The isolation of the farm, I suppose, and not having gone to school past fifteen. The only girls I ever saw regularly after that were the cousins, and that would never do. It weighs on my mind, this innocence, and I go quiet when the other men talk about their conquests back home in Ireland. Even if some of their stories are made up or yarns spun on lesser truths, they make me feel deficient somehow, and even more alone. I want a girl, but not someone I have to pay for. If only I could find a way to talk to that beautiful brown-haired one who watches us work from the shelter of the trees sometimes. She looks at us with such intensity, such longing, that she must want to know us but whenever she comes to watch us, she has gone into the woods again when I next look up from my digging. When I have seen her about the town, I have longed to go after her, to talk to her, but what would she, what would the townsfolk say about my following her? What exactly would I have to say for myself when I caught up with her?

* * *

August is my favourite month on the farm when our long labours are rewarded by the bounties of the harvest. Bringing in the wheat and the barley is the end of something and the beginning of something new. The cattle are out on their pasture, basking in what sunshine there is in County Sligo, and the grass in their fields has turned a brittle green before it is restored to lush vitality by the autumn rain. After the harvest, Niall and Joseph will be cutting the silage for winter feed once the grass has grown green again. Here in this valley the farmer has left his fields behind, and we have taken over. This is progress; this is who we are now.

The boy is on the path again as I make my way down to Much Purlock.

'Hello, Mister,' he says. 'You remember me? I'm Jack.' He glances round, just as he did before. There is something nervous about him, despite his friendliness, and his looking over his shoulders every few seconds makes me feel uneasy. It is as if he thinks he is being followed; by what I cannot say.

'Of course, Master Jenks. I remember you told me not to take it too much to heart if people around here weren't friendly to us. We mostly keep ourselves to ourselves, but people here aren't so bad.'

'I got a pet rat. Want to see it?'

'Why, sure. Does he bite?'

'Only when he's hungry,' the boy says and laughs. 'My Ma says not to put my fingers too near his mouth, but I keep him in my coat.' Sure enough, a pink nose tipped with twitching whiskers emerges from beneath his grey woollen collar at that very moment, followed by the surprisingly long body of the white rat. Its reddish eyes stare out into the fading light.

'I'm not too keen on rats myself. They try to eat all the corn on our farm back home. What's this little fellow called, then?'

'Sean,' the boy replies, as the rat climbs onto his shoulder, its scaly, pinkish tail reaching up under his ear as if it has a life of its own.

'What, but that's my name!'

'I know,' the boy says, glancing over his shoulder again. 'You told me last time.'

'But what on earth ...?'

He is suddenly off through the trees, as if pulled away by something that I cannot see, his rat scrabbling back down into the collar of his coat again. A rat called Sean indeed! I do not know what to believe, whether he is simply pulling my leg for a laugh or being serious. I am not sure that I want to see him or his rat again. There is something about him that makes me worry: that nervous energy and distractedness that looks like childishness but is not. He seems haunted somehow, damaged, if not by man, then at the hands of this self-enclosed place. Generations of inwardness make people like him: I have seen it before back home, too, and I do not like it. At least what we are building here will open things up, will end the isolation of this place.

The sunlight flickering through the trees at the edge of the path makes my eyes ache and I can feel a headache starting to build in my temples. This heat, subsiding slowly though it is as we come towards autumn, sucks the water from the sea, the rivers, the lakes,

Night Comes Down

and the sky and makes the air thick with it. It is hard to breathe with all this humidity: we need a storm to break the heat and to clear the air again. Until then, headaches and endless thirst and springs drying up to a trickle.

The roofs of Much Purlock shimmer in the heat as I come down into the town. It has grown familiar to me somehow over these last five months and no longer feels so strange. These buildings of weathered red sandstone now map out routes that I know without having to think about them: to the marketplace and the Star Inn, out towards Dereham, over to the Plough, the other public house on the edge of the town. It is a sleepy place, but not without its charm. It is squat and solid and surrounded by low hills, green fields, and woods. I would never want to stay here but I can see why it is hard to leave. Places like this trap you unless you are strong, or desperate. The men at the railway company want to change all that. Rutted roads and lanes will give way to shining rails as a means of escape for those who can afford it.

The locals are still wary of us and go quiet when we turn into the Star Inn or the Plough for a drink. Even without hearing our accents they know who we are, as strangers rarely come here unless they are passing through to somewhere else. That boy Jack troubles me, and I am not sure it is friendliness that makes him talk to me. It is as if he is compelled to somehow, perhaps by curiosity, perhaps by something else. It is hard to say.

The ancient stone cross in the marketplace, with patches of yellow and green lichen creeping up its lower parts where the damp from the ground has got into it, acts like the gnomon on a sundial and casts a dark line of shadow across the square on sunlit days. It draws me back, this cross: its great age roots it unalterably to where it is, makes it reassuring and comforting somehow. I sit down beneath the cross with my back against its base and take some bread and cheese out of my knapsack. The marketplace is quiet in the midday sunshine. Two pigeons are pecking around me, and I throw them some crumbs of my bread, but otherwise I am left alone, and the few passers-by do not even glance down at me as they cross the square.

Then suddenly there she is again! She walks past me not ten feet away and, for the briefest of moments, she looks down at me where I am sitting and smiles. Does she recognise me from the valley? It is all that I can do not to get up and follow her. She has pale skin and nut-brown hair and I think that her eyes are blue, or they could be green. Whatever the case, they are lovely. I would give anything to hold her, to kiss her, to have some human warmth. I wish I knew her name so I could say it to myself when I see her from afar again. Then she is gone out of the corner of the marketplace, and I am left sitting here on my own in the shadow of the cross.

It is at times like this that I miss Ma and Niall most of all. I wish I had had some word from them back home. Apart from Adam and Joseph, the men are not much company at all, and the hard work only amplifies my loneliness. My shift today starts at half past one and it will last until it gets dark: that is almost eight hours of uninterrupted, backbreaking digging before a late supper and turning in for the night. It is a little like how I imagine sentences of hard labour to be. There are some small mercies, though: the coins that the foreman drops clinking into my purse each Friday evening as I stand at the front of the queue outside the door of his hut; the chance to see her again; to come on walks like this; and to have a few glasses of beer at one of the pubs once or twice a week make it just about bearable, for now.

Chapter Twenty

This rain makes our work all the harder. The waterlogged footings and bed of the line threaten to slip over themselves as they turn from solid earth into liquid mud. We have to add in ballast and broken-up rock not just beneath the sleepers that will hold the rails, but also into the earth itself to try to give it strength and stability again. Everything will be easier once this rain has stopped and the ground has had time to dry out again. Until then, we labour away caked up to our knees and elbows in mud.

O'Donnell is walking around with a black eye and a deep cut to his cheek, which one of the men has stitched, but not very well. As much as they would like to, none of the navvies can lay claim to his injuries: O'Donnell says that he was attacked by two locals on the path on the other side of the wood, if for nothing else then only for his Irish accent when they addressed him as he walked past. This is the first such incident in the almost eight months that we have been here.

Yesterday I received a letter from home for the first time. It has lifted my spirits to read Ma's words and to hear that Niall is doing the best he can to keep the farm going. Pa's debts are far from being settled and Ma and Niall are a long way from certain that they will not have to sell the farm. Ma writes that I should try to stay on in England for at least two years from when I came over here last March. This endless work and the need for me to help Ma and Niall are the only things that will keep me here, that and my baseless, ceaseless hope that I will be able to find a way to talk to that girl, that fairy of the woods one day. Despite its beauty, I have little affinity with this place, and with a few exceptions I would happily never see most of these men again.

There is pandemonium down towards the bottom of this section of the line before it turns through a long curve, runs between the high cutting and comes out into the next valley over towards Gloucester. Mr Menzies is waving frantically and calling for shovels and spades and the men are running down the sides of the line from whatever jobs they are on and out from the camp towards him.

When I get there, I cannot understand what I am seeing at first. A great slew of earth and rock has slipped from the mound where it has been deposited after being excavated and moved there from the cutting, and two men seem to be standing in a deep trench amid all this debris, but all I can see are the tops of their heads. Mr Menzies is bellowing at all of us to dig, dig with all that we have got. Then I realise: they are buried up to their heads in the mud and stone and more of it is trickling and sliding down with every passing second. Neither of them seems to be conscious and their eyes are closed as we push our spades in around them and then reach in to pull the mud away from their mouths and noses. I cannot even tell which of the men they are. Joe and Adam are beside me now and we stand as near to them as we dare, but there is the real danger that we will be buried in this slip ourselves: it is already up to our shins.

After ten minutes of furious digging, we are down to their waists and buried in the mud almost up to our own waists. Other men crowd around as near to us as they dare, reaching in their hands and shouting advice, and they manage to pull the two men and us out of the mud and onto solid ground away from the dark mound behind us. They wipe the mud away from the two men's faces; one groans and shakes his head and then opens his eyes, but the other man is still unconscious. Jimmy is the one who is awake now and he is sitting up on the wet ground. The men splash water over his face and head from their flasks, and he groans again and wipes the last mud from his face.

'Fuck,' he says. 'Fuck. What happened?'

'The spoil heap from the cutting slipped and covered you,' Mr Menzies tells him, looking white-faced and suddenly exhausted.

Three or four of the navvies are crouching down beside the other man, who is lying on his back on the bare ground. I can see

Night Comes Down

now that it is Fergal from County Limerick. One man has his ear down to Fergal's mouth and has pulled back one of his eyelids, but there is no sign of life. They pour more water onto his face and try to hook the mud out of his nostrils and mouth with their fingers, but I think he is gone. They keep on trying to revive him, breathing into his mouth and massaging his chest, but nothing does any good, and after another ten minutes they give up. The men stand around not knowing what to do with that feeling in the pits of their stomachs. Fergal's is the second death that we have had here. It is beginning to feel like a cursed place.

* * *

The Irishmen dying on the railways over here have no chance of being buried back home: their bodies would have begun to rot in their coffins long before they could reach their native soil. The railway company has paid the undertaker in Much Purlock for Fergal's coffin, but Mr Menzies has only just realised that there is no Catholic church here. He has arranged instead for Fergal to be taken over by cart to Gloucester first thing tomorrow morning, where there is a Catholic church with quite a large burial ground, but none of us will be given time off to attend the burial, which the company will also pay for, or offer him our last respects. Fergal was only in his twenties, perhaps three of four years older than me, and his drowning in this red Herefordshire mud has left us all sleepless these last two nights. And Mr Sansom's bloody accident has hardly even faded in our memories.

The men are seething and muttering at not being allowed to go to the burial. There is talk again of getting rid of Mr Menzies, but it is all just hot air: if we protest too vehemently or down tools, we will find ourselves without pay or a place to live. We are held hostage by needing to be fed, housed, and paid by Mr Menzies and the railway company in a country where we otherwise have no place.

Rather than feeling that familiar relief of being free of the other men for an hour or two and the peace of nature here in the woods on the path down to Much Purlock, all I can do is to listen out for the sound of local voices coming my way. Most men would not want to risk attacking me on their own, or even if there were two of them, but I cannot take any chances. I do not want to damage my fists with so much heavy work to do. Perhaps it was O'Donnell's native rudeness that invited the attack, but it is hard to know where the truth lies with him.

The rain finally stopped falling yesterday afternoon and the sun came out this morning in a pale-blue sky. It is not market day, but the marketplace is busier than it was the last time I was here, and there is little risk of anything untoward happening with all these people around. It is good to be part of—at least a witness to—another life that is not the life of the men on the railway.

Oh, there she is again, that beauty, walking down the side of the square looking neither left nor right, with her brown hair flowing out from under her hat! She has a determined look on her face, as if she is walking somewhere with a purpose. She slows briefly to glance into the window of the butcher's shop, then carries on along the edge of the marketplace and out of sight. She lights up this landlocked place and looks as if she has no idea of her loveliness. I am tempted again to follow her at a distance to see where she is going, to see perhaps where she lives, but I do not want to draw attention to myself or to alarm her, and I stay standing where I am near the cross on the marketplace.

A woman's voice: I have not heard one close-to for so long; all my contact with my fellow man is rough-hewn and coarse-grained. Even the Star Inn is manned; there are no women working there. I am craving the softness of the way in which a woman speaks, the gentleness of her gesture, that fineness of thought and feeling. Until then, I am left with O'Donnell as an undesired bunkmate and all the other Irishmen working on the line in this rain-soaked and weatherworn place.

Chapter Twenty-One

The woods above Much Purlock, 1841

It was a bitterly cold December that year. My breath plumed in the air as I walked up through the woods after the Wednesday market, and I dug my hands deeper into the pockets of my coat. The woods smelled of decaying plant life and the woodsmoke that was swirling up from down in the navvies' camp. There was a slippery black carpet of leaves underfoot, slowly rotting down into the winter soil.

The bear-like Irishman had not been outside the Star Inn that morning, and I had felt a strange sense of disappointment at not having seen him there again. The navvies' shift on the line seemed to have finished for the day when I got to my place in the woods, even though it was not long after two o'clock and dusk was still some way off. I settled under my beech tree, well out of sight in the shadow of its branches, and watched the men come and go. One short, thickset man was cutting logs with an axe at the near end of the long row of huts, the dull ring of the axe reaching me a split second after the moment of impact of metal against wood, and a leaner man was stacking the logs beside the last hut as they fell from the chopping block.

The cold was creeping up through my legs as I sat with my back against the trunk of the tree, breathing in its ancient life and three centuries of weather. I had got up to stretch my legs and shake some warmth into them when I heard men's voices along the path that ran fifty yards from the beech tree. I thought they would continue down the path towards the camp but then heard them drawing nearer, having left the path. In some alarm, I scrambled up the tree as fast as I could, while trying not to make a sound. I climbed up about twenty feet and sat on a thick branch that reached up towards the next beech tree. It was the first time that I had climbed a tree since I was a child and it felt exhilarating somehow to be up high, away from the cold ground and the men.

They stopped in a small clearing no more than thirty feet away from me. There were five of them, and there he was! I was both relieved and very glad to see him again. They took out their clay pipes and lit them, smoking in a small cluster and talking animatedly to each other in their lilting accents, sending smoke up into the still air. I could not hear what they were saying but caught the odd word when they raised their voices: something that sounded like 'hangman' and then 'the bastard', which sent a jolt through me, and then 'pay him back'. 'Can't break the law,' the bearlike man interrupted the other men, who seemed to be in on some intrigue that he was not part of.

I kept very still up on that branch, the cold biting into my fingers as I held on to the rough bark and a fear rising in me that the men might turn to look up at something, the sound of a bird perhaps, and see me. It was, after all, still daylight. But they kept their hatted heads down and did not look around themselves much. Only once did the towering Irishman glance up, as if towards me; I shrank down as low as I could against the branch, and to my relief I did not think he had seen me. Before long they made their way back to the footpath and their voices grew fainter as they went down towards their camp.

I waited a while until I was sure that they had really gone and that no-one else was coming along the path, then climbed down the ladder of the branches to the ground. I was stiff from sitting in the same position on the branch and from the bitter cold, and I walked as quickly as I could towards home to get some warmth into my limbs again. There was still frost in the margins of the fields and in the shadows of the trees at the edge of the wood where the weak sunlight had not melted it away. The church bells in Much Purlock were ringing away across the fields, and I could only think that they must be announcing the funeral of some poor soul, perhaps one of the crones I saw hobbling through the market every Wednesday and whose deaths seemed to come each year when the cold arrived.

My father was in his consulting room with a patient when I got back to the house. The consulting room door was slightly ajar, which was unusual when my father was with a patient. I could hear the woman sobbing, and when she was not sobbing she was talking in a torrent of words that were muffled by the door and by her tears. I crept up closer without making a sound and was astonished to hear the unknown woman say, after further gasps and sobs, 'Oh, I'm so happy, William, so very happy.' How dare she call her doctor, my father, by his first name? How dare she?

I went out of the hallway, through the kitchen and into the back garden to gather my thoughts. Who on earth was this woman? A lone male blackbird was singing in the apple tree on that icy afternoon but could give me no answer. There was no sign of the insidious disease when I went up closer to the tree and looked up at his shiny beak before he flew away: the pestilence seemed to have passed over the local blackbirds for the time being at least.

I went back inside and met my father in the hallway, looking flushed but grinning from ear to ear like the cat that had got the cream. It was very strange to see him so gleeful: that was the only word I could think of. It made me angry to see him like that. Then *her*: somewhere around his age, slight and mousy, also smiling, more coyly than gleefully, as she stood in the hallway behind him as if she needed his protection. Who exactly was she, and why was she standing there like that in my hallway? She did not look as if much was wrong with her.

'Oh, hello Grace,' he said. 'I didn't know you were back already. I'd, um, I'd like to introduce you to Mrs Samuels. Her late husband Frederick was, ah, he was a very good friend of mine at Cambridge. Very sadly, dear Freddie died at far too young an age a few years ago.'

'Does Mrs Samuels live locally?' I enquired, not looking her in the eye and already knowing full well what the answer would be. I had never set eyes on her before.

'Ah, no, Grace: she's just come down from London—mind you, by stagecoach, you'll be glad to hear—and she'll be lodging at the Star Inn.'

'Please tell her, William,' the woman said. My father blushed beetroot red and looked as if his legs were about to give way. He held on to the hall table for support.

'Um, ah,' he said, looking at her rather than at me, as if he needed rescuing. He was usually such a loquacious man. 'A-as you know, Grace, I-I've spent quite a lot of t-time in London over the past year or two. You know I've been to medical conferences, b-but I've also been courting Josephine, ah Mrs Samuels.'

'William, it's nothing to be ashamed of,' mousy Mrs Samuels said, still smiling nervously and putting her hand on his arm to reassure him.

'I-I have asked Josephine to be my wife,' he said, still not looking at me, the smile quite gone from his lips.

'And has she said yes?' I asked him, utterly flabbergasted. Suddenly, my earlier idea of concocting a love potion and slipping it to him seemed to me like nothing more than stupid child's play. Now I could think of nothing worse than having another woman, some replacement mother figure, in my house. I would simply not be able to stand it. All the simpering and meddling and interfering would drive me to distraction.

'Of course, dear child,' she said. 'I'm absolutely over the moon. And Freddie would have understood. I've been too long a widow, as your father has a widower.' My father just stood by the hall table, looking down at his feet and stroking his betrothed's shoulder soothingly.

'Well, don't ever expect me to call you mother! And I'm no child—I'm seventeen!' I replied, anger rising in my throat. I knew that I would not be able to quell it before it reached my mouth and I ran down the hallway and out of the back door, into the garden and off down the road.

It was night-time before I went back to the house again. The curtains were all drawn across the windows and there was only one lamp behind the curtains of my father's study, glowing orange-red through the pitch dark. The house was quiet, and they were not there. I supposed they were dining at the Star Inn or further afield at the New Inn on the Ross road. It was a relief they were not there: I was still furious despite my long walk, and I would have not been able to contain myself if they had been there. Love potions be damned: I did not want another woman in the house. I did not want another woman taking the place of my mother. I did not want another woman taking the place of me. Unless my father saw fit to employ a cook or a scullery maid again, to relieve me of some of my dullening chores, I did not want any other woman in the house while I was still living there.

An owl was out hunting somewhere above the garden again and the bright moon was hanging high in the starlit sky. I stood in the kitchen doorway looking out into that perfect midwinter night and thought about leaving home right there and then, but I could not think of a single place that I could go. I had no living grandparents; no aunts and uncles that I had ever met, even though my mother had left behind a brother and a sister just across the Gloucestershire border in Coleford. I had no cousins that I knew who would be happy to give me a welcome and a roof over my head; no childhood friends in nearby villages with whom I had stayed in touch. I had no choice at all but to stay.

It was nearly eleven o'clock when my father came home. I was already up in bed, and I could hear him scraping his icy boots outside the door before he took them off, then lifting the latch and shutting the heavy oak door behind him as if it was a sunny summer's morning and he did not have a care in the world. He whistled to himself as he settled into his armchair in front of the fire and there was his echo a few minutes later as the whistling kettle came to the boil. I had not heard him in such good spirits for many months. I would have to increase his dose of ground mushrooms, that was for sure.

Chapter Twenty-Two

A pair of finely turned ankles and legs are hanging down from a branch high up in the beech tree near to whose mighty weathered trunk we have gathered. I do not think the others have noticed them, but I cannot help glancing up from time to time: I so want it to be her but cannot see her face from this angle with the winter sunlight streaming down from behind her and all the branches in the way. Being so near her for the first time, if it is indeed her, has made my heart beat faster and rather taken my breath away.

Are we the reason she has climbed up there, thirty or so feet above the icy carpet of leaves, or was she in the tree for some reason I cannot begin to imagine—perhaps simply for the joy of being up high, away from the world—before she saw us coming through the trees? She will hear me if I tell the others to keep their voices down, so they talk away, oblivious to the silent listener almost right above us. I can see her breath pluming in the air and wish that I could see her face.

We have come into the wood to talk where O'Donnell, Mr Menzies our foreman and some of the others cannot hear us. There has been ferment in the camp again: the men are still angry at Mr Menzies for the way he is with us and they want him gone. They seem to see me as a leader somehow, perhaps just because of my sheer physical size, and they think I should confront him, but I do not want to get involved in any of that. How can a man who is not yet twenty lead anyone anyhow? There is nothing to be gained by threats or violence, and I cannot lose this work now.

'Still with us, Sean?' Adam asks, prodding my arm and laughing. I realise that I have not heard a single word of what they have been saying. Nine months of working with these men—or, when not working, of listening to them seethe and simmer at the railway company or the food or the huts and now at Mr Menzies (it was never like this with Mr Sansom)—has left me unable to take much of what they say seriously. I would much rather think about the girl. I glance up again and she is shifting backwards now down the thick branch towards the trunk of the tree. I cannot risk looking up for too long in case one of the others follows my gaze and notices her.

'Joe was just saying that we should think about going on strike,' Adam says. 'Perhaps the company will listen to our complaints about that bastard then.'

'Don't any of you know which side your bread's buttered on?' I say. 'You're all really so stupid that you think they won't stop our food, turf us out of our huts, and send us packing if we down tools for even so much as an hour of our shifts?'

'What d'you suggest then, McClennan?' Nathaniel from County Cork asks. He has an abrasive manner that I do not much care for.

'Grit our teeth and carry on, unless you've got a better idea.'

I glance up again and catch the briefest of glimpses of the girl's face looking down, and my heart misses a beat. I cannot be sure as her head goes up again in half a second, but it is her, it must be her. From what I can see she has the girl's nut-brown hair and her pale skin. I do not think she has seen me looking, but she must be able to hear every word that we are saying. God knows what she must make of us and our petty intrigues. What must we look like from up above with our navvies' clothes, worn-out hats, and unshaven cheeks? A girl who looks the way she does is bound to be walking out with some lucky fellow already.

'Sean,' Adam says, 'are you still with us or off somewhere in your head again?'

'Sorry, lads, it's just too cold to be standing around out here doing nothing for much longer.' It was not that I was particularly frozen, but I realised that she could not climb down from the tree if she wanted to while we were standing no more than ten yards from it.

'We're not getting anywhere anyway, are we?' Nathaniel says. 'We should go back down. Menzies and the hagman will be waiting.'

'We can't go on strike and we can't take matters into our own hands, so what the hell can we do about Menzies?' Adam asks resignedly.

'Keep our heads down,' I say. 'Keep our heads down and hope he gets moved elsewhere eventually.'

I turn to look back at the girl one last time as we begin to walk between the trees towards the path. Her feet are feeling for the next branch down now, and they do so deftly and surely. She must have quite some courage to be so confident at that height. As she lowers herself down to the branch, I catch sight of the back of her head and her tangle of mahogany hair. I cannot be certain, but this girl, whoever she is, looks so like the girl in the marketplace. I wish that I could see her face. These men, these lumpen men. I just want the company of a woman.

When we get down into the camp, O'Donnell is standing by the fire, his hands on his hips and scowling at us like a loudmouthed scold. Although he has no authority over us anymore, he likes to poke his truffling Tipperary snout in where he is not wanted. I would very much like to punch that nose and shut him up one day.

'Where've you been, fellas?' he asks, sneering. 'Off conspiring somewhere again, were we?'

'Keep your nose out of our business,' Adam says, 'and try not to cause any more accidents.'

'Why you fucking —' O'Donnell says, then quickly trails off when Menzies comes out of his hut.

'What's all this chitchat about?' he asks. 'Why aren't you men down on the line?'

'Our shift was the early one today, Sir,' I reply, wanting to address him as anything but that. He should know that we were there, seeing as he was the one telling us what to do. I sometimes wonder whether he can even put names to our faces half the time.

'Well, keep it down,' he says, staring at the five of us but seeming not to notice O'Donnell at all. 'This isn't a ladies' tea party. Work or cook or sit in your huts, but save your chatter for elsewhere. Some of the men are trying to rest this afternoon, including me.'

'I wish he'd rest in eternal peace,' Joe whispers to me and laughs.

'What are you sniggering about, O'Shaughnessy?' Menzies asks.

'Oh, nothing much, Sir,' Joe answers. 'Just remembering an amusing anecdote.'

'I'm glad that nothing much can make you guffaw so. I don't see much to laugh about around here,' he says, swivelling his head round to survey the fire and the huts. 'O'Donnell, shouldn't you be down on the line with the hagman's team?'

'Y-yes, Sir. I just came back up because he asked me to set the water to boil on the fire for our four o'clock tea.'

It is good to see O'Donnell squirm. This is how Menzies is all day long: it is a wonder that the railway company sees fit to employ him as a foreman. Admittedly, he knows how to put the engineer's plans into effect, but he only gets us to do the work with scowls and half-threats and curses. Mr Sansom was an erudite gentleman, whereas Menzies is nothing more than a bully and a thug with a flair for making two-dimensional plans into three-dimensional reality.

Adam, Joe, and I have nothing better to do than to walk back into the wood and over the top down into Much Purlock. I am hoping I might see the girl again on our way through the town, but there is no sign of her. The Star Inn is quiet this evening, with just two or three locals propping up the bar and no-one about in the saloon. The public houses in County Sligo would be much busier than this at the end of a working day, with labourers and farmhands coming in from building sites or fields to quench their thirst for stout and talk of the prices of barley or brick. It is dead in here, as if all the menfolk of the town have been ordered inside by their wives.

'What'll it be, gentlemen?' John the innkeeper asks as we sit down at the table nearest to the window. He has never been unfriendly to us. Right from the first time that we walked in here late last March and the locals fell silent, hearing our Irish accents and seeing our rough navvies' clothes as we came in, he was never hesitant or wary with us. I think he even welcomed us with the very same words.

'Three glasses of Leominster's finest please, John,' Joe requests.

'Do you know a very pretty girl around here with dark brown hair and pale skin?' I ask John as he pulls the beer.

'You poor lamb,' Adam pokes me in the ribs and laughs. 'He's smitten with a girl he says he saw up a tree!'

'I know what I saw, and I've seen her before right here in the marketplace.'

John looks up from polishing the taps, flipping the white cloth that he uses for that purpose over his shoulder again, and then goes back to pulling the beer, the froth at the top of the glasses having bubbled and subsided away. 'The one with chestnut hair and a face like an angel?' he asks. 'If that's who you mean, it can only be Grace Matthews. She's quite a stunner, isn't she?'

'Grace,' I played her name around my lips. 'That must be her. What's she like?'

'She seems like a nice girl,' John says, 'but she mostly keeps herself to herself. She's the doctor's daughter.'

'Planning on trying to court her, are you?' Joe asks, winking at Adam and reaching up to take his beer from John, who has come over with the tray of glasses.

I really need this glass of bitter and take a long drink. 'Are we Irish not allowed to dream, then?' I say, joining in the laughter. 'I thought our very nation was built on myths and dreams.'

'There's no harm in dreaming, as long as you know it's only that—a dream,' Adam says. 'A local girl's never going to be interested in one of us.'

'Slàinte,' I say, raising my glass. 'Cheers and thanks for your words of encouragement.'

'I'm serious, Sean: a strapping farm boy like you should be courting a pretty country girl back home.'

'But we're here, not there, and I'm damned well not going to wait another two or three years, until I'm twenty-one or twenty-two to meet a girl.'

'I second that,' Joe says. 'The men—you two excepted—are beginning to make me want to leave this place. O'Donnell and Menzies might be the worst of them, but some of the others aren't much better. Now, if we had *girls* here that would change everything.'

'John,' I call, raising my glass, 'another three pints of Leominster bitter, please.'

'A fine ale this one, isn't it?' he says, already beginning to pull them. 'I'm always tempted to have a glass or two of it myself while I'm serving, but I shouldn't.'

'Have one on us,' I say. 'Surely it can't do too much harm.'

'Perhaps not this, but you should've tried their other bitter last year. That had some of the regulars tripping over the sill on their way out.'

It is bitterly cold and very dark when we leave the inn, and the air has turned thick with fog. As we climb the path up through the wood, the trees come at us as sudden and pale as ghosts when we get near them. Even the owls are not out hunting on a night like this.

I can just make out a shadow moving along the path ahead of us, and it seems to be going from tree to tree as we follow it about thirty yards back. Our footsteps are muffled by the damp leaves and the dense trees here, and I do not think that the figure, whoever it is, can hear us. It must be a child as it looks too small to be fully grown, even in this swirling, milky dark that distorts everything. The figure turns to peer back through the fog from time to time as we follow it up to the top of the wood. I do not know whether we have been seen, or whether this shape shifting on the path between the trees up ahead is looking back for something behind us that we have not heard.

'Have you noticed, Adam?' I ask.

'Noticed what?' he asks, breathing hard against the gradient of the hill.

Night Comes Down

'There's someone up ahead.'

'I've been trying to look where I'm going, keeping my eyes to the ground.'

'I thought I was seeing things,' Joe says behind us on the path. 'Seems that we're not the only ones out here at this hour.'

We are making our way slowly down the escarpment towards the camp when the figure stops again ahead of us on the path. It does not move off this time from where it is standing but seems to be waiting for something—perhaps for us. As we come nearer, I see that it is the boy, Jack, without a hat or a scarf and in only a thin-looking overcoat.

'What on earth are you doing out here so late and in this fog?'

'There's been a fox about and Ma asked me to guard the chickens, but I was freezing and didn't want to go back inside in case she scolded me.'

'How old are you?' Adam asks him, putting his hand on the boy's shoulder like an older brother.

'Twelve,' he says, quietly yet defiantly.

'We thought you were a ghost haunting our path,' Joe says laughing. 'Why choose such a foggy, cold night to come out here just so as not to go back inside to your poor Ma?'

'I wanted to walk to get warm and was curious about yer. I've met him before,' the boy says, pointing at me.

'I remember you, Master Jack. Here: take my scarf. You'll need it for the way home. It seems to be getting colder by the minute.'

'Thanks, Mister,' he says, shivering as he looks up at us like a waif abandoned in this wood. He wraps my woollen scarf tightly around his neck twice and then tucks its ends into the collar of his coat. 'I'll bring it back, I promise.'

'Don't worry, lad. You can keep it if you want. I have another one.'

'Watch how you go,' Adam says to him. 'You should get back to your Ma now. She'll be worried.'

'It's you who should be worried,' he replies, a hint of dark mischief playing across his face now. 'Ma says she'd curse you to hell if she could for what you've done to our land here. Course I said she never should. And that sickness in the rooks en crows. Who says it can't get to us, too, if it wants to? It's you lot who brought it here, she says, or it were all your digging en scratching at our soil.'

'What sickness do you mean exactly?' I ask, but he is already off walking into the night down the path towards the town, half blinded by the fog. I swear that it is getting heavier. It creeps around us, blown by the breeze, and reaches into the darkened trees. It is not a night to be out.

Chapter Twenty-Three

Much Purlock, 1841

Primped and preening Mrs Samuels was a visitor to our house every day for the eight nights she stayed at the Star Inn. I heard her giggling in the consulting room and her powdered face seemed to peer out from whatever room I was about to enter. It did not seem right that a woman of her age, and a widow to boot, was quite so jolly, and her simpering light-heartedness was infectious to those susceptible to the disease: my father went around that long week with a smile on his face and a chuckle in his voice. He would have to pay the price when she was gone.

He took to wearing the embroidered purple velvet waistcoat that he usually reserved for special occasions. It had bulged over his stomach at my confirmation in a hushed and gloomy St. Andrew's church when I was fourteen and it had been the centrepiece of the party at Chard's Olde Bookshop in Hereford to celebrate the publication of his monograph on diseases of the blood. The waistcoat's mother of pearl buttons seemed to wink in the candlelight at Mrs Samuels as we ate in near silence at the dining table, and its effect was of a theatrical opulence quite unsuited to an isolated stone house in the wintry middle of nowhere.

'Grace, I'm going to accompany Mrs Samuels back to London tomorrow,' my father announced suddenly. His voice was too loud after the quiet scraping of our cutlery over the China plates of beef stew and dumplings that she had prepared. I had had to go out while she was preparing the meal, so annoyed was I by her looking in all the wrong cupboards for the utensils, pots, and pans and by her complaining to my father that we still had no cook.

'William, as we're getting married in the new year, Grace should probably call me *Josephine* now,' Mrs Samuels said, touching my father's arm and beaming at me across the table with her too-white face. 'We'll be familiar, after all. I'll be her stepmother.' My mind curdled at those words.

'I'll call you Mrs Samuels,' I replied. Only the evening outside was icier still. My father looked down, vexed and abashed, at his second helping of stew.

'We'll take the train from Gloucester tomorrow, Josephine,' he said, as if to provoke me further. 'It'll be so much quicker and more convenient than the stagecoach that brought you here. I don't mind bearing the expense.'

'As you wish, dear,' Mrs Samuels said, as if replying to the both of us at the same time.

A brilliantly black sky sewn with the pearls of a million stars greeted me when I went up to the well. I wished on those stars, oh how I wished, that my mother was there with me: she would have known how to comfort me, how to distract me from my father's selfishness and his merry widow's painted-on glee; but of course things were as they were because my dear mother was gone. After her death, the world had tilted on its axis somehow, and this tittering widow now sitting at our kitchen table was the result. If only my herbalist's skills could conjure a falling-out-of-love potion.

They left the next morning, and it was a relief to have the house to myself: I could go wherever I liked without the spectre of Mrs Samuels haunting me, or of my father's amorous whispers and giggles following me from room to room. The frost crunched underfoot as I walked over the grass, and a pale sun shone in the sky. On winter days such as those it is quite possible to believe in magic and the divine. I walked up into the icy woods and went up over the other side to my usual beech tree. The tree trunks around me were all still white with frost where the sun had not yet reached into the wood, and it was too cold to stay under the branches of that tree for long.

I wanted to watch the camp, but there was no-one about down below me among the huts; I thought that the men must all be at work on the railway line, as it was not yet noon. I waited for perhaps half an hour, stamping my booted feet trying to keep warm and keeping my hands deep in the pockets of my coat, but the only figure that I saw was a small thin man with a pronounced limp going between the towering woodpile and the fire and back again. My feet were tingling with the cold and beginning to go numb standing on that frozen ground, so I left the cover of the beech tree and walked through the still wood back to the path. A web of sunlight was up above me, but it was quite dark beneath those trees.

Suddenly, as if from nowhere, a man was coming towards me along the path. I looked up and saw him properly when he was perhaps only ten yards away from me and realised with a shock that it was my giant of a man, the one I had followed from the Star Inn back to the camp, narrowly missed being seen by when I climbed into the beech tree that time to hide from him and the others, and dreamed about more than once up in my lonely bed. I blushed at the very thought of it all but had no time to leave the path again or to turn around and go back the other way down towards the camp. I stumbled on a tree root in my confusion and almost fell as he was about to go past me, having raised his cap in greeting.

'Watch yourself!' He laughed as he caught my arm and steadied me. 'Careful where you step.'

'Th-thank you, sir,' I stuttered, embarrassed and ashamed by my own clumsiness. 'I wasn't looking where I was putting my feet.'

'It's easy to do,' he said. Even in the half-light of the winter wood I could see that he had twinkling eyes and a kind smile as he looked down at me. He was clean-shaven and, despite the cold, his skin was weathered deep brown by all the work outdoors.

'You're from the camp down there, aren't you?' I asked, already knowing the answer of course.

'Yes, I'm one of the navvies working on the new line. My name's Sean McClennan,' he said, reaching out his hand. It was rough and huge when I shook it, my small hand also no stranger to hard work. 'What are you doing out here all on your own?'

'I've been exploring these woods since I was a small child. I have always felt they were mine somehow,' I replied, still flustered by my coming face to face with him so suddenly. 'Well, I'd better be on my way.' I did not know what else to say now that he was standing right there in front of me.

'Was it you that time?' he asked, his eyes bright and the smile still there on his lips.

'Was it me where?'

'Up in the tree on the edge of the clearing,' he said, pointing behind me and laughing a deep laugh.

'You saw me?' I asked, going redder still. 'I didn't think you had.'

'Your legs dangling down from that branch rather gave you away,' he said, and laughed again. 'Although the other men didn't seem to notice.'

'I was there first,' I said, managing only a shy smile. 'Well, I really had better be on my way down to Purlock now. I've got chores to do before it gets too dark.'

'So long then, I hope we meet again,' he said in his thick brogue, walking off at a brisk pace down the path behind me, the sound of his footsteps dampened by the fallen leaves. 'Oh, you didn't tell me your name,' he called back after me, as if as an afterthought.

'It's Grace, Grace Matthews,' I replied, with a sudden fluttering lightness in my chest and a quickening of my step towards home. I did not know if he had heard me.

* * *

My thoughts kept returning to him as winter tightened its grip on the land. That lightness in my chest, the feeling that I was floating somehow when I thought of him, did not leave me as the days became shorter and darker. I did not know him, but I knew

I felt something for him even if I could not yet put that feeling into words. But how could I care for a navvy working on the railway line? It made me recoil at my own weakness. I despised my father for using the railway from Gloucester; I had attended the Anti-Railway League and town hall meetings; I had stood waving banners on street corners; but I could not stop myself thinking about one of the workers on the branch line. It did not make any sense. It turned out that I was just as hypocritical as everyone else.

My father came back from London the week before Christmas, after four or five days in the capital with Mrs Samuels. I was cleaning the dishes in the bucket with the stiff brush when he walked in fresh from the pony and trap from Gloucester. It could not go on like this, and I had decided I would have a word with him at the right moment, make him advertise for a scullery maid at the very least. It had been almost seven years, and Mrs Samuels's arrival had changed everything. He could no longer say that he did not want another woman in the house.

He looked in ruddy good health: his cleanshaven cheeks were aflame with the cold, and he had pomaded his dark hair so that it gleamed in the winter light. He was still wearing his velvet waistcoat with the mother of pearl buttons and looked like nothing so much as a superannuated dandy come down to the countryside to take the winter air.

That night when my father took his pep, after my fine lamb casserole and two glasses of Bordeaux wine before his port, it was equal parts snuff and ground mushroom. At first, he sat there in his armchair smiling benignly into the crackling fire, then his expression slowly began to change: he looked haunted, as if he had seen a ghost.

'They're going round and round,' he murmured to himself, his chin sunk down into his chest and his glazed dark eyes reflecting the light of the fire.

'What are?' I asked. He did not look up or even acknowledge my question.

'Round and round,' he said again. 'Look at their glinting eyes and their teeth.'

'There's nothing there, Father. There's just us, this room, and the fire.'

'Growling and pacing round and round,' he said, before slumping down further into his armchair and seeming to fall into a stupor. His eyes were still open, looking at nothing that I could see, but they barely blinked and did not move.

After a while his eyes closed, and he started snoring softly. A thin trail of saliva ran down from the corner of his mouth onto the collar of his shirt. I sat mending the hem of my dress with a needle and thread and staring into the fire, which was slowly ebbing after its earlier vigour. It was approaching nine o'clock, and the night was windless and black. The ticking of the grandfather clock in the hallway sounded loudly in that stillness.

Suddenly, my father sat bolt upright, his eyes as wide as saucers, and shouted at the top of his lungs. 'No, no! They're coming for me! They're snapping at my legs!'

Before I knew it, he got to his stockinged feet. Then he was off walking like a somnambulist, looking neither left nor right, his arms thrust out in front of him, up the hallway and out through the kitchen into the back garden.

'Father, where are you going?' I called after him, but he did not seem to hear me. After a minute or two, I followed him out of the back door and up through the garden with the lantern. He was trying to climb into the well when I found him, the lantern's flickering light picking him out of the dark.

'Father, stop! What on earth are you doing?'

'They're frightened of water. There's water down there,' he said like a simpleton, with one now-bare leg over the low wall of the well and a hand holding on to the crank handle. I pulled hard at his sleeve and took hold of his arm and, although he tried to resist me, got him away from the well.

'Father, what the devil were you thinking? You could have killed yourself!' He said nothing but let me lead him meekly through the dark garden down to the house, his head turned all the while back towards the well, me holding the lantern with one hand and his arm with the other.

I locked the back door and slipped the key into my pocket, and he went silently up to bed, his bare feet leaving a trail of damp leaves and mud on the runner in the hallway. I sat there in the kitchen long into the night with only the light of the lantern for company. I wondered with some unease, I must admit, what if anything of this strange and disturbing episode he would remember in the cold light of morning.

Chapter Twenty-Four

Herefordshire, 1841

After another bitter night, a bitter day. The frost cracks under my feet as I walk, even though it is already past midday. I woke up frozen through and needed to thaw my hands and feet by the stove before I could even begin to pull on my boots and a second pair of gloves. Mr Jones promised us a better stove for our hut, and for every other hut here, but nothing has arrived. O'Donnell moans about the lack of proper heating and says that things were so much better when he was working on the canals back home in Ireland, but he will not say anything against Mr Jones or Mr Menzies themselves. His unspoken guilt at Mr Sansom's death seems to have cowed him to authority somehow; it is either that or he is hoping to be made hagman again one day.

This path between the camp and the town, going up through the wood and down the other side, has become almost as familiar to me as the one between Rose Farm and the western edge of Binn Ghulbain, although I do not love it nearly so much, despite the beauty of the trees here and the stillness of this place. The icy cold has muted all the creatures in the wood, and there is no sound except my footsteps and my steady breathing as my breath plumes out into the frozen air. I am making my way down the path about half a mile from where the wood ends and the first of the houses of the town begin when I see a flickering movement deep in the trees off to my left. There is something or someone in there, I am sure of it, but they are obscured by the trunks and the branches and the gloom. Something glints in the half-light and there is that flickering movement again.

I pick my way carefully between the trees, trying not to make a sound and looking out for branches and sticks that might crack under my weight. As I edge nearer, I can see a figure bending down then straightening back up again beneath the bare branches of an oak tree. The figure looks small, but it is so hard to see in this gloom. There is that flickering glint of something metallic again and then the sound of scraping and digging at the earth.

I creep nearer still and hide myself behind the trunk of a beech tree. Whoever it is does not seem to have heard me, as the scraping and the digging has masked any sound that my footsteps might have made over the icy leaves on the frozen ground. The figure has its back to me. It must be a child, it is so short. It bends forward again to peer into the large hole that it has dug, and then I see them: three rows of black rooks and crows that are laid out on the bare earth beside the hole. I know that figure, the way it holds itself. I have seen it before.

It half twists to look up at something in the sky above the bare trees but does not turn round fully in my direction. When I see the silhouette of his face, though, I know who it is at once: it is that boy Jack again.

He puts down his spade by the side of the hole and gently pushes the carcasses of the dead birds with the side of his booted foot one by one into the blackness of the soil. It is the strangest thing that I have ever seen in my nineteen years on this earth. I do not know whether to come out from behind the tree and go over to him to ask him what he is doing, or to leave him alone in his sad and unsettling task.

Then I remember his talk of a sickness in the rooks and crows when we met him along the path deep in the fog that time and decide to leave him well alone. I walk back through the wood to the path without turning round even once.

***

I really want to go into the Star Inn for a pint of bitter, to warm myself in front of the fire and just to sit for a while trying to understand what I saw back there in the wood. I do not know if I should feel sorry for that strange boy or horrified by him. It makes me wonder whether there is something I am missing about this place. My shift starts at two o'clock, though, and Mr Menzies always gives us such an earful if he finds out that we have been drinking before we turn up for our work. 'The company doesn't pay you lazy bastards to waste your money on drink and then waste my time,' he said to Adam last week when he smelled whisky on his breath one morning. 'This is precise work that needs precise minds, not brains pickled by alcohol.'

'It was last night, and you'd be a fool not to drink in a place like this,' Adam replied, gesturing around at the rain-soaked huts as we stood by the spitting fire.

'Who are you calling a fool?' the foreman said, his hackles rising.

'It was just a turn of phrase, Sir, nothing more,' Adam replied. And then as a whispered aside to me: 'And you'd be a fool, too, to believe that.'

Rather than going into the inn, I make my way through the market. There are more stallholders than customers here today, blowing into their gloved hands and stamping their feet to keep warm. They stand behind their stalls for hours on end for little reward on days like these, when all that people want to do is to stay inside out of the cold. I never feel unwelcome here. Coming from all over the county as the stallholders do, the town is not their home either, and they have little reason to object to us navvies going around the market and buying what we need. I need to get some twine and a needle and thread from the haberdasher on the other side of the marketplace and some leeks and onions somewhere here. Our diet is far too lacking in the bounties of this country: we are given an excess of meat, starch, and fat but hardly any vegetables and fruit. If we were at sea, the captain would be worrying about scurvy by now. These large red onions will do, and those leeks look well-grown to me. If I was at home, I would cut them up and add them to a beef stew, but we have no beef here apart from tongue, only sinewy mutton and fatty bacon.

Before I set off back to the camp again, I go and stand for a while under the cross on the edge of the marketplace to see whether Grace, her name newly minted on my tongue, will walk past again. Two starlings are fighting over a scrap of bread not three feet from my boots, apparently unaware or unconcerned that I am here. While the stallholders are never unfriendly, the townsfolk of Much Purlock still stare at us whenever they see us, and the men in the Star Inn start talking in low voices whenever we go in. John's friendliness towards us does little to persuade them to do otherwise. I do not feel uncomfortable standing here, and God knows I could handle myself if one of the local men taunted me or squared up to me, but this cold does not exactly make you want to stand around doing nothing for too long.

She does not seem to be about today. I wonder what it would feel like to touch her, to hold her, to kiss her—to kiss any girl for that matter? Kisses from Ma on my forehead or my cheek are all I have ever known of a woman's lips, and her kisses stopped after I was confirmed when I was thirteen. O'Donnell still tries to tell us about his conquests back in Ireland, but none of us will listen to him now. We are all in the same boat here: huddled in our huts in the camp, completely lacking in female company, apart from those men who buy it from the widow Mary. We are a stew of men thrown together, all sweat and brawn and unkempt hair, clothes washed at best in buckets of cold water and bodies only washed where clothes give way to the skin on our hands, faces and necks. If we are lucky, we go for a dip in Cuckoo Mere a mile's walk from the valley, but only every ten days at the most.

* * *

There is no-one about as I come to the edge of the wood, and I can see no movement between the trees now as I walk further along the path. The boy must have gone. I probably would not be able to find the exact spot again where he dug the hole even if I tried to look for it. How many oaks are there in this part of the wood alone?

The peace of this place is the tonic that I need. When I was still too young to work on the farm, Niall was usually far too busy to keep me company, so I was left to my own devices while he and Ma and Da were out in the fields. Once I had grown old enough to join them in their work before and after school each day, much of what I did was still solitary—mucking out, turning the hay, less strenuous tasks such as those. Some of my unhappiness with life in the camp comes from the fact that I can never be alone. I retreat in my sleep, but when I wake up the three pairs of eyes of my hut-mates are always on me or, if they themselves are still asleep, they soon wake up at the sound of my moving about. After that, I am not away from the men again until I go to sleep the following night, unless it is to run errands or out on walks like this.

I am looking down as I walk and simply do not see her. Before I know it, she is coming towards me along the path and my ox-heart leaps in my chest. She is dressed in a thick woollen coat that is wrapped tightly around her and her hair is hidden away under a fur hat, but that lovely face is hers. I am not sure whether to keep on looking at her or to lower my eyes so as not to alarm her; but as she comes nearer, as she is about to walk past, she stumbles suddenly over something, a tree root or a stone, and instinctively reaches out her hands towards me to stop herself from falling.

'Watch out!' I say, laughing and catching her arm to steady her. 'Mind where you step.'

'Thank you, Sir.' ('Sir?' No-one has ever called me that before!) 'I wasn't looking where I was going.' She seems slightly embarrassed; she has a sweet-sounding voice and a gentle but self-assured smile.

'It's easy to do on this rough path.' I still cannot believe that I am talking to her. I wish my heart would stop beating so hard. Her eyes really are as cornflower blue as I hoped they would be.

'You're from the camp, aren't you?' she asks, looking up at me. She must remember me from overhearing us talking under the tree that time as she was sitting on the branch almost directly above us, otherwise I do not see how she can know. I am not dressed in my navvy's clothes today. She surely cannot remember me from watching all of us men working on the line.

'Yes, my name's Sean McClennan,' I say, reaching out my hand to shake hers, which is small and soft through her woollen glove.

'I'd better be on my way,' she replies, letting go of my hand too soon. I wish she would stop a while longer. Seeing her up close is the best thing that has happened to me since I came here.

'Was it you that time?' I ask, hoping that this will keep her talking.

'Was it me where?' She looks at me, not understanding.

'Up in the tree.' I laugh again because I am nervous and because I want to reassure her.

'You saw me?' Her cheeks blush a coral pink unless it is the cold air on her skin. 'I didn't think you had.'

'Your legs dangling down from that branch rather gave you away.'

'Well, I was there first,' she says, smiling both with her mouth and with her eyes. 'Well, I've got chores to do before nightfall and really should be on my way.'

'You didn't tell me your name,' I call after her as she starts off again towards the town. I already know it, of course, but want to hear it from her mouth.

'It's Grace, Grace Matthews,' she turns back to me and smiles.

My heart is singing as I stride the last half mile through the wood before dropping down the steep escarpment towards the camp. My mind has not yet caught up with my heart: the thing that I have been longing for these last hard months has happened when I was least expecting it. Then there is the strangest thing: all the birds in this wood that were silent have suddenly started calling and singing again.

Chapter Twenty-Five

Much Purlock, 1841

A crackling frost and a patient I did not recognise greeted my father when he came down to breakfast. The man coughed in the consulting room while my father drank a cup of tea and ate a slice of bread at the kitchen table, saying nothing other than a brief 'Good morning, Grace', and then searching distractedly around the kitchen and his study for his spectacles. He looked perhaps paler than he usually did in the morning, before fresh air and food brought the colour to his cheeks, but there was no other obvious physical sign of the disturbance of the night before. But something was not quite right with him: he looked blank behind the eyes, deadened somehow, as if he was half out of this world and half in it. I wondered what he would see when he looked in the mirror, how he would diagnose himself.

He went into his consulting room and closed the door. I left him to his patient and went out into the icy air and the sunshine. The first thing that greeted me on the lane was a rook up in the bare apple tree behind the Jennings' wall. Its beak appeared to be untroubled by the rot, but there was something strange about its eyes: they were milky-looking and blind, although the bird did not look old. It jerked its head up and down and from side to side when it heard my footsteps on the lane, but it could not see me. I stopped and watched it for a while. It jumped from branch to branch but did not move far from the tree; it cawed and bobbed its head and cawed again. It was as if it was trying to tell me something, but I could not understand it and it could not see me. I took it as a bad omen, that rook, and left it behind in its apple tree with a sense of foreboding. The outside world had been let in, the railway was coming, and this is what we got for it.

It was Wednesday and market day again. I went between the stalls with my mother's wicker basket over my arm and bought some winter greens and two fresh trout from the river Wye. Perhaps it was just my tiredness, having gone up to bed long after midnight, but I began to worry as I went around the stalls that my father would start to question things before too long, that he would begin to put two and two together, and that I would be found out. He was a man of science, after all. He always had to know the *why* of things, to look for a cause and a diagnosis.

The stallholders huddled under thick coats, blowing on their cupped hands and stamping their feet to keep warm. Mrs Jenks was there selling her eggs and I bought half a dozen from her, white ones that she laughed shyly about when I handed over my silver sixpence. There was no sign of Sean McClennan. He was not outside the Star Inn that morning nor with some of the other navvies who were walking around the marketplace, so I went with my basket of provisions up into the woods, hoping to see him on the path again or to spy him down in the camp.

The day had started out sparkling and bright, but by midday the sun had become a ghost of itself behind grey, snow-laden clouds and the air felt heavier somehow. Now a sudden sleet had begun to fall. The leafless trees in the wood gave little shelter from the sky and the sleet got into my eyes, down the nape of my neck despite my hood, and into the sleeves of my coat. Advent time brought with it such changeable weather, sunshine one day and snow flurries the next, but I had never known it to change so quickly from morning to noon. It looked as if it would snow over Christmas.

I did not find Sean on the path up through the wood and I could not see anyone down in the camp. I stood under my beech tree avoiding the worst of the sleet and waited until the damp and the cold got too much to bear. Then, rather than walking back to the path and following it home, I went down through the wood towards the camp. I am not sure what made me do it: curiosity about the navvies, I suppose, and the desire to see him again. It was perhaps a foolhardy thing to do, but I was driven by some impulse quite beyond my control and I could not stop myself.

The fire was lit on the square of bare earth between the huts, but no-one was about. There was a group of men working on the bed of the line about half a mile away up the valley towards Much Purlock, but the sound of their labours did not reach me at that distance. Otherwise, the valley was completely still and empty. The sleet had finally stopped falling, but the sky remained ashen grey.

I gently pushed the door of one of the huts and it swung open with a creak on uneven hinges. A damp, earthy smell came out of the dwelling, as if it was as much outside as in. It was a sparse place with four poorly built bunkbeds, a rough-hewn table with some chairs around it, and a small stove in the corner giving the hut some warmth. I stepped in just for a moment, but there was little clue to who lived there: only two or three coats hanging on hooks and some cups and tin plates on the table. A candle had burnt itself down to a congealed mass of wax on a low shelf in the far corner.

'What're you doing here?' an Irishman said behind me, and I span round fast, my heart doing somersaults. An unpleasant-looking man in a peaked cap was standing there outside the hut, holding a shovel over one shoulder.

'I-I was j-just having a look around,' I stammered. 'I-I've come over from Much Purlock.'

'This is no place for a girl,' he said, staring unblinkingly at me. 'You must leave.'

'I-I'm not intending to stay,' I said, my cheeks aflame.

'I think Miss Matthews is here to see me, O'Donnell,' a voice that I recognised said behind the gruff man. 'Step out of the way and I'm sure she'll come out to join me.'

'Oh,' said the older man. 'Well, she can't be here, McClennan. You should know that.'

'She's *from* here, O'Donnell. She's from the town, from these valleys. I'd say that gives her every right to be here,' Sean said.

'You'll cut yourself on your sharpness one day,' O'Donnell replied. 'You watch yourself.'

'Don't worry, I will. You should watch yourself too, O'Donnell. It's no way to talk to a lady.'

With that, O'Donnell walked off and I stepped out of the hut and shook Sean's hand. His grip was icy cold but firm. I was so relieved, and happy, that he was there. 'Who on God's good earth was that?' I said. 'I'm sorry to have caused such an upset.'

'Oh, he's what's called our hagman, the man in charge day-to-day under the foreman. And to think I thought he was fine, a good man when I first met him back in Liverpool!'

'Well, I'm sorry if he's in charge of you, he seems such a sour, ill-mannered man.'

'Oh, he's certainly that and more,' Sean said.

We walked out from among the huts and up the path through the wood. Sean was beside me but kept at a respectful distance. I wanted to move closer to him, for warmth if nothing else, but dared not do so. The sun was trying to break through the grey cloud and the wind had dropped a little, but it was still bitterly cold.

'What made you come down and have a look around our gloomy little camp?' he asked in his lovely lilting voice. He looked over at me, his cheeks radiant with the cold and his blue eyes shining.

'I was just curious, I suppose, and I wanted to see where you lived.'

'In County Sligo my family has a beautiful old farmhouse, but what I have here's not much to write home about, is it? I wouldn't waste money on one of those Penny Blacks.'

'The countryside around here's magical at least,' I said and laughed. I felt sorry for him, all the same.

'Yes, and we work out in it in all weathers, come rain or shine, frost or thaw.'

'How do you bear the endless hammering, digging and lifting all day long?' I asked. 'And out in the cold like this.'

'I'm used to physical labour from the farm: I'm as strong as a shire horse after years of such work.'

'You're certainly nearly as big as one.' I laughed again, embarrassed at my silly words as soon as they had come out of my mouth. I suddenly sounded like nothing more than a fawning schoolgirl.

'And you keep out the cold with the heat of the work,' he said, as if he had not heard me. 'We lose so much sweat even in this cold weather—sorry to speak so crudely—that we have to drink jug after jug of water every day.'

We had reached the heart of the wood, the path uphill levelling off amidst the densest stands of beech, sycamore and ash trees and meandering over the gentler ground like a lazy stream made of earth, roots and stones. We had walked for some minutes side by side in a comfortable silence, matching our strides in the cold air.

'Would you like me to accompany you down into Much Purlock, or shall I turn back now?' Sean asked. 'I've the afternoon free, as my shift was early today.'

'Come with me then if you'd like. I can leave you outside the Star Inn.'

'Ah, there'll be no beer for me today, alas. Our gangmaster Mr Jones has banned us from drinking in the town during the week now. Too much rowdiness over the summer months.'

'That's why I haven't seen you when I've been round the market on Wednesdays recently,' I replied.

'Were you looking out for me, then?'

'Well, I did wonder where you were when I didn't see you, as I had got used to seeing you around. So, I suppose I was in a way, yes.'

He looked pleased then and smiled at me again, his eyes sparkling brightly against the greyness of the day.

'I'll be sure to be outside the Star Inn next Wednesday morning at ten o'clock if you like. My shift does not begin until noon that day. We could go for a walk together if the weather isn't too wet.'

'I'd like that very much.' We had reached the marketplace, and I did not feel it was right or proper that he came all the way to my front door with me. 'Well, I'd better get back home. I've got work to do and supper to make for me and my father.'

'It's just you and him; you've got no mother or brothers and sisters? And you've no cook to prepare supper for you?'

'I'm an only child, and my dear mother died seven years ago. The question of the cook is a rather longer story.'

'I'm very sorry for your loss,' he replied, looking at me with a furrowed brow. 'Losing a parent is hard on the young.' He was the first person who had said that to me in all those long years. 'Until next Wednesday morning, then.' And he went off, walking at a brisk pace back towards the wood.

* * *

My father had no patients that afternoon and he sat in front of the fire nursing a toddy of malt whisky and hot honeyed water. He seemed to be suffering from a head cold after his antics out in the garden the night before, and he sat in silence as I did my chores and prepared our evening meal.

'Grace, it's strange,' he said as we were eating at the kitchen table that night, 'but these *episodes*—I don't have any other word for them—only ever happen when I'm here in this house. I've never had anything remotely like them when I'm away in London.'

'Yes, that is strange,' I replied, my stomach tightening, 'though I don't see how this house could have any bearing on them. I'm sure it's just a coincidence.'

'I don't believe in coincidences,' he said. 'They're in the same class of things as superstitions and old wives' tales. There's measurable, quantifiable science and then there's common nonsense.'

'If you say so, Father,' I said and sighed under my breath.

'No, something here in this very house must be causing these things if their origin isn't in my head.'

'Has the good Doctor Gillespie ruled out a lesion of some kind?'

'My pupils are even, and I don't have severe headaches or nausea or problems with my vision. Such a cause seems vanishingly unlikely to the both of us.'

'What do you—what does the good doctor—think might be the cause of these episodes, then?' I needed to know how close he was to the truth, whether I should change course now or could afford to wait a while.

'I've no idea yet. But I do know that my visions, my episodes, are very unpleasant and frightening. I'll get to the bottom of them, I can promise you that.'

Those words, said through a mouthful of baked river trout and fresh winter greens, sounded almost like a threat.

Chapter Twenty-Six

Herefordshire, 1841

A letter arrived from home yesterday, with one paragraph written by Ma and the other by Niall. It has lifted my spirits and depleted me at the same time. It is heartening to have news from home again, the more so now that the desperation of their situation seems to be easing a little, with one of our best fields having been sold to our neighbour John Byrne, but it makes me miss the place even more. I cannot see a way of getting through. How am I supposed to keep going here for the next year or even longer, with the men being the way they are and the work so hard? There is nothing to leaven any of it, except for Grace.

I cannot stop thinking about her. I wake up with her lovely face in my mind's eye and I go to sleep and her face is still there. She is the only thing that is keeping me here: the weather is bitter outside, and inside the hut it is little better. If I were to turn up back at Rose Farm, Niall would have nothing to reproach me for after these nine hard months. Once I had explained to him how desperately hard, how harsh, it has been here, he would understand why I had to come back home. But I cannot leave now, not now that I have met her.

Since Grace turned up here in the camp a week ago and pushed open the door to one of the huts, O'Donnell has been relentless in his mockery of me. 'Did you say *grace* back in Sligo like a good mama's boy before your soup and potatoes?' he asks me in a stupid, put-on child's voice. 'Hail Mary, full of *grace*,' he intones over and over at me like some deranged priest. It is as much as I can do not to hit him. If he carries on much longer, I do not think I will be able to stop myself.

Our work has slowed with the coming of this icy weather. Mr Menzies curses and swears at the earth that is too hard to dig; at the snapped shafts of shovels and pickaxes; at the frozen water that we cannot drink without melting it first in the cauldron hanging over the fire. Everything is taking three times as long as it did. The mood is always sour whenever Mr Menzies is in earshot. Only O'Donnell seems to find him a foreman worth working for, and he hangs onto every word that he says. There is no chance O'Donnell will be made hagman again, though: Mr Jones would never allow that to happen.

My shift ends at three o'clock. I will walk into town while it is still light. They are too miserly to give us a lantern each, and finding my way back to the camp through the woods in the pitch dark is bad enough. I do not want to have to go into Much Purlock in the half-dark as well. Seeing that boy Jack and the dead birds has left me feeling rather less comfortable in these woods than I was before. It as if something unpleasant, some trace of death has been left hanging in the air here, even with the birds buried deep in the soil.

Grace and I walked through here into town together after she visited our camp. O'Donnell started mocking me about her as soon as I had come back; he thinks that I do not stand a chance with her. My nerves disappeared, though, once I had talked to Grace again, and I felt at ease walking beside her. To look at her, you would think her beauty would make her believe she is above everyone else, but that is not how she is at all. I am meeting her in the marketplace in two days' time, and it feels as though I am rather holding my breath until then.

At first, I think my eyes must be deceiving me. The boy is leading a fine-looking cockerel on a long leather leash as I come down through the last of the trees to where the path meets the first cottages of the town. The bird's orange and black feathers are puffed out and he is strutting proudly along the path ahead of me like one of the Queen's own guards out on parade in London. Talking to Jack again is the last thing I feel like doing, but I cannot resist asking him about the cockerel.

'Who's this handsome fellow, then?' I say, catching up with him.

He has not heard me or noticed me walking behind him, so intent is he on the bird, and he starts in surprise. 'Oh, oh hullo Mister McClennan, he's called Tom Finery,' he says, looking round. 'Ma got him for me a few days ago.'

'I've never seen one being taken for a walk before.'

'Ma says Tom's henpecked, that he needs to get away from the girls for an hour or two.' He laughs and pulls on the lead. The cockerel's eyes glitter like polished jet and his bright red comb wobbles as he walks. He definitely has something of the devil about him.

'Well, he seems to be enjoying his walk. Perhaps your Ma's right.'

'I'm taking him over to the marketplace and round Purlock before the sun sets. He has lots of energy in those legs of his.'

I do not know why for certain, but I decide to broach the topic of the disturbing matter of the crows. 'Master Jack, I saw you that time in the wood. There was something moving between the trees, and I walked in to see what was going on and saw you digging that hole. Why were you burying those birds? Where on earth had you found them?'

'I been burying them here and there for months now, Mister McClennan. I find them in the hedgerows and thickets and on the verges and don't like to see them just lyin' there. I collect them up in a sack and bury them where I see fit.'

'You find them lying dead, just like that?'

'They're mostly pretty far gone, with mouldy beaks an' all. Summins got to them.'

'Any idea what it might be?'

'My Ma says it's summin to do with you lot, the outside coming in. I don't believe her, though. I think it's always been here, lurking somewhere.'

With that, they are off on their way again, the cockerel now leading Jack rather than the other way round. He really is the strangest child I have ever met. There is something uncanny, something unlikeable, about him and it leaves me feeling unsettled every time. I am hoping to be away from here before I see him again.

I leave the last of the trees behind and take the path that runs past back alleyways and over rough ground to the sparse garden of the Star Inn. The inn is not yet open, as it is not quite four o'clock. I am the only person sitting out here, half frozen in my thick woollen coat, huddled at the wooden table with my hands stuffed deep into my coat pockets, waiting for a pint of Leominster bitter in front of the fire. The sun is setting over the dark wood and the trees are lit up by its slanting light until it sinks below the hill, and everything goes black. As black as the feathers of those dead rooks and crows lying in the winter soil. I cannot get that image out of my mind. Was it really us that brought this sickness here, whatever it is, was it really us?

'Sean, hullo, you're bloody miles away!' Adam says suddenly. I had not even heard him coming through the gate and over the garden's flagstones.

'Don't creep up on me like that! You'll give me a heart attack.'

'Joe's on his way,' he says, laughing, 'but Mr Menzies was giving some of the men an earful about something or other when I left, and Joe got caught up in that.'

'The bastard.'

'He really is, and I'd swear he's getting worse.' Just then, the back door swings open, casting lamplight and flickering firelight onto the garden.

'You lads coming in?' John asks, looking out. 'Or are you staying out there in the cold?'

* * *

Grace is wrapped up in the thickest of woollen coats when we meet in the marketplace, and she still looks frozen through. The stallholders have small braziers over which they can warm their gloved hands, but when the new year comes it must bring milder weather with it, otherwise people are going to start to want to stay indoors and retreat from the world. Food will run scarce, and communities will be frozen in on themselves.

'I've been worrying about you down there in that rickety hut of yours,' Grace says. 'Are you and the other men managing to stay warm?'

'Barely. We're all praying for a change in the weather soon. If it doesn't come, I think some of the navvies will up and leave. The work's hard enough as it is. I would leave, too, but I'd rather like to stay now …'

'Really?' Grace says and smiles up at me. She has the loveliest smile: her cheeks flush and dimple slightly, and her teeth flash white between her pink lips. I would like to kiss those lips, but I do not dare try yet.

'Let's get some warmth into us,' I say. 'What about a walk over to the Wye?'

'Yes, let's go out that way and I'll walk back with you through the woods afterwards. I'm in no hurry today.'

She puts her arm through mine, seemingly completely unafraid of people seeing her like this and what they might say. Perhaps they will assume that I am some distant cousin of hers newly arrived in Much Purlock, but I doubt it given my navvy's clothes and the fact they surely know her and all of her family's business. Despite the cold, I feel this warmth when she is beside me: there is a giddy elation inside me, a surging heat that I cannot name, but it is part pride and part love and part lust. I would like to know what she is thinking, what she is feeling, about having me by her side, but she is silent for a while as we walk through the quiet outer streets of the town.

On the lane that leads to the field path over to the Wye there is a great beech tree, its bare branches raised against the frozen sky. Icicles have formed on its lower boughs, and they sparkle in the light as if some winter god has reached down his icy fingers and rested them there. I reach up to break off one of the icicles and look at its tapering length more closely.

'Don't,' she says. 'Leave it hanging there with the others. They look so beautiful.'

I take my hand away and leave the row of icicles intact and glittering beneath their branch. 'I haven't seen those for a while. Not since the winter before last in Sligo.'

'It wasn't as cold as this last winter here,' she says. 'It's rather magical in this bright sunshine if you don't have to be out in it for too long.' She pushes her hands deeper into her muff and we continue on our way over to the river.

I have half a mind to ask her about the rooks and crows here and the disease that the boy mentioned, but then think better of it. What on earth would she think of me bringing up so gloomy a topic on so beautiful a day? What interest could she possibly have in such a subject? It is only now that we have left the town behind and are on the field path that I have noticed just how quiet it is out here. The cold has silenced all the birdlife and there is not even the faintest rustle of creatures moving in the undergrowth. It is a world stilled by winter. Back on the farm, there was always movement and sound even in the coldest weather: the cattle lowing in the barn; the sheep huddling around the feed that we had put down in the corner of their field. Here, every mammal has scurried underground and every bird that has not left for warmer skies is roosting in the trees that still have some cover on them. The Wye is the colour of old bronze in this light.

'Race you there!' she says suddenly and laughs, and before I have taken in what she means she is off down the path running as fast as she can, one hand holding up her long skirt above the frozen mud of the field. She is surprisingly quick, despite the icy ground, and I have to run until I am out of breath to catch up with her. When I do, she is laughing, clouds of her hot breath filling the frozen air around her, and her cheeks are aflame from the exertion and the cold. It is as much as I can do to hold myself back from trying to kiss her right there and then. I grab her arm to steady myself after coming to such a sudden stop, and we both lose our balance and fall into a heap of well-wrapped bodies and limbs on the path.

'So much for me holding up my skirt!' she says, lying on her back on the cold earth not two feet from me, and laughs again. She looks radiant in this light, so full of life.

I get onto my knees and stand up awkwardly, then take her hands in mine and pull her up beside me. 'You're as fast as a hare!' I say, still a little breathless.

She brushes the earth and twigs off her skirt and coat and puts her hat back on her head. 'What does that make you—a lurcher?' she says and smiles up at me.

'Perhaps a rather overfed one.'

'Oh, no. You're a fine specimen: any hare-courser would be proud of you.'

She holds my arm again as we half slide and half walk down the slippery bank to the river's edge, the dark green water flowing fast and silent. Up right is the Wye's source, somewhere far off deep underground in dark hills soaked with rain. Down left, miles away over fields and woods and counties that I have never seen, beyond the swirling pool where trout flicker against the pull of the current, is the Celtic Sea that will take me home again one day. For now, though, I am here; and for the first time, it is not just iron and mud and men and money that are keeping me.

Chapter Twenty-Seven

Hereford Insane Asylum, 1849

Days without a beginning or an end. Winter is here and night bleeds into day, day bleeds into night. It is a time of half-light and smoke from the stoves hanging in the damp air. The ward has been quiet over recent weeks, but we are all stewing in our own juices, fermenting like cider apples in a jar, and the lid will blow off this place before too long.

Mrs Swain the orderly has grown a second purple wart, this time in a fold of her neck just below her chin. It is larger than the one on the tip of her nose and it bobs up and down when she talks. What she has to say is never pleasant, but her warts so undermine any authority that she thinks she has over us that we all snigger into our sleeves when she has gone.

'You there,' she says, as if she does not know my name after all these years. 'The Warden has a letter for you.' She looks angry at having to tell me this, her bulging eyes staring right through me and her warts aflame. And, still, they tell us that we are ill, that they are trying to cure us.

'Oh,' I say. I cannot think of anything else: it is only my second letter since I have been imprisoned here.

'Well, are you going to go and get it or not?' she asks, still glaring at me.

'I suppose I will.' I smile my sunniest smile back at her: that usually does the trick of really riling her and she stomps away.

The Warden, grey Mr Chillingham, is frowning when he opens the door to his office. There are white flecks of dandruff on the shoulders of his black coat and one shirttail has become untucked and is sticking out from beneath his waistcoat. He always looks as if he has battled his way through a storm to get here, with his ashen hair unkempt and his clothes askew. On the infrequent occasions that I have spoken to him, however, he has never been unpleasant to me, only seeming to be rather overworked or perhaps unhappy in his role. I wonder if he even knows how most of his orderlies treat his patients.

'Ah, Miss Matthews,' he says, pressing the fingers of his left hand to his forehead. 'Forgive me, I've got something of a headache today.'

'I'm sorry to hear that, Mr Chillingham. You've no doubt got a lot to do.'

'Yes, always,' he says. 'There are reports to write and the city's mayor and its illustrious elders to satisfy. And you patients always keep us on our toes! So, what can I do for you today?'

'I was told there's a letter waiting for me.'

'Oh yes, it's somewhere here,' he says, and starts rummaging in the drawer beneath his desk. I glance around his office while he is looking for the letter, but it is not much to look at: there is only the desk and his high-backed wooden chair and a shelf behind him that holds box files and folders. The only concession to decoration here is a large oil-painting of plain-faced Queen Victoria, facing left with a brilliant diamond diadem on her head, large diamond earrings hanging pendulously from her earlobes and a diamond necklace encircling her thick neck. All that glittering opulence in this place!

'Do you sing "God Save the Queen" to Her Majesty every morning when you arrive?' I say under my breath.

'I'm sorry, Miss Matthews?' He sounds perplexed, still searching for my letter. 'Ah, here it is,' he says, holding up a small white envelope with a Penny Red postage stamp in the top right-hand corner with the Queen's portrait on it. It is an odd feeling to hold something from the outside world when he hands the letter across the desk to me.

'Thank you, Mr Chillingham. It's a surprise to receive it.'
'Is there anything else?' he asks.
'There is one more thing, Mr Chillingham: all the letters that I wrote to my father, were they ever actually sent?'

He looks sheepish for the briefest of moments, as if he has been caught out, found cheating, and puts his hand to his forehead again, then quickly restores his face to a reassuring expression. 'Why, of course, dear child,' he says, speaking as if he is a parish priest and I am one of the sheep in his flock. He looks at me unblinkingly across the desk. 'Of course. I can vouch for that. Just because you haven't received any replies doesn't mean the letters were never sent.'

I leave his office clutching the small envelope, addressed to me in an unknown hand, not knowing whether he is telling me the truth or not. The power always lies with the liar when you have no way of knowing the truth.

***

The letter is from Mrs Samuels! She who would have been my simpering stepmother if things had turned out differently. Her handwriting is full of loops and flourishes as affected as any that I have seen.

3, Sydenham Hill
London SE
13th November 1849

Dear Miss Matthews,

I admit that I had some pity for you when I first learned from Mr Matthews – William – that you were in a place for the insane, but that quickly faded when I recalled, so very bitterly, the reasons for your having been incarcerated there. You were the agent of your own misfortune.

William and I could have spent these last eight years happily together as husband and wife. We both deserved that much, and you robbed us of that happiness for a long time. You cruel child. How dare you do that to him? How dare you do that to me?

William is faring much better now, and he has even begun to see patients again and to tend to his beloved garden. His recovery and his restored faith in life and in me have allowed us to see each other again in London and in Much Purlock for the last couple of years. We are even talking once more about marriage, so you did not break us, and you did not win.

William and I are still struggling to forgive you, but we will continue to pray that we can find that within us one day. Whether God has forgiven you I cannot say, for I am only one small voice in this great world of ours.

If you are ill, I pray that they will find a way to cure you, but I fear that it is not a sickness that afflicts you but that there is a streak in you, some malignity, that can never be erased.

Yours sincerely,

Mrs. J. Samuels

The ward is quiet, as all the women are out for their hour of walking the grounds. I go through her curlicued letter three times, propped up on my hard bed, and I feel nothing but rising anger. Her impertinence is astounding. She has got everything back to front and upside down: for all the wrong that I did my father, it is also *me* that should be forgiving *him*, which I simply cannot do. I crush her letter and the envelope in the hard fist of my hand and throw it into the open mouth of the stove. Fire is a cleanser like nothing else. I want some fresh air, despite the rain. I need to get away, to get out of this place. I will, I will find a way to escape from here.

Chapter Twenty-Eight

Much Purlock, Advent 1841

Carollers were singing in the marketplace on the last Wednesday before Christmas and snow was falling silently, settling on every surface that lay prone to the sky. Footsteps were muffled as people walked through the town, and even the sound of the church bell that rang out for a funeral that morning was dampened by the snow-laden air. Cartwheels left deepening ruts in the drifts.

I waited for Sean in the shadow of the Star Inn, huddled in my winter coat that was lined with rabbit fur. Three other navvies went past me into the inn, talking in low voices in their heavy accents and laughing together, but I had to wait for almost half an hour in the gently falling snow, my hat pulled down low, until Sean arrived just after midday.

'I'm sorry, Miss Matthews, um Grace,' he said. He was slightly out of breath and had obviously walked over as fast as he could from the camp. 'Mr Jones our gangmaster's on one of his visits to us and he always has so many things to go over. He kept us all talking this morning, between shifts.'

'I was thinking you might have got lost somewhere in the snow on the way here,' I joked. 'But stamping my feet and keeping my hands in these deep pockets of my coat helped.' I smiled up at him. My cheeks felt flushed pink, and not just from the cold air. I had half expected that he might not come.

Night Comes Down

'Shall we walk somewhere?' he said.

'Yes, please, let's do that. I need to get some warmth into me. Where should we go?'

'What about over to the river? It somehow reminds me of home.'

'Do you miss it that much?' I asked, as we left the marketplace and walked past the church, whose belltower was now silent, out towards the fields before the river.

'When I have the time to stop and think about it, it makes me very sad to recall the farm and my Ma and brother there.'

'I'm sorry, Sean. How long's it been now since you left Ireland?'

'About nine months. It's gone by in a flash, mind, with all the work. Just look at these hands!' He held them up in front of him, red with the cold, their palms and fingers calloused and cracked.

'I hope you'll be able to see the farm and your family again before too long. You've come all this way and I've never even left Herefordshire!'

He helped me over the stile that led from the path into the fields, his cold, rough hand wrapped around mine, and then climbed over the stile himself behind me. I had never held a man's hand before, and it felt so strange and so wonderful at the same time.

'I hadn't gone much beyond County Sligo myself until I came over here.' We stood at the edge of the sloping field of untouched snow in front of us. 'Then there was Belfast, Liverpool, Hereford: all those cities that I hardly got to see anything of, and then this beautiful place.'

'I'm glad you came,' I said.

He smiled down at me again in that way of his but said nothing for a while.

We half walked and half slid down the field, holding hands where it sloped most steeply, our boots and ankles soaked by the foot-high snow. A flock of seagulls had come inland up the river and they wheeled and shrieked above us. Then there was the Wye ahead of us, flowing silt-brown and fast between its high banks. It always lifted my heart to see it: that river's untamed wildness and unseen depths were a quiet mystery snaking through our landscape.

At least all those men who wanted change could do nothing to destroy the river.

I remained at the edge of the field, my feet getting colder and colder in my frozen boots, while Sean climbed down the bank towards the water. I feared for a moment he might slip and fall into the current, but he was sure-footed and stood right by the river's edge. He picked up a large stick that was lying there and threw it arcing out over the water, where it landed midstream and was pulled away by the current.

'You need a faithful dog to bring that back for you,' I said, laughing.

'I don't think any dog could withstand that current. They'd be swept downstream before they knew what was happening to them. The river's swollen with all the rain we've had, and now this snow.'

'I've hardly ever seen it this high: it really is raging. Please be careful.'

He stayed there for a few moments longer, then climbed back up the steep riverbank, and we stood huddled side by side in the icy air. The snow was falling less heavily now and there was a brightness in the sky away to the east. Sean slid his hand into mine as we looked out silently at the river, which made hardly a sound as it flowed downstream, only the swirling eddies at the very edge of the water fizzing and bubbling as they caught the frozen earth of the bank. His putting his hand in mine did not seem at all forward or presumptuous, it simply felt right. It was a friendly, safe thing, nothing more than that.

'We'd better start back towards Much Purlock before too long,' he said. 'A few of us are meeting with the gangmaster again later this afternoon. The huts are completely unsuitable in this weather, and we need to know what he plans to do about it.'

'Will he actually listen and do something?'

'Well, he's a fair man, but of course it's the railway company that holds the purse strings. But if we down tools in protest, they'll have to make some changes to our living conditions. No-one wants to freeze to death in their sleep!'

'It's really that bad? I'm sorry, Sean. What about the stove I saw?'

'When the weather's as cold as this, it doesn't give out enough heat in our hut, and it's the same in all the others. They need to get us bigger stoves and more bedding, at the very least, and cover the outside of the huts in another layer of timber.'

'I hope your gangmaster will listen. It seems he must.'

'We're all getting restless and some of the men want to go back to Ireland. I need to stay on working on the railways for another year at least, if I can.'

'Why exactly?'

'Things were very hard on the farm when I left. My father had almost bankrupted us before he died. I need to earn a living and look after myself for a while.'

He was quiet after telling me this, and we climbed the stile that led back onto the lane in silence. The lane was deserted and the bare trees on either side cast dark shadows on the snow, now stained with mud and grit where the carts and carriages had driven. It was the shortest day of the year and the sun was already sinking towards the horizon in the west, even though it was not yet two o'clock in the afternoon.

'I'd better be going,' he said, speaking at last when we got back to the marketplace. 'Will I see you here again at midday the Wednesday after New Year, Grace? I'll bring you a belated Christmas gift.'

'I would like that very much.'

Sean was a gentle, kind soul, whatever his towering physical presence and fists like sides of meat might say to those who did not know him. I could see that from the few times that I had met him. He had a stoicism about him, and a thoughtfulness and fragility, that was hard not to warm to. He was one of those people who were so very different from how they looked; this hulking man would frighten anyone who encountered him on a dark night on a lonely road, but he would probably be the first to rescue an injured bird that he found there. As soon as he had walked off towards the wood that afternoon, I wanted to see him again.

* * *

The snow delayed my father's return from his Advent-time adventures with Mrs Samuels in London, and he did not get home until late on Christmas Eve. I heard the pony and trap draw up outside. I stoked the fire so it was blazing brightly when he came in, then went to check quickly again that the powdered mixture of mushroom and snuff was in his pep jar in the study and that there was no hint of anything untoward in its appearance.

'Hello, Grace. Grace, are you there? Help me in with my bags, will you?' he called through the open door, an icy wind blowing into the hallway. 'The man has had to turn around straightaway because of the weather and deposited me and my luggage on the doorstep.'

'Sorry, Father,' I said, coming into the hallway from the kitchen. 'I was just out the back fetching in some more logs from the woodpile for tomorrow. Let me help you with those bags. How was the journey?'

'The part by train from Paddington went without a hitch,' he said. 'The final leg here from Gloucester was truly ghastly. The road's barely passable.'

'There's still some supper left on the range, Father. I'll bring it to you on a tray in front of the fire once you've changed out of your travelling clothes.'

'Thank you, Grace,' he said. 'I haven't eaten even a morsel since I left London.'

While he went upstairs to change into his nightgown and long bed socks, as it was already past ten o'clock, I set his food on a tray and put it on the low table by his favourite armchair. He came down the stairs like a white apparition in his nightgown and cap and devoured the meal in silence, looking into the fire and flicking without any obvious interest through the pages of the newspaper he had brought back with him from London.

'Father, would you like a nightcap?' I asked when he had scraped his plate clean and put his knife and fork down together. 'We've still got some Bordeaux wine left, or there's a bottle of sloe gin that the Jennings left for you as a Christmas present the other day.'

'Thank you, Grace, but no. I'm off to bed: it's been a long day,' he said, yawning into his sleeve. I hid my frustration behind a smile and bid him goodnight: I had hoped that his taking a drink would soften him up and he would then retreat into his study to snort his pep.

* * *

The next morning there was a hard crust of ice on the snow, and frost bloomed on the inside of the windowpanes. I built up the fire, bringing it back to life after its night's slumber, and before long the room was habitable again without my outdoor clothes and coat on. I had bought a goose from a smallholder's stall in the market after Sean left for the camp, and it had been hanging headless on a hook in the cold store in the garden waiting to be plucked and cooked. I went and fetched it and sat at the kitchen table while my father was still in bed, holding its body against my knees and yanking out its long white feathers one by one. They made a sort of puckering sound as they left the skin. I plucked the bird quickly and carefully and could not help smiling to myself, sitting there in the first light of morning, as the words 'his goose is cooked' ran round and round my head.

Father came downstairs just after nine o'clock, still in his nightgown and cap. He had no patients to see over Christmastime and he always slept in late whenever he could over the festive season.

'Morning, Grace, and a happy Christmas,' he said, kneading his eyes. 'That smells delicious. What bird is it?'

'A goose from the market. It's good and plump. I plucked it myself. It'll be ready at about noon.'

We ate our Christmas meal in near silence, my father sipping from his glass of Bordeaux wine between mouthfuls of goose, roasted potatoes, and vegetables while I ate without much relish, despite the goose being tender and good, and looked out of the window at the snowbound lane. There was no-one about and it was as if we were at the very end of the world. Even the Jennings family's garden gate remained firmly shut: all the people of Much Purlock were locked away behind closed doors for Christmas Day while I wanted to be anywhere else but there at the table. I knew that before too long he would want to toast mother's memory and I would not be able to stand it. He poured himself a second glass of wine and tucked his napkin more firmly under his chin into the collar of his shirt.

'Grace, you know that this is now our eighth Christmas without the nourishing presence of Mary, your dearly-missed mother,' he began, looking relieved to be unburdening himself of this annual duty. His cheeks were flushed pink and there was a hint of perspiration on his upper lip. 'May her soul be resting in eternal peace and bliss in Heaven as we sit here. I'd like to propose a toast to her cherished memory on this holiest of days, a day of birth and new beginnings.'

Something inside me shrank as he said that, and he raised his glass of wine as I lifted my water glass to clink its rim against his. 'I still miss her every day,' I said, not looking at him but out at the lane again. I did not want to cry in front of him.

'I know,' he said, 'and it's my great regret that she's not here with us. But please think of Mrs Samuels, erm Josephine, as someone who can bring some much-needed light and laughter into this gloomy household of ours.'

'But she's not my mother and I can't think of her like that. I never will.'

'Please, Grace, *please*,' is all that he could say, before forking his last slice of gooseflesh into his mouth.

After I had cleared the table and washed the dishes, we went for a walk through the town and up into the woods. It was the only time that I had been anywhere but the house and garden with my father since our walk together on Christmas Day afternoon the previous year. We went right to the heart of the wood, despite the foot-high snow on the ground, which was trampled to a sheet of glassy ice on the pathways that were regularly used but still pristine, and soft where no-one had trodden among the denser stands of trees.

The further we went, the more anxious I became that we might encounter Sean on one of the paths, but there was no other living soul about. My father had suggested that route and insisted that I join him: I was torn between not wanting to spend the afternoon out walking with him and wanting to see if I might catch a glimpse of Sean. But having my father beside me on those lonely paths made the anticipation fearful rather than pleasurable. How would I explain Sean and I knowing each other if we met him on one of the paths?

As we came to the far side of the wood where it dropped down into the next valley, before we turned to head back towards Much Purlock, we saw the navvies' huts down below us at the edge of the trees. They were snowbound, with ice-laden roofs and drifts on the windward side of each hut, but the path between them and out of the camp had been shovelled clear.

'There's smoke coming from their chimneys,' my father said, 'so I suppose those shacks must be occupied.'

'That's where all the men working on the railway line live.'

'How do you know that?'

'I've seen them coming and going when I've been out for my walks in these woods.'

'They're nothing but common riffraff, those men. Make sure you keep away from them. Haven't you heard about all the commotion they've been causing at the Star Inn, at the Crown and elsewhere around the town?'

'I've heard nothing about any of that, Father. They've probably just been letting off steam. Looking at them, most of them are still young, even boys almost.'

'They need to learn a thing or two about how to behave in a place that's not theirs.'

'But you'll still be happy to use what they're building here, won't you?'

'The railway's how we'll all get around the country before too long. But that doesn't mean I want the navvies living on my doorstep.'

I bit my tongue and said nothing further to him as we made our way home in the twilight. My feet were freezing cold and wet when we got back, and the fire had almost gone out.

Father drank two more glasses of Bordeaux wine with his supper of cold goose and bread and butter. I watched him from the other chair as he sat looking into the fire and peering over his glasses at a book on diseases of the tropics. He had that self-satisfied way of smiling to himself while he read, as if he already knew what the author would say before he had come to the actual words on the page. As I got up to clear away the dishes and to fetch in more logs for the fire, he stood up from his armchair and went into his study. I knew then that we would have an eventful evening in that otherwise quiet and lonely house.

He came back after a few minutes and sat down in his armchair again, wiping his moustache with his hand and sniffing forcefully. He was smiling to himself as though he had heard a particularly good joke. He picked up his book and seemed to be trying to force himself to concentrate on the printed words on the page, but his eyes kept wandering to the fire, then towards the darkened window onto the lane, then over to me sitting in the other chair darning some stockings. His mind did not appear to be on the distant diseases of the tropics that cold Christmas night.

'Do you hear the church bells ringing?' he asked suddenly.

'I can only hear the wind in the trees, Father, nothing else.'

'No, St. Andrew's bells are sounding out tonight. Surely you can hear them. The ringers are going up and down the scales. Always such a joyous sound!' His eyes had glazed over, and he went to the window to look out into the darkness, as if he would be able to see the sound travelling towards him through the ethers of the night. There was, of course, nothing to see or to hear other than the wind and the pitch-black lane.

By nine o'clock he had started to sweat profusely, his forehead glistening in the firelight and drops falling from the tip of his nose into his lap. He rolled up the sleeves of his nightgown and took off his cap, placing it on the arm of the chair beside him. He was still smiling to himself but had begun to mutter unintelligibly under his breath and to cast furtive glances over at me and at the stairs that led off the corner of the sitting-room up to the bedrooms.

'No more logs on the fire: it's too hot in here already,' he said. Then: 'She's here in this house.'

'Who is?' I asked, but he did not answer me.

'Footsteps running along the floorboards up there!' he exclaimed after some minutes of silence, pointing to the stairs.

'It's probably just mice in the wainscot,' I replied, trying to calm him. 'I can't hear anything unusual.'

'No, no!' he shouted, white spittle flecking his lips. 'She's here, she's here!' He levered himself out of his armchair and looked like he was about to run to the stairs, but then slumped back down into the chair, utterly depleted, his eyes shut tight and a low moan coming from his lips.

After a while, his shoulders shook with great gusting sobs, and he buried his face in his hands. It was pitiable to see my father like that. The ground mushrooms, I had learned, had such varied effects on him: one moment apparent joy, the next spasms of sorrow, the next an unbridled mania that made him chase his own shadow across the garden. His eyes saw apparitions that were not there, his ears heard sounds that could not be heard, and his mind tried to fathom things that were beyond understanding. If he could have become his own patient, my father would have presented himself with a medical case that might have taken years of close observation to solve, were it not for my bag of mushroom powders high up on their shelf in the kitchen.

PART TWO:

STEAM AND STEEL

Chapter Twenty-Nine

Much Purlock, 1842

I woke from a dream in which rooks had been pecking at my eyes. I could feel the searing pain very distinctly. When I awoke, I could not see the birds and thought I was blind. I had a headache behind my eyes that took all morning to lift, and I could not get that awful image of the birds out of my mind.

New Year's Day brought fresh snow with it. For a while on that first morning of the year, the mud and grit that had been churned up in the snow over Christmas by cartwheels and hooves on the lanes and roads of Murch Purlock was covered in a fresh layer that made everything white and pristine again.

My father had retreated into his study since the morning after Christmas, leafing endlessly through his medical books. He would not find the answers he was looking for within their pages. I had taken the adulterated powder of ground mushroom and snuff out of his pep jar in the study and replaced it with his pure brown snuff that I kept hidden in its bag up on the kitchen shelf where my father never looked. I would not give him another dose again until I was as sure as I could be that he would not make a connection between his pep and his episodes of mental aberration. The more often I put the admixture of ground mushroom and snuff into his pep jar, and the more he snorted the concoction and suffered his episodes, the more likely it was he would connect the cause and the effect.

After the snowfall came brilliant sunshine that lasted almost the whole of the month. The snow and ice slowly melted away from roofs, gables, gutters, and roads, leaving brick and tile and earth and stone behind, all clean and new. It was as if the sky had been scoured and burnished clean, with the whites and greys of Christmastime polished away.

I met Sean outside the Star Inn at midday on the first Wednesday after New Year, as we had arranged. He looked tired but happy to see me and was done up in a great woollen coat that I had not seen before. He was carrying a cloth bag with him that seemed to be holding something quite heavy.

'Hello, Grace,' he said, his eyes twinkling down at me. He seemed to be growing his sideburns longer, but he was otherwise still clean-shaven. His breath hung in the air between us like smoke. 'How have you been since we saw each other before Christmas?'

'There's not much to tell you, I'm afraid. It's always such a quiet time of year with just me and my father cooped up in our house together.'

'It's surely better than spending Christmastime in a camp full of half-frozen and half-starved men,' he replied, laughing but not altogether happily.

'I'm sorry, Sean. Of course, you're right. It's just that my father and I don't enjoy one another's company much.'

'He's not proud to have such a lovely girl as his daughter?' I felt my cheeks flush at his words and lapped them up like milk.

'I'm mostly just the cook, the maid, and the charlady in our household. I've had to look after myself, and after him, ever since my mother died. He won't have anyone else do it—he got rid of our cook and our help. I was only ten and still at school. I wanted to stay on there much longer than I did.'

'And what does he do with himself all day while you're hard at work?' Sean's eyes weren't twinkling now, and he was frowning down at me.

'Oh, he's busy seeing his patients in his consulting room, or going off to London to visit his simpering wife-to-be. He never used to mention her but now he can't stop.'

'You'll be gaining a stepmother then?' he asked, a smile playing on his lips and his frown gone now. 'Perhaps she'll help you around the house a little at least.'

'She's as flighty as a winter pheasant and won't be any help at all. I don't want her anywhere near me. I thought I wanted someone who might be a mother to me again, but I don't, I really don't. I don't even like her touching our pots and pans, let alone sitting at our dining table whenever she's in Purlock.'

'Then perhaps you'll have to consider running away to the circus or going into service somewhere if they're really set on marrying each other. Or you could join me on my travels ...' He tailed off and laughed but looked as if he at least half meant it.

'I suppose we'll have to wait and see what happens. Perhaps she'll have a change of heart before the summer's upon us.'

'If she's as flighty as you say she is, perhaps she will. But, then again, if they're really in love ...'

'Well, they do giggle like schoolchildren and whisper sweet nothings into each other's ears whenever she visits from London. I find it dreadful and can only think of my poor mother. How dare she even think of replacing her? I go for long walks whenever I don't have chores to do and simply can't wait to get out of the house.'

'My Ma and Da were married for almost thirty years,' he said. 'They loved each other very much, but Da made a mess of things at the end.'

'How so?'

'He invested the money he'd saved from a lifetime of work on the farm in schemes that left us with nothing, only the farm and the house and a stack of unpaid debts. That's why I came over here. I would've just been a drain on Ma and my brother.'

'I'm sorry, Sean.'

'But England's not so bad, despite all the hard work, particularly now that I've met you! I've long been wanting to, from afar.'

'Oh, is that so?' I asked and blushed again but was so happy.

'Here, I've made something for you,' he said, handing me the cloth bag, which was heavy in my hands. 'I had to while away the long winter evenings in the hut somehow, didn't I?'

I pulled open the bag and there was something wooden in it. I lifted it out and held it up to the sunlight to look more closely at it: it was a carved wooden cross in a circle, with intricate woven decorations cut into each cross arm.

'It's beautiful. Thank you, Sean. Did you really carve this yourself? Is this oak?'

'Yes, it's cut from a branch I found in the wood. I whittled it over Advent in the evenings. There wasn't much else to do apart from stoke the stove and try not to listen to O'Donnell.'

'I've never seen a cross like this before. It's quite different from our plain ones.'

'It's Celtic,' he said. 'It's what the old ones look like where I come from.'

'Well, I don't know what to say. It's really lovely, Sean.'

'I'm just happy you like it, Grace. Shall we go somewhere, perhaps out towards Dereham? I've been out that way once or twice, and this weather's perfect for a good walk.'

Once we had left Much Purlock behind, we headed away from the Wye along a footpath that ran across a field of winter wheat. I had never been that way before. Crows strutted and pecked at something at the edge of the wheat on the far side of the field and they took off cawing, their ragged wings beating low over the hedge, as we came nearer. I wondered what was lying there out of sight, what dead thing they had found on that cold ground. They went back to whatever it was as soon as we had climbed over the stile into the next field, which was ploughed ready for the spring, leaving only the grassy path that ran untouched through its heart. We walked in comfortable silence in the sunshine, and I slid my gloved hand into Sean's. He smiled down at me again with those eyes that matched the clear blue sky.

'I'm sorry I didn't bring you a present,' I said, then plucking up all my courage, 'Would a kiss make up for it?' Before he could even answer me, I went up on tiptoes and kissed him on the cheek.

'Oh!' he said, and blushed crimson. It was the only time I saw him like that, flustered and a little shocked. 'W-why, thank you,

Grace.' He looked down at me, smiling and happy and proud somehow.

'We'd better not be seen doing that by anyone in Purlock. No kissing in town!' I said and laughed giddily. I felt so full of joy. I had never kissed anyone before, not since I was a small child.

Dereham lay low in the distance, nothing more than a small hamlet of cottages set between trees. It did not have its own church, and the parishioners had to walk the two miles across the fields to Much Purlock to attend services at St. Andrew's. We did not go all the way into Dereham but instead skirted round the edge of the last field before the houses and then made our way back over the fields towards Much Purlock again. The winter sun was still shining down, but a biting easterly wind had started to blow, and we could not stay out in it for long. We went hand in hand all the while, huddling together for warmth. I did not kiss him again, not then, but I wanted to.

'Does your father ever ask you who you meet when you're out and about?'

'He doesn't take much interest in what I do,' I replied. 'Generally, he only notices me when I'm standing in front of him or when he wants me to do something.'

'But he must feel some affection for you as his daughter?'

'If he does, he finds it hard to show it. My affection for him also went rather cold when my mother was ill and then died. I blamed him in part, as I think children often do.'

He squeezed my hand tight and pulled me closer to him, and we walked the rest of the way back to Much Purlock in silence. We unlocked hands and edged apart as we came to the first of the houses, even though the road was deserted. When we reached the marketplace, the stallholders were packing up for the day, collapsing trestle tables and beginning to load up their carts for the journey home. Their horses chewed on hay from nosebags, stamping impatient hooves and snorting clouds of vapour from flared nostrils into the darkening air.

We were about to part by the Star Inn when I saw my father

walking quickly across the other side of the square. My heart jolted so hard that I thought it must surely stop beating, but he was walking away from us with his head down against the wind and he did not see me.

'Why're you so pale all of a sudden, Grace?' Sean asked.

'Oh, it's just the cold. I need to get in front of a good fire!' I said and laughed, although I did not feel much like laughing. I did not want to leave him and go back home again.

My father was already in his armchair when I got to the house, humming a tune to himself that I did not recognise. He had thrown his boots towards the fireplace to dry, and his overcoat was draped over the arm of his chair. The fire was nothing more than a dying pile of orange embers that was giving out little heat.

'Father, didn't you think to build up the fire?'

'I've not been back long. Can't you fetch some logs in from the shed, Grace?'

'Do it yourself for a change!' I said and stomped up the stairs to my bedroom.

'Grace,' he called up after me, 'I won't be spoken to like that, not in my own home. While you're living under my roof, you'll keep a civil tongue in your head!' I answered him by slamming my door and locking it.

When I went downstairs again towards midnight to fetch some water for the night and to have some bread and cheese for a late supper the fire was dead, and my father was not there. I had not heard him come upstairs, but I was not sure I had not drifted off to sleep for a while. The stars were out in the black sky, but the moon was hidden behind the trees and the starlight was not strong enough for me to see far into the garden. I went out to the woodshed to get a basket of logs for the morning and heard a sound that I thought at first must be a fox or a badger: *scratch, scratch, scratch* it went, then a pause, then *scrape, scrape, scrape,* pause ... I stood in that dark shed and listened. It went on and on. Something was at the far end of the garden digging at the cold earth. The clang of metal against stone gave it away in the end: it was the sound of a shovel, not of claws.

The wind had dropped, and the night was still. Not even the owls were out hunting. Only that intermittent scraping and digging sound broke the silence. I left my basket of logs by the back door and walked up the garden path, my lantern swinging as I went over the uneven ground. The candle sent its warm light into the dark corners that the starlight did not reach, but the far end of the garden was in darkness as thick as ink. What was he doing out there at that hour? I did not like walking into that darkness; it made me feel vulnerable and alone.

Someone looking out of the dark into the light always has the advantage over someone looking out of the light into the dark. The scraping sound stopped as I was halfway up the garden, just past the well. It felt as though I was being watched as I carried my flickering lantern up the path and that feeling of unseen eyes looking at me out of the darkness sent shivers down my spine. I stopped at the top of the garden where the apple tree is, waiting for the sound to start up again, but there was absolute silence, and no-one was there. Perhaps my father, or whoever it had been, had slipped quietly away through the hedge and out onto the back path that leads down to the lane when he saw me coming.

I went all around the hedges and the trees, the pear, the cherry, the damson, in that thick darkness, the candlelight making the trunks and branches flicker and glow, but there was no sign of a disturbance of the ground. I could not understand how there could have been the sound of digging with no-one to make it and nothing there. When I went back down to the house again, my mind was in a turmoil, quite unsure of what to think about what I had just heard. My imagination must have been playing tricks on me. When I went upstairs to bed, I pushed open my father's bedroom door and he was in there snoring away, oblivious to everything.

I lay in my bed unable to sleep through the dark hours of the night until just before dawn, when I finally fell into a dreamless slumber as sunlight broke over the horizon. Sean's carved oak cross, leaning against the leaded windowpane up on the windowsill above my bed, gave me some comfort and hope through that long and lonely night.

Chapter Thirty

Mrs Samuels came to lodge at the Star Inn again in early February. It did not seem that she had told my father exactly how long she would be staying for this time. Rather than taking her breakfast at the inn, she came to the house each day for it and mooned around inspecting my dear mother's trinkets and curios while my father saw to his patients in the consulting room. The weather had turned grey and rainy, with rolling and roiling clouds being blown across the sky by an endless wind, but I could not wait to escape each morning when I had made the breakfast then cleared it all away again. The more that I tried to keep away from her on those mornings, the more she followed me from room to room around the house. She even came up and tried to make conversation through my bedroom door as I was getting myself ready to go out.

I still could not explain the digging sounds I had heard in the depths of that January night. I went around the garden several times in the daylight, looking carefully under the hedges and the trees, but I could see no disturbance of the ground. I even went more than once behind the hedge at the far end of the garden where the path down to the lane begins and squeezed through a gap in the neighbouring hedge into the abandoned garden there. Apart from waist-high weeds and a fallen apple tree that was already well rotted through, there was nothing there. Then finally I saw it in a far corner of that ruined garden that I could have sworn I had looked in before: a rectangle of disturbed soil where the weeds and grass had been cut away. I pushed at the soil with my boot, then when I saw nothing but more half-frozen and half-sodden soil, I got a stick and picked away at the earth.

Three or four inches down, things that were blacker than the soil began to show themselves in the loosened earth. Then the muted stench of rotting flesh hit me, my stomach clenched, bile shot up my throat and I gagged over that foul-smelling hole. There was a haphazard row of a dozen or so stubby black beaks on heads with dead black eyes down there and body after body with fans of mud-smeared wing- and tailfeathers. I realised with horror that it was a grave for rooks and crows in that frozen February ground. Someone had been burying the diseased birds of the neighbourhood—and I had thought that the sickness had passed. I went away from that silent, abandoned garden with a shudder, cleaning my boots on a tussock of coarse grass, and vowed never to go back in there again.

Mrs Samuels was still in the house when I came back from the garden that morning, even though it was almost midday. I held my tongue as she dipped a ladle into the beef stew that I was cooking on the range for lunch, slurped loudly with apparent relish at the meat liquor, then dipped the ladle back into the pot for a second ladleful. I could hear my father in his consulting room with another patient: I did not want to be trapped in the kitchen with Mrs Samuels and her hunger without my father to divert her. I told her to mind the stew and serve it to him when he came out for lunch, and then I went out for the afternoon.

I walked up through the woods less often than I had done before, and now only rarely went over to the far side where it dips down into the next valley to watch the navvies' camp, but the pull of the trees still took me out that way sometimes. A half-hearted rain had begun to fall, but to be out of the house and away from my father and Mrs Samuels was a blessing. The lanes and footpaths were deserted once I had left Much Purlock behind me, and I walked alone with only the rain, the birdsong, and the clouded sky for company.

And then into the woods where the trees were so familiar to me that they were like my childhood friends. I had not visited my beech tree for many weeks, and I went to find some meagre shelter from the rain beneath its bare branches and to see what life there was down in the camp. The woods smelled of the slow decay of damp leaves and of wild garlic and the spores of fungi clinging to fallen tree-trunks and branches, a whole world of dead trees beneath my feet. I knew that I would have to find some more of those mushrooms again before too long.

Rain pocked the surface of a large puddle by the fire down at the camp, the flames leaping and dancing in the wind despite the rain. Those men that were not on their shifts on the line must have been huddling in their huts to keep out of the weather. I was longing to see Sean again, but no-one was about. I would have gone down through the trees to get closer to the camp, but the rain was becoming heavier now and I wanted to go somewhere—St. Andrew's church porch or one of the barns out in the fields—that I could find some shelter and not be disturbed by anyone.

I went back up the path the way that I had come, through the denser stands of beech and oak, and then left the path and walked between the trees over the undulating ground, the carpet of leaves and wild garlic muffling the sound of my feet. The rain was even heavier now, its cold darts getting into my clothes and down my neck, but the trunks and the branches gave me some protection at least from the worst of it.

I heard voices in the distance after a while and saw a fire between the trees. I wanted to see who the people there were but did not want to be seen. I crept closer over the soft ground: the voices were all male and Irish and the men were dark shapes gathered around the orange glow of the fire between the trees. I managed to get very near to them without being seen or heard; they were the other side of a high and broad holly bush, and they were throwing sticks and branches onto the fire. The wet wood hissed and popped angrily in the rain as it burned.

'Menzies is an arrogant cunt and he needs cutting down to size,' one man said. I had never heard that word used before but could guess what it must mean.

'But how're any of us going to do that?' another man asked.

'No idea,' the first man said again. 'But that's exactly what he is and what he needs.'

There must have been seven or eight men there around the fire and they all grunted in agreement when he said that. Two or three of them wandered off to look for more wood, but by pure chance none of them came around the back of the holly bush and found me. So far as I could see through the leaves, Sean was not there, but it was hard to tell in the gloom of that wood and with the bush right in front of me. I did not want to move position in case I gave myself away.

They went quiet after that, passing around a couple of flagons of something and muttering to each other as they stared into the fire, laughing now and then. I lost interest after a while, for there was nothing much to see or to hear, and I crept off back the way I had come. I did not know why I had thought that Sean might be there; and I now faced the prospect of having to return rain-soaked and disappointed to my father's and Mrs Samuels's den of delights, not having even seen Sean, let alone talked to him.

While I was walking back towards the path, I saw something flickering between the tree trunks up ahead. I stopped as still as I could and held my breath: there in the shadow of an oak about fifty yards away was a red deer stag. He must have been at least a ten pointer, although his antlers were half obscured by the dappled light. He heard me or scented me on the wind and turned his head with those magnificent antlers to look at me: what magic and darkness was in his gentle eyes. Then, having seen me and sensed danger, he was gone before I knew it, racing and leaping away across that wet and silent wood. I had only seen deer a few times before in the wood, and never one as large and as beautiful as he was.

My eyes seemed to be playing tricks on me: where the stag had been only moments before there was Sean. My heart leapt! I closed my eyes and opened them again and he was still there. He did not see me at first, but then as I came nearer, he looked up and saw me through the trees. I guessed that he must be on his way to join the other men around the fire.

'Grace!' he called out and waved over to me. 'What're you doing out here all alone on a day like this?'

'I didn't want to stay at home with those two lovebirds. It's so much better being out here, whatever the weather. I just saw the most beautiful red deer stag. Did you see him, too?'

'I must have just missed him. I'd have loved to see one out here. How are you, Grace?'

'All the better for seeing the stag and for seeing you.' I went up on tiptoe again and kissed him on the cheek. He did not blush quite so fiercely this time but smiled at me happily and stroked my damp cheek with the back of his hand.

'I was on my way to see some of the men over that way,' he said, pointing towards the part of the wood that I had just come from, 'but you've given me an excuse—I mean a reason—not to go. Who wants to stand around in the rain talking about our intrigues when I can spend time with you?'

'I saw their fire through the trees and overheard them talking. Apart from complaining crudely about someone whose name I didn't recognise, they seemed to be having a fine old time.'

'You *overheard* them, did you?' he asked and laughed his deep laugh. 'Were you eavesdropping, by any chance?'

'I might have been just a little. There wasn't much else to do in this wet wood.'

'They were probably complaining about Mr Menzies. The men like him even less than they do O'Donnell.'

'They'd like to get rid of him, as far as I could tell.'

'Only the railway company can do that,' Sean replied. 'But he does a good job, he's just not got a nice way of going about it. He's nothing like Mr Sansom was. He puts our backs up almost every time he opens his mouth.'

We went down the path towards Much Purlock hand in hand, our heads bowed against the wind and the rain. Being by his side made me feel like a woman, despite being only seventeen. I went up on tiptoe to kiss him on the cheek again before he left me to walk back up through the wood and over to the camp. He bent down to kiss me then, too, on the lips this time, but with our mouths closed. I did not know any other way then.

'I wanted to go back home again last summer, I missed it so much, but I'm so happy I stayed,' he whispered in my ear.

My heart was singing as I walked home. I was sure that I loved him.

When I went in at the back door, Mrs Samuels and my father were sitting at the kitchen table sharing a pot of coffee. The rain tapped at the windowpanes and the wind came down the chimney, threatening to blow out the ash from the fireplace. They looked up at me as I came in, secretive and smiling like naughty children.

'Grace, we've set our wedding day for the last Saturday in May. Oh, the happiest of happy days!' Mrs Samuels said. 'I'd like you to be one of my bridesmaids, along with my three daughters.'

'I-I can't, I *won't* do that,' I said, refusing to look either of them in the eye now. I ran upstairs to my bedroom and slammed the door. How quickly my pure joy had turned to anger. It was news to me that the ghastly woman even had children. What, would they come to live with us as well? That simply could not, would not happen. I had to find a way of stopping them getting married. I had no choice now, no choice at all.

Chapter Thirty-One

The Three Graces came to visit Much Purlock with their mother in early March. Mrs Samuels fussed and clucked around her brood as they sat at our kitchen table, and it was the first time I had seen her really acting like the matriarch of our house. It made me want to get up and leave the table right there and then. Her girls were all a little older than me, and three of the plainest I had ever seen. One had teeth like a rabbit and startled eyes, as if she had been caught at night in the light of a hunter's lantern; the other two had moon faces, as if they were looking at themselves in the backs of spoons. They were done up like proper young ladies, though, wearing pretty silk dresses, bows in their hair and rouge on their cheeks. The echo of my unspoken nickname for them with my own name was not lost on me.

'You're so naturally pretty,' one of them said to me when she first saw me, after I came in from a walk in the spring air. Gracious reciprocation was expected, but I simply could not muster any.

'I don't have much time to look in the mirror,' I replied to none of them in particular. Mrs Samuels introduced me to her girls, but I did not really take in their names. I thought of them only as Myxy, Moon and Half-Moon, the youngest one.

My father sat at the head of the table, smiling delightedly but saying little. He peered over his glasses at me, his mutton chops, moustache, and beard oiled and combed smooth, and he seemed to be weighing up whether to criticise me in front of the girls and their mother for my unwillingness to engage in the appropriate manner or to hold his tongue instead.

'Grace likes to walk more than she does to talk,' he said at last. 'She's always been that way.'

'Never mind,' Mrs Samuels said. 'We've got plenty of conversationalists in here.' The Three Graces smiled crookedly up at me from their places at the table, and I went upstairs to change out of my outdoor clothes.

'No, you stay sitting down and I'll finish clearing away,' I overheard my father saying when I went back downstairs again in my best dress. My ears took in the words, but I could not believe what I was hearing. I had never known him to do anything at all around the house in recent years, other than chop wood in the garden now and then and rake over the beds and the vegetable patch.

'While the master of the house washes the dishes—what world are we living in!—I'll show you round,' Mrs Samuels said, and laughed gaily. 'The first thing I must do is to reacquaint your father-to-be with a cook and a domestic. It's more than high time!'

They went off to peek into my father's consulting room, gawping no doubt open-mouthed at the full-sized plaster model of a human skeleton that hung in the corner there and staring uncomprehendingly at the anatomical prints of interior worlds on the walls, and they then tried out the armchairs in the sitting-room.

'This is a snug little place,' one of the two Moons said. (I could not tell their voices apart.)

'Yes, it's really most quaint,' Myxy replied. 'I could well imagine retiring to somewhere like this when I'm in my dotage.'

'That's not so very far away for some of us,' Mrs Samuels said, and chuckled to herself. I stood in the hallway all the while in my blue satin dress with bows on its sleeves, feeling as if I was a stranger in my own home.

'Ladies,' my father called from the kitchen, 'it'll soon be time for me to walk you back to the inn. We can take some afternoon tea there before I come back and see to my next patient. He's due here at four o'clock.'

'Will you join us, Grace?' Half-Moon asked me as they came out of the sitting-room and found me standing there in the hallway. 'You look so lovely in that blue.'

'I need to prepare the evening meal. Perhaps another time,' I replied, trying hard not to be too stand-offish. It was, after all, not this girl's fault, only a year or two older than me as she was, that I could not stand my father or her mother.

'It would be nice if you could join us just for half an hour or so,' Mrs Samuels chipped in. 'Isn't that so, William?'

'Yes, do come over to the inn with us for a cup of tea at least, Grace,' my father said too airily from the kitchen, amid the clinking of dishes and cups as he put the crockery away. There was a defeated undertone to his voice, as if that was the very last thing that he wanted.

'Well, if I must,' I replied, suddenly glad to be intruding on his happy gaggle of guests. I went to fetch my coat from the hook by the back door.

The afternoon was overcast, and a strong breeze was shaking the bare branches of the trees all around. We walked in single file down the side path and along the lane, with Mrs Samuels up in front, followed by her three girls, then my father, and with me making up the tail. The Moons and Myxy chatted away, while Mrs Samuels and my father walked on in silence. I had to lift the bottom of my dress away from the mud. I had not worn it since I had last been to a Sunday service some years earlier, but it still fitted me quite well. I had not worn anything nice for a very long time. I imagined that the Samuels girls were rather more accustomed to dressing for the occasion up in London than I was down in Much Purlock.

At the Star Inn we went straight up the back stairs to their two adjoining rooms, avoiding the few daytime drinkers in the saloon bar who peered at us curiously through the windows as we went past. God knows what they made of us. Much Purlock had rarely seen such an overdressed group of people parading through its streets than in that afternoon gloom. My father and I were obviously well known to the town, but the Moons and Myxy and Mrs Samuels must have presented quite a sight: strangers in silk and furs tottering through the streets before disappearing into the inn.

My father had asked for two pots of tea and a tray of cakes to be brought up by the serving girl, Sarah. The girls and their mother all nibbled carefully around their teacakes and sipped daintily from their teacups with their little fingers sticking out. I had never seen anyone eating and drinking quite like that before: it was as if they were tiptoeing around their food and drink for fear of offending it. I ate one teacake with currants and hard icing on it as quickly as I could, then put another one in my coat pocket, wrapped in a piece of the inn's letterheaded paper that was set out in a stack on the desk in the girls' bedroom, to take home with me. We hardly ever had sweet things to eat, and the cakes were sugary and delicious.

My father settled into the high-backed chair in the corner of the girls' room, with Mrs Samuels sitting next to him on a lower, blue-painted stool, and smiled out at his new-found family as if this was the most natural thing in the world. And I had not even met three-quarters of them before that very day! I felt completely out of place, redundant somehow, and I could not wait to get away.

After half an hour or so, Sarah came in to clear away the trays and to stoke the fire in both fireplaces. Before she left, arms laden, she smiled at me with her eyebrows raised as if to say: 'And who exactly are these people, Grace?' She and I had been in the same class at school, and she was always a kind-hearted, thoughtful girl.

'D'you know her?' Half-Moon asked when she had left, obviously having noticed our unspoken exchange. 'She seems a little forward for her position.'

'It's not so big a place, this. Most people know each other here,' I replied curtly. 'I suppose it's quite different where you come from.'

'Well, yes,' Myxy said, interrupting us, staring at me with her unblinking rabbit eyes. 'There are almost two million people in London. We know our friends and the local shopkeepers, but most people are strangers to us.'

'You're lucky to have each other,' I said. 'I'm on my own.'

'You have your father at least,' Half-Moon, the friendliest of the girls, said. I almost laughed, but managed to hold it in.

'Well, we live under the same roof,' I said. 'Not much more than that though.' Mrs Samuels and my father were talking and laughing away together, and they did not hear me. The girls looked at me enquiringly but said nothing further on the subject.

I made my excuses soon afterwards and walked home in the dusk. I was glad to be on my own again and much preferred it that way. Sean was the only person who by being with me made my life happier rather than sadder or lonelier. I wanted to be with him or with no-one. I was glad to have got away from my father, at least for an hour or two, and from the Samuels girls and their awful mother.

That ache of missing my own dear mother was resurfacing again, and I could not stand it. I tried to push it back down again, to keep it at bay by keeping busy. I was making beef stew and suet dumplings for supper that night, and I put a bottle of claret on the table next to my father's place. One glass of red wine would lead to another, and two glasses of red wine would lead to him going into his study after supper and taking a pinch or two of his pep.

Once the stew was simmering away on the range, the steam from the pot clouding the kitchen windows, I reached up for the bag of adulterated snuff behind the jars on the top shelf and went into his study to empty the pure snuff from his jar and put in my admixture. It had been a while since I had done that, and I was curious to know whether the effect on him would be all the stronger now because of his unwitting abstinence from the powder of dried mushrooms.

He came home just after seven o'clock, and he had barely taken off his coat and gloves before he started sniffing the air in the kitchen and asking when supper would be.

'I'm going back to the Star Inn later to wish the ladies goodnight,' he said. 'Let's eat before it gets too much later, Grace.'

'It'll be ready when it's ready. You could try sounding a little more grateful that I cook for you every evening.'

'You cook for *us*, Grace. Don't you eat as well?'

I did not deign to answer that question. 'Perhaps your new wife will be taking over these duties in the summer unless you see fit to get a cook in again once you're married? I've had a bellyful of doing it all since I was just ten years old, Father! And where exactly will Mrs Samuels be living?'

'Why, right here with me—with us. She's fond of the idea of a change of scene and the healthier air away from the smog in London. And I can't exactly give my practice up at forty-five.'

My heart sank into my stomach. 'And what about her girls? Where will they be?'

'They'll come and go between the two places, between her townhouse and here.'

My heart fell into my boots. 'You mean here as in this house, or at the inn? You know there's no room for guests here, Father, unless you're expecting me to sleep in one of the outhouses.'

'I expect they'll all be married off before too long, in any case,' was his only reply. I somehow strongly doubted that, having just spent part of the afternoon with them.

He devoured two helpings of the stew and dumplings, despite his round of teacakes earlier in the afternoon, and looked as if he was sitting on pins and wanted to get back to the inn as soon as possible. I thought that my plan had failed, but after first drinking down one glass of claret and pouring himself another, which he drank in two large gulps, he got up, put his napkin down on the table and went into his study.

He was in there longer than usual and I wondered if he was reading one of his medical treatises or had nodded off. He came out at last, sniffing and brushing off his moustache with the back of his hand.

'There's something slightly off about my pep,' he said to no-one in particular, and he did not seem to be expecting a reply. My heart jumped and thumped in my chest, and I felt my cheeks flushing. 'But it certainly gives me quite a kick.'

He left to walk back to the inn a few minutes later, looking rosy-cheeked and very pleased with himself. There was that smile on his lips again that I recognised from before. That smile seemed to lead inextricably to other things, to visions, hallucinations, aural intrusions, mental aberrations; and I had high hopes that his night ahead would be anything but uneventful. Mrs Samuels and her girls might find that the future head of their household was rather more than they had bargained for.

I heaped more logs onto the fire, as the night was a cold one, and settled into my armchair to read by the light of my lantern. I had taken to leafing again through my father's edition of *The boke of secretes of Albertus Magnus of the vertues of herbes, stones, and certayne beasts* and was beguiled by the mysterious and strange language of this mediaeval German friar and philosopher who later became a saint. Much of it made little sense to my eyes and ears as I read the words out loud to myself, but this man from six hundred years ago understood so well what gifts nature can give us and what it can take away.

My father may well have read the book, or at least the parts of it where the pages had notes scribbled in their margins, but he had not learned how precious the natural world is. He had welcomed the coming of the railway; he had not railed against its destruction of nature. By giving him my mushroom powders, I could teach him just how powerful nature is and what it can do to you. If I increased the frequency with which I gave him the adulterated pep and it had its desired effect on him, I might also, as an additional boon, manage to make Mrs Samuels think twice about going ahead with the wedding in the summer. I could not stomach the idea of her and her girls spending even one night under our roof.

* * *

I longed to see Sean on that dark and starless night, to have him near me. I wanted to kiss him again, to have his mouth on my mouth, to feel his warmth on me. He was my light in the darkness and my hope. But I went up to bed alone and lay there in the cold dark, my body slowly giving away its warmth to the sheets and the pillows.

A strange noise coming from downstairs woke me in the middle of the night, sometime after two o'clock judging by the height of the moon in the sky behind broken cloud. I crept onto the landing and the house was in darkness, with only the faintest glow of candlelight coming up from the sitting room. I listened carefully and all was quiet, but then there was a great gasping sob and another, as if my father was trying to suck in all the air in the room down there.

'Why, oh why,' I heard him whimper to himself; then, 'I wasn't myself. I can't have been.'

He went silent for a minute or so, before I heard him sobbing to himself, quietly at first and then more and more loudly, as if he would never stop.

'What will they make of me?' was the last thing I heard him ask into the night air between great gusting sighs before I went back into my bedroom and quietly closed the door.

CHAPTER THIRTY-TWO

Hereford Insane Asylum, 1850

I am paying for it now. There is no proper rest here: the women shuffle around late into the night, and cry and moan in their sleep. Even with the thin pillow over my head, this animal noise burrows into my brain and my sleep is always broken, night after night after night.

Mr Osney accompanied me on another of my walks through the grounds today. Spring has arrived in full force, pale buds pushing out from slender branches towards the sunlight and green shoots breaking through the soil everywhere. All this renewal of life and here I am in the same old place. Year after year of these blank walls and these bars on the windows, even though we are not prisoners, as we are reminded by the Warden and the orderlies when we protest at out treatment. 'Patient' and 'prisoner' are interchangeable words here: they call us patients when we say that we are prisoners here in the asylum, held against our will, and they treat us like prisoners while calling us patients. This year I will get out; I have sworn that to myself. But even if I could escape, or persuade them of my sanity, that I am harmless to others and to myself, where would I go?

A new girl called Lorna has arrived here. She reminds me of how I was almost ten years ago: all defiance and passion, thinking that the world must listen to her, when it is she who needs to listen to what the world has to say. She comes from the Shropshire borders, and she has an accent as thick as cream. 'Why're you in 'ere then?' she asks me on her second day here, having spent her first day on the ward in total silence. I had thought she was completely mute until I heard her speaking to one of the orderlies.

'My father accused me of trying to poison him and the magistrate believed him.'

'En did yer?'

'I wasn't trying to poison him, only to teach him a lesson.'

'What were the lesson, then?' she asks.

'It's hard to put into words. I was trying to show him that progress isn't always good. Make him see that the natural world's more important than any of us. We can't exist without it. And I didn't want him to marry again, at least not the woman he had chosen.'

She looks at me as if I am speaking in tongues and sidles off to stare out of the window into the evening light over the garden.

This place after night comes down is like a farmyard slowly settling. The women low and moan and yawn, and the orderlies clank and clang the pots and pans as they clear them away. The ward's main doors are then slammed shut and bolted from the outside as the last orderly leaves. We are left to our own devices until six o'clock in the morning, when the whole thing starts again. Sometimes one or another of the more disturbed women on the ward turns violent during the night, threatening to harm themselves or others, and there is no-one to intervene but us inmates. We have to hold them down or lock them in the latrine until their rage or mania has passed. The orderlies never leave anything sharp on the ward: all the knives and forks are locked away overnight in the kitchens of the asylum, far away on the other side of the building near the men's wing.

Apart from Mr Osney and the Warden, I have not spoken to another man since I came here: the men are only allowed out for their exercise when we are locked back inside, and there is no getting into their wards. The women stare out of the windows at them longingly as they take their exercise, but I have no eyes for them. I still only want Sean.

Chapter Thirty-Three

Much Purlock, 1842

Mrs Samuels was absent from Much Purlock throughout the month of March, and my father went listlessly about the house, cancelling appointments with his patients where he could and spending long hours in his study or consulting room leafing through his medical books. In his pining, he often did without lunch, leaving me to eat it on my own in the kitchen or, if the weather allowed, to take it with me on my daily walk.

I met Sean outside the Star Inn on the second Wednesday of the month. It had been more than a week since I had last seen him, and I had done my own pining in the interval between our seeing each other. The sun was shining down, spring was in the air, and I no longer cared what the townsfolk might say about our walking out together. We stayed close to each other as we went around the market stalls, and one or two of the stallholders smiled knowingly at me but said little. I smiled back at them but offered no introduction or explanation. They knew, in any case, that Sean was one of the navvies and thus a stranger to the town, even though they themselves were not from Much Purlock but from the countryside beyond.

Once we had left the edge of the town behind, we joined hands and walked in the afternoon sunshine along the path to Cutstock, the birds singing in the trees on either side of the path and the smell of damp earth drying in the new warmth of spring filling our nostrils.

'Look up over there,' Sean said, pointing above the sycamores to our left. 'That's a red kite. I haven't seen one of those birds in a long time.' It circled on the thermals, rising higher as we watched, and called out with its plaintive, shrill cry.

I have never understood why they call when they are hunting, as if to warn their prey of their approach. I would stay silent myself. 'Some farmers call them pests and poison them around here,' I replied. 'They say that they take the lambs still suckling from their mothers in the fields. I think they're majestic creatures myself. I often wish I could fly up and away like that.'

'Please don't: I'd miss you.' Sean looked down at me and smiled. He bent and planted a kiss on my lips, and I went up on tiptoe before we continued our walk and kissed him back.

'It's just that my father …,' I said, and then did not know quite how to carry on.

'Your father what?' he asked, frowning down at me now.

'The widow he's marrying this summer, Mrs Samuels, has three dull daughters and they're all threatening to come and live here with us. I just can't bear the idea. I won't be able to stand it.' I felt myself flushing with anguish at the very thought.

'Run away with me then!' he said and laughed his hearty laugh.

'Where to?'

'I've no idea. Depends on where the railway will take me next.'

'I've never even left the county. I can't really imagine going anywhere else, and I'd never take the train.'

'We can go by coach, then. Just come away with me later this year.' He smiled and looked as if he really meant what he was saying.

'I suppose we'll have to see how things go over the next few months,' I replied and smiled back at him encouragingly. 'We've hardly known each other for very long, have we?'

'It may have only been a few months, but I feel I know you well already.'

'There's much more to know.' I kissed him again. 'You'll just have to wait to find out what that is.'

'If I had to hazard a guess, I'd say you were a beautiful white witch who casts her spell on man and beast alike,' he said, laughing and pulling me closer to him.

'Perhaps,' I said, laughing. 'Perhaps.' I held tightly onto his arm. I did not want to ever have to let him go again, as if our parting would break the magic.

The hamlet of Cutstock nestles in a bend of the Wye about four miles from Much Purlock, just far enough from the bank of the river to be untouched by the winter floods. The brown river was in spate after the rains and spilled over the bank onto the pasture fields between the village and the water. Sean and I walked as near to the river as we dared, the water swirling only a few yards from our feet, and we saw the blue flash of a kingfisher as it dived for a fish from the branch of an alder tree on the far bank. It could have been a scene from 1500 or 1600 or 1700: there was no sign of the modern life that had crept into my world only two valleys and a dozen fields away. Sean was from that other world; but he had slipped over into mine, if not quite by accident, then also not by design.

'Have you ever met any of the men from the railway company itself?' I asked.

'No, only their mouthpieces Messrs Jones, Sansom and Menzies. Two out of the three of them are, or were, good men. Why d'you ask?'

'I like you really very much, Sean, but I hate the company you work for. I like you even though you're employed by that corrupting enterprise.'

'I came over here to work on the railway because I had no other choice, none at all,' he said with a vehemence to his voice that I had not heard before. 'It was either that or staying on in County Sligo to watch our farm slowly drown in debt and sink without a trace. You know that we navvies aren't building the railway for people like us.'

'I'd rather die than ever use it. It's wrecked the valley where the line is. What kind of progress is that?'

'For the railway companies, progress just means money and nothing else, Grace,' he said and laughed a hollow laugh. 'Anyway, I've had enough of this gloomy talk. Let's see if the inn's open. I need a glass of strong ale.'

The River Inn was a low-lying, ancient whitewashed building with a black timber frame. The sunshine allowed us to sit in the garden, and I waited at a table while Sean went inside to fetch me a glass of water and himself a glass of beer. He came out almost as soon as he had gone in.

'The man says he won't serve me because I'm Irish,' he said, looking angry and embarrassed at the same time. 'As soon as he heard my accent, he told me to get out of his inn.'

'Leave this to me,' I said, and marched inside.

The inn was empty and my bootheels clacked on the bare wooden floorboards as I went in search of the innkeeper. He was drying glasses with a cloth in the dimly-lit back bar, expecting perhaps a rush of drinkers from the outlying farms at the end of the day. He looked as if he had been caught red-handed when he saw me marching over to his counter but stared defiantly straight back at me all the same.

'I sent my friend in here to fetch me a glass of water and himself some beer,' I said, 'and he came out with nothing. What's the meaning of this?'

'As soon as he opened his mouth, Miss Whoever-You-Are, I knew he was an Irish navvy. I don't want them in here. They've caused nothing but trouble.'

'He's a good man; no doubt far better than you are, you stupid bigot.' I glared at him angrily, the heat rising in my throat. I was about to demand the drinks from him, in any case, but decided that my money was too good for him, and I stamped out of the inn, slamming the ancient oak door behind me.

'You had no luck either?' Sean asked when I walked back round to the garden empty-handed.

'Let's just say that he and I didn't see eye to eye. Let's go back to Much Purlock now instead.'

We walked in near silence back over the fields the way we had come, holding hands and staying close together but each of us lost in our own thoughts. It was the first time I had witnessed such bigotry first-hand. The wind was picking up and the sun's light carried with it less heat as the cold air blew in.

'Have you had much of that kind of thing here?' I asked.

'Not me personally, but some of the other men haven't fared so well. I tend to keep myself to myself, and usually only go to the Star Inn, where they know us and tolerate us now. But some of the other navvies have gone a bit further afield and they've had a spot of bother here and there.'

'People here have been cut off from the world for so long that they often haven't met anyone from much beyond Gloucestershire or Shropshire or Wales,' I said. 'That's no excuse, of course.'

'I hadn't found people here to be unkind until today. And look at you and me!' He laughed. 'O'Donnell was attacked on the woodland path a while ago, but I wouldn't hold that against anyone.'

'From what I saw of him when I came down to the camp that time, he seems a very unsavoury fellow.'

'He's certainly that and more.'

Sean stopped to kiss me on the lips just before the path across the fields from Cutstock came out between the first houses of the town. The softness of his mouth sent electricity down my spine and a rush of blood into my cheeks. I wanted to kiss him again and again and so much more, but I had to get home to begin the supper. I wished that I was making the meal to share with Sean rather than my father: how lonely he must have been going back through the woods and down to the camp to sit long into the night around the fire or in his hut surrounded by those worn-out men. We walked to the marketplace together, no longer holding hands, and then went our separate ways, promising to see each other again the following week.

My father was still in his study when I got back to the house, and I could hear his muffled, sepulchral voice through the door as he read passages from his medical books out loud to himself. I wondered how long it would be before he realised that he would never find the key to unlocking the mystery of his aberrations in the pages of those books. I would have to give him another dose to see if that brought on the beginnings of an epiphany in him. Until then, he locked himself away like a hermit in pursuit of knowledge that would never be his.

Chapter Thirty-Four

Spring has always been my favourite time of year: all that hope in the burgeoning of new green life as it thrusts itself through shoots and unfurls itself in leaves, before fading in the summer sun, falling shrivelled from the bough in autumn and rotting in the frost-bound earth of winter.

I went foraging in early April with mother's wicker basket over my arm. I was looking for henbane, which I knew from my father's medical books had been used in ancient times as an anaesthetic and to temper diseases of the nervous system. From Albertus Magnus, I had learned that it was also used as a hallucinogen: henbane's effect all depends on the dose given. If I was the cause of my father's episodes of mental aberration, I could also feed him their balm, their cure. I could be both the sickness and the medicine, with the mushrooms of autumn and the henbane of spring.

I went over the fields to a copse on the low hill near the path to Denscombe, where some weeks earlier I had seen a clump of the pale-yellow flowers of henbane, shaped like bells with starburst ends. I found them again sheltering beside the trunk of an ash tree and picked some of their veined leaves and delicate flowers, putting them carefully in my basket and covering them with a cloth. It was a fine day, the spring sun burnishing the sky, and I sat in the heart of the copse on the stump of a tree. There was birdsong all around and the breeze played with my hair, blowing it over my face and into my eyes, as I ate the piece of rye bread and the cheddar cheese I had brought with me. I was happiest on my own and, if not on my own, then only with Sean. Sitting there in the copse all alone, I knew, or thought I knew, that I did not need anyone else for my happiness: nature and the sound of my own thoughts were enough for me.

There were women's voices in the distance, and they slowly became more distinct as they came along the path towards the copse. I got up from the tree stump and hid myself behind a sycamore on the far side of the trees, as far away from the path as I could get without going back out into the open field. There were three of them, carrying large rush baskets of laundry on their shoulders away from Denscombe out towards the river, laughing with each other and talking away despite their heavy loads. I had not had that friendship with other girls, other women, since my schooldays and seeing them so happy together, despite the mundanity of their task ahead, quite took my enjoyment of the day away. The men at the mill were the nearest I had to friends, and they were hardly that. The only one I had was Sean, and we both wanted so much more from each other than just friendship.

I walked home with the girls ahead of me in the distance for a while, until they turned off down a field path towards the river. Despite the spring sunshine and the birdsong, my mood had become low: seeing the washerwomen so happy in each other's company and carrying my mother's basket over my arm had served to make me miss her, miss female company itself, even more strongly. I could not help thinking, I could not help cursing fate, that everything would have been so different if she had only not got ill, if she had only lived.

My father was in his consulting room with a patient when I got home. I decided to make the richest supper that I could muster, serve him strong wine, and then test my herbalist's skills with the ground mushrooms and the leaves, petals, and stems of henbane. Perhaps practising my art would alleviate the bitterness of my mood. I chose the plump chicken that had been hanging on its hook in the cold store since market day and stuffed it with finely chopped sage and onion, then put it in the range to roast in its own juices for two hours. Cutting up potatoes, carrots, and leeks for the soup to start the meal worked out some of my anger through the clenching of my palms and the pressure on my fingertips. I added the larger chunks of potato to the roasting pan for the chicken, which was browning well and gave off such a fine aroma that my mouth watered. I roughly chopped the cauliflower and the cabbage to boil them just before the chicken was cooked through and had made a suet duff with currants that morning for pudding, now simmering under a muslin cloth in its pan on top of the range for as long as the chicken roasted.

My father came out of his consulting room long after his unseen patient had left through the front door and as the meal was almost ready. He was wearing his purple velvet waistcoat with the floral embroidery again and a pair of charcoal-grey trousers. I sensed a special occasion of some kind coming on: he was humming a tune to himself and seemed suddenly full of the joys of spring. It was quite a difference from his recent gloom.

'Why, Father, you look all spruced up, as if you've got somewhere else to be.'

'Didn't I tell you? Mrs Samuels, erm Josephine, is at the Star Inn for a much overdue visit and she's coming over here in a little while to eat with us.'

'Oh, is she now?' I replied. 'No, you didn't say a word about it. It's just as well that I've cooked a large bird for supper tonight.' I was amazed to hear that she had forgiven and forgotten quite so quickly whatever it was that had unfolded at the Star Inn that night when she was last there with the Three Graces. My work was obviously far from done.

'Well, she'll be here by seven o'clock, so let's make sure the table looks presentable: please put the linen napkins out. After last time, I need everything to go as well as possible over the next few days.'

Mrs Samuels knocked at the kitchen window just after the grandfather clock in the hallway had struck seven. When I opened the back door to her, she glanced at me and then tried to peer round me to look for my father, whom she had not seen in weeks. She had a steely look in her eyes, as if her mind was set on confrontation.

'Hello, Grace,' she said somewhat coolly when she breezed into the kitchen, offering me her hand. 'That smells delicious. I haven't eaten anything since Sydenham Hill. Is your father not in?' There was a whiff of something floral coming off her: verbena or crushed lemongrass or another herbal extract with a citrus scent.

'He's gone into his consulting room for something. I'm sure he'll be out again in a moment.'

'I thought he'd be raring to see me.'

'Oh, he's certainly that! He's been talking about nothing else for days,' I said lying. He had barely spoken at all, and when he had spoken, he had done so only to himself and not to me.

My father came out of the consulting room a few minutes later and smiled sheepishly at her, bowing his head before her as if she were Queen Victoria and kissing her outstretched hand.

'William darling,' she said, 'I've missed you so.'

'Not nearly as much as I've missed you, dearest,' he replied, sounding like a lovestruck balladeer. He had blushed a shade of puce beneath his whiskers, remembering no doubt his indiscretions at the Star Inn. I saw that my father was on probation now: one more mishap and he would surely no longer be affianced to this metropolitan madam.

I served my thick vegetable soup in our best blue-and-white China bowls, and they drank it hungrily from their spoons, casting nervous smiles at each other and dabbing at their mouths with their napkins. The chicken came out brown and spitting from its pan, and I set it to rest on the wooden cutting board for a few minutes while I sharpened the carving knife and took the cabbage and cauliflower off the boil.

My father and Mrs Samuels sipped their red wine and talked to each other hesitatingly in subdued tones. In my mind all the while, far more than that atmosphere of awkwardness and tension in the room, was the jar of adulterated pep in my father's study. I had sneaked in that morning while he was still asleep and tipped out his pure snuff into a bag, then poured in an equal measure of my mushroom and snuff powders. It was pure good fortune that Mrs

Samuels had arrived that evening to witness the effects of his taking it. If an episode of delirium and aberration followed, as it always seemed to do, just as night follows day, then I would offer my father a cup of coffee with some henbane stem and leaf steeped in it with his breakfast in the morning. Perhaps that would bring some calm and balance to his disturbed mind.

'Thank you, Grace, that was a fine meal,' Mrs Samuels said, putting her knife and fork down together on her plate and wiping her lips with her napkin again. 'The bird was most moist and perfectly cooked.'

'Excuse me for a moment, ladies,' my father said, getting up from the table, his napkin still tucked under his chin into the collar of his shirt. 'I'm just going into my study for something.' There was no word of thanks for the meal. He made his strange half-bow towards his fiancée again and my pulse quickened as he headed down the hallway.

Rather than stay sitting at the dining table alone with Mrs Samuels, I got up and busied myself with clearing away and washing up the dishes and the pans. Mrs Samuels just sat there staring into space and smiling to herself, as if she could hear all the angels singing. She did not lift a finger to help me clear the table or to wipe it clean after our meal.

My father sneezed into his sleeve as he came back into the dining room and brushed his moustache with the back of his hand. He sniffed powerfully once or twice, as if he wanted to force all the oxygen in the room into his lungs, and then sat back down next to Mrs Samuels. I was not sure that she knew about his pep habit, and he certainly did not explain what he had been doing in his study.

'Some business to attend to?' she asked.

'Oh, nothing important. Just looking over one or two things.'

'Shall we head to the Star Inn, then?'

'Let's just have one more glass of this fine red wine, then I'll take you back over there.' He had a faraway look in his eyes, as if he was not really with us in the room. He poured himself another glass, but she put her hand over her wineglass and would only drink what she had left in it.

He chuckled to himself suddenly, with his chin down into his chest, the fold of fat beneath his beard rippling and jiggling with his mirthful heaves of air. Then, before he could put his hand over his mouth, he guffawed loudly.

Mrs Samuels's eyes nearly popped out of her head. 'Whatever's tickled you so?' She looked at him goggle-eyed and half-smiling, not getting the joke.

'Don't you see it?' Laughter spurted from his lips along with flecks of spittle.

'See what?' she asked, frowning now. She was, no doubt, expecting some witty observation of something she had missed.

'That billy goat over there,' he said, pointing into the darkest corner of the dining-room farthest from the light of the candles. 'His yellow slitted eyes are like the Devil's. He's laughing away at us, I can tell you.'

'Are you pulling my leg, William?' she asked. 'It's really not funny, if so.'

'Ha-aa, ha-aa, ha-aa, he's looking right at us,' he said loudly in the voice of a bleating goat. He had a glazed look in his eyes now, and I was delighted to see that my powders were working so well again.

'Father, are you feeling quite alright?' I said, pouring some water from the stoneware jug into a glass and passing it to him. 'Here, have a drink of fresh water. It'll revive you.'

'I want to go now,' Mrs Samuels said icily, staring at my father as if he were a creature from the farthest reaches of the cosmos. 'William, if you can't, or won't, escort me back to the inn, perhaps Grace would be so kind.'

'Ha-haa,' my father bleated, getting up and walking over to the corner of the room, where he crouched down as if to look the 'billy goat' in the eyes. He seemed completely indifferent to Mrs Samuel's anger. 'Old Nick,' he said, smiling strangely and attempting to shoo the invisible beast out of the corner. 'Leave us be. We've done nothing to harm you.'

Mrs Samuels gathered up her coat and made for the back door. 'The last time was awful enough, William,' she said, spitting out her words. He was still peering into the corner, oblivious to her. 'And now *this*. I can't, I simply won't, stand for it.'

I took my coat from the hooks by the back door and went out behind her. She had stepped out without even turning back to look at him and barely said a word as we walked the quarter of a mile to the Star Inn, me leading the way with the lantern in the dark. She bade me a crisp goodnight and then went inside.

My father was sitting in his armchair and smiling serenely into space when I got back to the house. He did not look unhappy or in any way upset at what had happened that evening, and he did not ask where Mrs Samuels was, or indeed say anything at all. The fire was blazing nicely in the grate: it would be one of the last ones we had before the spring weather turned warmer towards the end of the month. I retreated upstairs to bed early, and he did not even look at me as I went past his chair to the stairs; he just carried on staring towards the darkened window that looked out onto the lane. The billy goat seemed to have quite gone out of his head now.

When I got up in the morning his bedroom door was shut tight, and I could hear him snoring away. He did not stumble downstairs—still wearing his nightgown and clutching at his head, groaning quietly—until I was already clearing away my breakfast things almost one hour later.

'What happened last night? Where did Josephine go?' he asked, looking as if he had just come up for morning air after sleeping the night at the bottom of a haystack.

'Don't you remember? Mrs Samuels asked to be taken back to the inn and, your being rather indisposed, I did what she asked and took her there.'

'Did we even finish supper? My mind's completely blank after leaving the table to fetch something or other. Did she say anything at all?'

'She's really not best pleased, I can tell you.'

'Oh, God,' he said, moaning. 'Oh, God.'

'Let me make you some coffee to clear your head. Go and sit in your armchair in the sitting-room and I'll bring it to you.'

While he sat in his chair with his head in his hands, still moaning and groaning quietly to himself, I boiled a pan of water on the stove with two leaves and two stems of henbane. That seemed to be the right sort of dose to me, but I was relying on instinct rather than science. Albertus Magnus had made no mention of dosages, only talking about henbane in the magical language of an alchemist of his age. I ground up the roasted coffee beans with our cast-iron grinder and tipped the powder into the pot, then added in the boiling water through the sieve that removed all traces of the henbane pulp. The coffee smelled of exactly what it should; there was no hint of a foreign scent that would alert my father to its added herbal ingredient.

He cupped his hands around the mug and drank the coffee greedily as if it were mother's milk. He looked more pallid than usual, greyer somehow, but the hot liquid seemed to bring some of the colour back into his cheeks. He gestured for a second cup, and I was only too happy to fill it again. He did not seem to have noticed any difference in taste to his usual morning coffee. The quiet groaning had stopped by the first cup, but it started again not long after the second and his grey cheeks became suddenly greyer.

Just then there was a rapping on the door, as though the person knocking was working out their anger through the knuckles of their hand or the tip of their cane. I went from the sitting-room to the backdoor and saw the sour face of Mrs Samuels through the small kitchen window beside the door.

'Is William about or is he still in bed?' she asked without even greeting me when I opened the door.

'Father,' I called. 'Mrs Samuels is here for you.' There was the creak of his armchair as he got up and then the sound of shuffling feet. His face was ashen and there was a sheen of sweat on his forehead and upper lip.

'Josephine,' he said, looking down at his slippered feet. A great rumbling came from somewhere deep inside him. 'Y-you came back.'

'Only to give you this,' she said icily. She yanked the gold engagement ring off her finger and dropped it into his outstretched, trembling hands. He reminded me a little of a supplicating beggar. 'Consider our engagement broken off.'

My father had gone deathly pale now and a drop of sweat hung trembling from the tip of his nose. His whole face seemed to be in movement, he was shaking so. Suddenly, with a gurgling groan and another series of guttural rumbles, a great gout of vomit shot out from the O of his mouth and spattered the hem of Mrs Samuels's dress and the tips of her boots as she stood facing him in the doorway.

'Urgh, urgh, no!' she gasped in horror, turning on her heels and starting to run down the side of the house towards the lane. 'First Frederick and now you,' she wailed. 'What is it with you Cambridge men and drink?'

The dose of henbane that I had given him must have been too strong: it was hardly the balm for an agitated mind I had expected it to be. I had read that it could act as an emetic, a purgative, if too much was administered in one go, and I would have to be more careful with it the next time.

My father leaned ashen-faced and gurgling against the door frame, gazing after Mrs Samuels as she went, then stumbled off back towards the sitting room, clutching at his stomach and groaning loudly again. If there was ever a better image of a completely depleted and broken man, I have yet to see it. I began to feel truly sorry for him; but then I thought of his gleeful journeys on the railways from Gloucester, of my poor dear mother, and of the foolish, preening creatures that Mrs Samuels and the Three Graces were, and I buried any feelings of pity deep down.

Chapter Thirty-Five

In late April, rain shook the leaves of the trees in the garden for days on end. Pools of water gathered on the roads and the lanes, and what was once compacted gravel and earth became sliding mud. The thundering wheels of carts and the hooves of horses shook the ground so that the thoroughfares turned here and there into what felt like jelly. Through all this mud and liquefaction came the good doctor from Gloucester, Gillespie, again.

'Ah, Grace,' he said when he emerged from the consulting room and found me just returned from the marketplace, 'I trust you've been doing your best to look after your dear father. He's faring rather less well than I had hoped after my last visit.'

'I give him peace and quiet and nourishing food. There's not much more I can do.'

'Loving kindness always goes a long way when someone is suffering so,' he said.

'And what exactly does he pay you for? The love or the kindness?' Doctor Gillespie looked as if he had been slapped hard in the face.

'I-I beg your pardon?' he stammered, as my father opened the consulting room's door and came out to join him.

'Not causing our dear old friend any offence, are you, Grace?' he asked.

'I was just asking Doctor Gillespie what treatment he's giving you, what cure for your malady he has in mind.'

'You didn't quite put it like that,' the older doctor frowned. 'Perhaps your dear father needs to remind you how to speak to your seniors, if not your betters.'

'Please apologise to Doctor Gillespie, Grace, if you said anything uncalled-for,' my father said.

'I've nothing at all to apologise for.' With that, I put mother's basket down on the kitchen table, picked up my coat again and went out without bidding either of them goodbye.

'The imprudence, nay impudence, of youth is sometimes something to behold,' my father said as I went out the kitchen door. I heard Doctor Gillespie murmuring his agreement as I closed it behind me. And then I was off down the lane and out towards the woods, the rain having eased somewhat by the late morning.

I had not planned to see Sean again until later that week, but I decided to walk over to the camp just in case I could find him. The woods smelled of fresh rain on mouldering leaves and the green tang of the white-flowered wild garlic that was everywhere under the trees in springtime, growing right up to the edge of the path. The rain finally stopped while I was in the wood but drops still fell on me from the branches and the leaves of the trees, small cold darts that went down my neck and into the seams of my clothes.

No-one was about and the birds started their singing again once the rain had stopped. I did not want to be anywhere else but right there under those oak, ash, and beech trees, despite their dripping the last of the rain on me. The spring breeze brought with it not just the garlic, but also the smell of new life above last year's leaves rotting down. It was exhilarating and it got into my blood. I wanted to see Sean right there and then. There was an urgency about that feeling: I wanted him to kiss me again, hard on the lips.

The camp was empty when I scrambled down to it from the steep edge of the wood, but the damp logs on the fire were crackling and hissing in the breeze. It must have been built up not long before I had got there. It was as if someone had been there not a moment before but had seen me coming and slipped away.

'What are you doing here again?' a belligerent Irish voice asked suddenly. It made me jump almost out of my skin. I turned and saw an ill-shaven man coming out of one of the huts and recognised him straightaway as the one who had accosted me the last time I was there.

'Mr O'Donnell, isn't it?' I asked, already knowing the answer. 'What business is it of yours where I choose to go? I've been coming over to this valley since I was first able to walk.'

'It's my business when you're right here in our camp,' he said. He had a hard, unpleasant accent, nothing like Sean's musical lilt. 'Our foreman would be interested to hear that you've been visiting again.'

'Then tell Mr Menzies. Or I'll tell him myself if I see him,' I thought that it might wrongfoot him a little that I knew the foreman's name.

'You're here for McClennan, are you?' he said, scowling at me. 'He should go back to his farm or his barn or wherever it is he comes from.'

'How dare you talk about Mr McClennan like that?' I retorted sharply, the heat rising in my throat and my cheeks flushing with anger. No-one apart from O'Donnell had ever spoken to me like that. 'He deserves your respect, not your sarcasm.'

'I answer only to the railway company, Mr Menzies, and God, and no-one else,' he said, and then turned his back on me to wipe out with a rag one of the greasy-looking iron cooking pots that were lying on the ground not far from the fire.

The flames made the logs spit and hiss and the breeze had picked up again, threatening to bring more rain with it. There did not seem to be anyone else around but O'Donnell, and he went back into the hut that he had come out of and banged the door shut behind him. I felt only sorry again for Sean that he had to share his sleeping quarters with such an odious man.

The bed of the line was no more than a hundred yards away from the huts, but no-one was working on the section of banked earth and stone nearest the camp. I walked further up the valley towards Much Purlock between the line and the edge of the wood, hoping I would find Sean working somewhere on the section that ran past the first of the houses. I did not care that the navvies and

Mr Menzies would be surprised to see me there and that they would no doubt want me gone as soon as they saw me. I just wanted to see Sean and had little thought for anything else.

The line curved round a long bend that led to where the railway ended about a quarter of a mile from the marketplace. A low stone building was being built to mark the start and end of the line; the mayor, almost as ancient as the town itself, had laid its foundation stone on a dull March day when I was down at the mill and then out in the woods. I could not bring myself to watch the stone-laying because of what it marked, and because the arrival of that stage in the construction of the railway meant Sean's leaving Much Purlock for some other part of the country would not be too far away.

There was the heavy, echoing thud of sledgehammers up ahead, and I crept from the sloping meadow back into the wood, walking in the shadows between the last of the trees. When I came opposite to the section where the men were working, I could see that perhaps fifteen of them were setting thick, squared timbers into the bed of the line, each timber spaced about three feet from the next like the rungs of a giant ladder going all the way up to the top of the valley and round the long curve towards the town.

I could not see Sean at first. A man who I took to be Mr Menzies, wearing a tall, somewhat dilapidated hat and carrying a long measuring-stick, seemed to be directing the work and mouthing orders that I could not hear from fifty or more yards away. All was industry and busyness and labour, with hardly a glance cast around at the beauty of the landscape into whose heart they had carved this scar. The railway company had no care for the land because they did not know it, other than through their surveys and charts and maps, and therefore they did not love it. Not loving something allows you to do what you want with it. I knew that from what I had done to my father, from how he was with me.

Suddenly, Sean's head, arms and shoulders seemed to climb out of the ground beyond the raised bed of the line on a body and legs that I could not see. He was holding a muddy shovel over his shoulder, and I realised that he must have been digging in a deep hole.

He came back to earth, as it were, and said something to the other men who were going about the laying of the timbers.

Seeing him, even from that distance, did something to me physically. It made my stomach flutter and my heart beat harder and faster. That intense desire for the touch of another human being, for Sean, made me feel almost delirious, but he did not look over in the direction of where I was standing under the trees. Despite my urge to abandon caution, I did not dare to go nearer the line or to try to call over to him, as I would have attracted the attention of the other men, and I knew how that would be; my presence would make things difficult for him. I just had to stand there in the shadow of the trees then, the occasional raindrop still falling on me, and watch him at work with the other navvies while he did not even notice me.

The disappointment left a bitter taste in my mouth that needed sweetening somehow, but what was I to do with those lips that wanted kissing, with all that yearning? Going home meant chores and silence punctuated only by my father's preoccupations with his malady. But I had nowhere else to go, and so I walked back up through the wood with my head down against the wind, which blew at me now full in the face as I followed the path over the hill and down the other side.

My despondency only grew as I made my way back to the house on that grey afternoon, the leaden sky weighted with more rain. I needed something to divert me, and I hit on the very thing. It had been a fortnight since I had last given my father a dose of the powders, and it was high time that I gave him another one. Watching the evening unfold might just take my mind off Sean, if only for a few hours.

CHAPTER THIRTY-SIX

Hereford Insane Asylum, 1850

High summer in the asylum and the ward is heating up. Lorna seems to have lost her mind, and she is down on all fours all day long looking for it in the cracks in the wainscot, where the rats and the mice play and listen to her breathing.

I went for my walk with Mr Osney at noon today when the sun was at its hottest. He strode beside me all the way round the grounds with one hand raised above his eyes to shield them from the glare and his other arm linked through mine. I do not know why he and the Warden insist on thinking that I will try to run away again, given half a chance. Bitter experience has shown me I would not get too far before they found me again. And I have no money and no change of clothes that they do not keep locked away in the cupboards to be handed out on laundry day. Still, escape is never far from my mind.

'Miss Matthews,' he said, turning to look at me and watch my reaction, 'I spoke to Mr Chillingham about your case again yesterday. It seems he's thinking you might be moved to somewhere more, er, *conducive* before too long.'

'More conducive, Mr Osney? What exactly does he mean by that?'

'He's been reading through your file again and he's now of the opinion that you're not insane. He agrees with what you've been saying all along: that you've been here on a false pretext based on a misunderstanding of some kind, when you could have been paying for what you did somewhere else instead.'

'And where might that somewhere else be exactly?' I asked, not without some trepidation after that bolt from the blue.

'He's planning to send you to the workhouse. Can't have these strong arms of yours going to waste.' There did not seem to be any malice in his voice, but when I turned to look at him, I could swear that I saw a glint of amusement in his eyes.

'Let me go!' I cried, the anger rising in me. I tried to uncouple my arm from his, but he would not loosen his grip. If anything, he tightened it.

'I'm not allowed to when we're out, you know that. It's not been so long since you ran away, has it?'

'I wasn't running away. I just wanted to be somewhere else than this godforsaken place for a few hours.'

'It looked like an attempt to escape to us, Miss Matthews. We can't have that happening again.'

'But you just told me that Mr Chillingham no longer thinks I'm insane, and I'm surely no danger then to anyone now, am I?'

'Even so,' he said. 'Even so.'

Having been upright for some hours, Lorna has now gone back to walking around on all fours. She whines at the wainscot now and then, but otherwise she is silent and in her own world. Gone is the defiance of the girl who came here only four months ago; this place seems to have rendered her as mute and cowed as a circus bear. Still, the orderlies had better watch out for her teeth if they provoke her. Whatever is wrong with her, she can still scratch and bite.

Chapter Thirty-Seven

Herefordshire, 1842

The thaw has set in, and we have begun to lay the rails. This stage of our work requires the greatest care, and all of our measurements have to be perfect to the hundredth of an inch. Mr Menzies has become even more dour and silent with the weight of the work, and Mr Jones is coming down from Birmingham more regularly now. There are rumours that the railway company board will be visiting us and inspecting the results of our labours in two or three weeks from now.

All the men are wondering where we will be sent next and whether we will be kept together or split up into separate teams. Unlike them, I have someone other than myself to think about now and I cannot countenance the idea that the work that brought me here and allowed me to meet Grace will take me away from her. We have so much to see, so much to do together. I think that I have quite fallen in love with her.

For weeks now, O'Donnell has been even more belligerent and unpleasant than usual. We all suspect that he thinks Mr Menzies will make him hagman again before too long. The position has been vacant since it was taken away from him last year, with Mr Menzies having assumed direct control of the men with no-one to intervene on his behalf. Mr Menzies is bad enough but having O'Donnell telling us what to do again would be the final straw. If we are all to be split up, I pray that he will be sent somewhere far away from me.

The section we are working on now is towards the bottom of the valley where the railway turns round a wide bend, leaves the valley through the cutting, and runs out into the flat land towards Gloucestershire. We can see the other team of navvies working on their section of the line about two miles away across the fields, and we should meet them by late March or early April. It is slow work, this, and very exacting. We have been told by Mr Menzies that we will be made to work double shifts from the spring when the days are longer, and we will be given time off during daylight hours less frequently. How am I supposed to see Grace if I cannot get into Much Purlock at least every Wednesday afternoon?

After the thaw there is the mud. We all go trudging off to work in it and come back in the evening towards dark caked in it and wet through. What I would not do for a bathtub full of piping hot water. Going off to wash ourselves in Cuckoo Mere is not at all pleasant in this weather. The surface of the water is agitated by the wind and impenetrable to the eye. We dip our toes in, then edge in further up to our waists, without really knowing what is lurking in the water there. I cannot help thinking of the snagging jaws of pike and the writhing bodies of eels whenever I am in the water.

But Grace, oh Grace! She makes all this rough living bearable. My heart sings whenever I think of her. Perhaps it is because she is the first girl that I have ever kissed, but I want to marry her, to make her my wife. I felt that desire even before I knew her name.

What will I do when Mr Jones and Mr Menzies order us out and away from here? I do not know; I only know that I cannot leave her behind. I will have to find a way to take her with me or, if not that, then get her to follow me when I have settled down in some new place for a while. With the railways being built all over this country now, it is hard to know where we will end up. It would be a hardship too far to have had her and lost her only because of my being taken away from her by the railway company.

John the innkeeper is washing glasses when I come into the Star Inn. He looks up from behind the bar and smiles when he sees me.

'Hello, Sean. How've you been keeping? A pint of the usual?'

'Thanks, John. It's been hard, the work we're doing now. We're all exhausted by it.'

'Only a few more months to go, I've heard.' He has put all the clean glasses up on the shelf behind the bar now and he pulls a pint of bitter, stopping halfway through to let the foam settle.

'And then exactly where'll we be?' I wonder, looking down at the dirt under my fingernails.

'Somewhere off down the line,' he says with a laugh.

'I suppose so, but I don't really want to leave here.'

'I've seen you walking out with Miss Matthews. There's been some talk about it in the town, as you'd imagine.'

'I'm sure there has, but it's not really anyone else's business, is it?'

'You know how people are. You can't stop their tongues from wagging.'

'Well, they need to find more important things to talk about. They should work in my boots for a day or two. That would give them something to think about.'

'They'd probably be too exhausted to say much at all then,' John says.

* * *

It is the last Wednesday in March and the weather has turned milder now: on some days over the last few weeks, the sun has even come out from behind the clouds and its rising warmth is slowly drying out the mud in the valley. Grace is late meeting me today, and I wonder for a moment whether she has changed her mind about coming, the devil of doubt creeping into me when it is least wanted. What would I do if she simply did not come at all? I do not even know where she lives, so I could not go looking for her.

I would just have to hope that I would see her about one day by chance again, as I did before.

Then suddenly she is here, running over the marketplace with her hat in her hand. She is wearing her long woollen coat and her cheeks are flushed with the running. My heart leaps in my chest and my pulse quickens. I look round at the stallholders and their customers, but they do not seem to be paying us even the slightest attention. A whiskered man walks right past me carrying a heavy-looking hessian sack, but he does not look at either of us as Grace runs up to me, beaming, and clasps my hands in hers as she comes up to kiss me.

'Sorry I'm so late, Sean,' she says. 'My father was unwell earlier, and I had to tend to him before getting away.'

'I hope he's feeling better now. Without your mother, I suppose you're all he has by way of help if he's not well.'

'He would have Mrs Samuels around if she hadn't abandoned him to go back to London for the time being.'

'Oh yes, I remember you telling me about her and her daughters. Aren't they getting married sometime soon?'

'It was supposed to be this summer. We'll see about that.'

We leave the marketplace and walk hand in hand along the narrow, winding lane that leads out towards Denscombe. A few people come past us, but this part of the town is mostly deserted today. Grace seems happy to see me, but she is preoccupied with something. It is hard to say how, but it shows in her face; there is a slight frown above her smile, and her eyes are smiling less than her lips.

'Is everything alright, Grace?'

'Oh, I'm just thinking about things with my father. I wish I could find a way to live somewhere else, away from him.'

'You know what I've been saying these last few months. Come away with me!'

'Where are you going?' she asks, a shadow of sadness in her eyes now.

'I don't know yet, but I do know that I want you with me more than anything, Grace. I don't want to leave you behind, to be without you.'

'But they're just words, aren't they? Where would we live? I can hardly lodge with you when you're living in a hut somewhere with the other men.' There is a rising frustration in her voice that I have not heard before.

'I'll find somewhere for just the two of us, I promise you that.' I put my arm around her shoulders and draw her to me, kissing the top of her head where her hair is all whorls and warm softness. With the spring sun shining down on us now, she is still holding her hat.

'I know you'd always do your best for us, Sean, but it's all rather uncertain and unknowable, isn't it?' she says.

'I'm at the mercy of the railway company, Grace. Surely you see that.'

'Yes, I know that and do understand. I just need something, some hope to hold on to.' She turns to me to kiss me again: her lips are so soft and so warm on mine, but it feels like she is holding something back; that some part of her is resisting until I come up with a plan for the future.

The Wye is slate grey today and flowing high and fast between its banks. All that weight of water: whatever I did to swim against it, I would be pulled down towards the sea. The railway company will take me away just like this river would, and I will have no way of resisting it. What use are hope, love, and desire when the power lies in someone else's hands?

When I get back to the camp the men are working the late shift on the line, or they are off collecting wood to build up the fire before it is time to cook the evening meal. The camp needs cleaning up before Mr Jones comes down from Birmingham again tomorrow: greasy pots and pans are lying around the fire and smoke-filled washing is hanging wet on the lines that are strung up between the trees. This place looks as if it has been left abandoned even while we are still living here. I kick some of the pots into a pile to take them over to Cuckoo Mere later and sweep up around the fire with the besom.

'Got past your first kiss yet?' O'Donnell's gloating voice says suddenly.

'What?' I spin round to see where he is, but he is not out here anywhere. Then he pushes open the door of our hut and comes out.

'I saw you in town, you two little lovebirds, all cosy and coy together,' he says mockingly. 'But she's out of your class, fella.'

'What, were you bloody spying on us?'

'No, just out for a walk and a little look around,' he says, sneering at me. 'You got something to say about that?'

'My life is none of your damned business, you stupid fool.'

Something in his face, that malicious glint in his eyes and the smirk on his lips as he comes towards me, pushes me somewhere I have not been since I was a boy at the village school. Before I know it, I have unfurled my fists and let them fly. O'Donnell is down on the ground from my right hook before my stronger left hand has even hit his chin.

Chapter Thirty-Eight

Much Purlock, 1842

My father moved around the house as if he were walking through treacle. A weariness seemed to be weighing down his limbs, and he yawned loudly behind the door of his consulting room whenever he was alone in there. I had stored away the henbane up on the kitchen shelf; dosing him with it so soon again, having seen its emetic properties, might have an adverse physical effect on him that I was not intending. Instead, I would increase the frequency with which I dispensed his adulterated pep.

My unrequited longing the previous day to see Sean, *for* Sean, was not relieved that night by watching my father stare fixedly at the shapes he said were moving across the sitting room walls after he had taken the snuff and mushroom powder that I had put back in the pep jar in his study. Despite his belief that his affliction emanated from some physical malady within him, I could see he was in good health: all ruddy-cheeked, his waistcoat almost bursting at the seams, and his hair and beard thick and lustrous with pomade. No, it was not a strictly physical thing: the powders might have been snorted up through each nostril in turn, dusting the lining of his nose and throat and going deep into his lungs, but as they were absorbed into his body, his bloodstream, it went from the physical to the alchemical to the mental. For a man of the mind, it surprised me that this was the one realm of his being that he least suspected.

There was something distasteful in the amount of time he spent focussing on himself, on his affliction, now that Mrs Samuels was no longer on the scene. He now often saw only three or four patients each day—farm workers or shopkeepers or housewives with seemingly mostly minor ailments—and whenever it was quiet in his consulting room, he would write letters feverishly to Doctor Gillespie or colleagues in London; or he would devour his medical books in search of answers, sitting behind a half-open door. If he was the question, then I was the answer, but of course he did not know that then.

* * *

The weather became gradually warmer in early May, the unbroken banks of grey cloud finally giving way to a pale blue sky. I met Sean outside the Star Inn on the first market day of the new month and did not want to tell him how much I had missed him the previous week. He already had enough on his mind with his labours on the railway, and with Mr Menzies and O'Donnell. It seemed to me that all these concerns were distracting him from me, from us, and I resented the very reason that he had come to Much Purlock in the first place for taking him away from me. He smiled down at me with his twinkling eyes, so far as I could tell not suspecting that I was feeling a little abandoned.

'This sunshine's given the men a bit of a lift,' he said. 'Even the damned mud's finally drying out!'

'There's a nest of bullfinches just outside our kitchen window. New life's bursting out everywhere here now that spring's arrived at last.'

'What about you and all of this new life?' he asked, that sweet, slightly mischievous smile playing on his lips.

'What do you mean?'

'Have you ever thought about having a child of your own?'

'I'm still only seventeen, Sean. There's really no hurry for any of that, is there?'

'My Ma had me at nineteen. She's not yet forty.'

'Well, I'd like to see something of the world before I settle down and have children. Even going beyond Herefordshire would be something.'

'Come away with me then!' he said, his eyes bright. 'Come away with me and we can see something of the country, something of the world.'

'I'd like that, Sean, I really would, but your work's here for now, and the only money of my own that I have is what I earn from my errands for the mill—and that's not much.'

We had left the town behind, and we were walking over the fields towards Denscombe again. He held me close to him as we walked, the sun shining down on us for the first time in months. The Wye glittered in the light over at the far edge of the field, which was sown with wheat that was still only a foot high and dark green from too much rain and too little sun for the months since it had been planted.

'Say that you'll at least consider it,' he said, then bent down to kiss me on the lips. He smelled of fresh air and good Herefordshire soil, and it was the most wonderful thing in the world to have his arms around me and his mouth on mine. I had to admit that my feeling of being abandoned by him was slowly melting away, the more so when I went up on tiptoe and kissed him back. It was always that way with Sean: because of his work, we were only able to see each other once or twice a week, and never in the evening, given my duties at home and his having nowhere that I could visit.

We did not go into Denscombe itself that day but turned instead towards the Wye, skirting along the edge of the field where its unsown margin met a tall hedge of hazel. The river was running high and fast, pushing at the tussocks of grass, the trailing brambles and the branches that leant from its banks into the green water. Sean took my hand and led me towards a clump of willows whose branches were trailing in the river, their leaves like slender silver-green fish swimming against the current. He seemed eager to get me under the cover of those trees and pulled me close when we were behind the shimmering screen of leaves to kiss me hard on the lips.

'I wish we could be man and wife,' he said into the nape of my neck, his breath hot on me.

'Are you asking me to marry you?' Something in the way he had said it was more confusing than intoxicating.

'One day, when I've made something of myself,' he replied hesitatingly but obviously sincerely. 'But I meant something else.' He kissed me passionately again.

'What then?'

'I want us to do more than kiss,' he murmured into my mouth and moved his hands over the contours of my breasts. I was inclined to let him continue and he moved his hands over my breasts again, caressing them gently through the cloth of my dress, and then downwards on to my belly, but my nervousness got the better of me.

'Sean, Sean,' I said, gently pushing his hands away. 'I want us to be together but not like this. If you're going to touch me, to see me, it can't be out here in the open. We're not cattle.' In truth, it was nothing to do with where we were, the riverbank and the trees, but only my coyness and inexperience. He suddenly seemed so much more forward than I had expected him to be.

'I'm sorry, Grace,' he said, pulling away from me and looking defeated and crestfallen. 'I thought it was what you also wanted after these past months of walking out together.'

'It is, and I do, but I need more time.' I clasped both of his hands in mine and went up on tiptoe to kiss him. I missed his mouth and brushed his cheek with my lips as he turned to look out through the curtain of leaves. 'We've only known each other since the winter and it's hardly even summertime yet.'

'I understand, I really do,' he said. 'I'll wait. It's just that I've already waited my whole life.'

We left the cover of the willows and retraced our route along the river and over the edge of the field. The sun had begun its slow descent over the Welsh Marches and the shadows were getting longer as we went over that field and into the next. Sean held my hand as we walked, but he did not hold me as close to him now. He was silent for a while, but smiled at me from time to time, his eyes sparkling in that way of his.

'You're not upset with me are you, Sean?'

'No, Grace. Why should I be?'

'Because I didn't do what you wanted me to do back there.'

'Now if we lived in a world like that, where would we be?' he replied, forcing a laugh. 'I was just a little disappointed, that's all, but I can only hope that it'll happen one day.'

After a while he seemed to regain some of his confidence again. There was a swing in his step once more as we walked the final mile of the field path back towards the town, and he kissed me again when I was climbing over the stile into the last field before Much Purlock, my lips level with his for a few brief moments. But still he did not hold me as tightly to him as he had done on the way out towards Denscombe, and I worried that we would perhaps go our separate ways less close now than we had been only two hours earlier when we had left the town.

I had known all along that he would not be content with just holding me and kissing me, that men always wanted to take things further in the end, but I had not thought it would happen quite so soon. I was not prepared for the sudden shift in our relations and felt that I would have only myself to blame if things went wrong because I had resisted. As it was, he left me in the marketplace with a smile on his face and the promise that we would see each other the following week. My longing to see him again as soon as we had parted was now tempered by the worry that he would want me to do things for which I was not ready.

Chapter Thirty-Nine

In the middle of May, my father announced that he would be giving himself a holiday the following week to go to Bath and take the waters, believing they would be restorative and therapeutic to him. I was not convinced by his reasoning, but I welcomed the news as I would have the house to myself for a while. Before that, I would increase his dose of powdered mushrooms to see him on his way. Spring is always the strangest as well as the most wonderful of seasons, and there would be nothing stranger than my father with his head full of visions and dreams going out into the world again to find his cure.

While he was out for a walk on the Monday before he left for Bath, I added two more handfuls of dried mushroom powder to my admixture of snuff and mushroom, increasing its potency by perhaps a third. Although the adulterated powder now had a mustier, lighter brown hue, I knew that he was unlikely to notice the difference in the half-light of his study where the pep jar was kept. I poured out his pure snuff into a cloth bag and put it away up on the kitchen shelf, then put my doctored powders into the jar instead. It would be interesting to see what the increase in concentration of the mushroom powders would do to him. I would have to gather more of the slender-stemmed, brown-capped ones again in the autumn. I could not let my supply run too low.

My work for the mill was busy that month, and I ran errands up and down Channers Lane and out to the most far-flung parts of the town and the surrounding farms. The iron-rimmed wooden wheels of my handcart squeaked against their axles as I pulled it up the hill from the mill and over the stony roads, carrying sacks of cornmeal and flour for the farmers' wives and the inns. I had not seen quite so many of the corpses of rooks and crows that had infested the waysides and the hedgerows the previous spring and summer, but I was not foolish enough to think the disease had simply gone away. Some of the infected, rotten-beaked birds had surely fallen into thick undergrowth where they were not so easily seen. If not that, then the sickness was perhaps simply lying dormant, waiting to strike again.

Once the line was finished and the Much Purlock railway halt was opened, it was not too hard to imagine that all sorts of diseases and afflictions of man and beast hardly known about in those parts would arrive with the influx of visitors to the town. There would be more birds falling from the trees, from the sky, and that would be just the start of it. Who could tell what the railway would bring with it? It certainly would not bring opportunity and prosperity for most people in the town. I for one would no doubt have to keep on choring and cooking for my father, if he had his way and did not get a cook and a maid again, without seeing any benefit at all from the so-called progress that the Hereford, Purlock and Gloucester Railway Company had tried to sell us. No, the whole endeavour was about nothing more than money, and with it would come—had already come—untold harm to our natural world.

I had not yet asked my father how he intended to travel the seventy or so miles to Bath, but I suspected that I already knew part of the answer: he would doubtless take a pony and trap to Gloucester, and from there go westwards by train. He would pay for the latter part of his journey when he got home; in fact, he would pay for it even before he left. I had to be careful not to incapacitate him completely, however, as he was not a man of large private means and he relied on his work as a doctor for income. Without his paying patients, we would soon not eat unless I foraged for food in the woods and the fields. A diet of nettle soup and roasted puffballs, enlivened by the occasional snared coney, would not keep us going for very long.

At least the mill paid me for the errands that I ran. It was not much but it was something, and it made me feel less tied to my father to have coins in my pocket that I had earned myself. I intended to get more work eventually, so I could make myself less dependent on him. Until then, I would have to go on being his dutiful cook, servant, and housemaid, a silent shadow moving about the house, ensuring that everything was shipshape and cooked on time. I was his daughter but somehow no longer his daughter since my beloved mother had died.

The handcart's wheels squeaked and squealed as I pulled it up the gradient of Cobb Hill. It was one of my favourite errands, that one: taking two mid-sized sacks of oatmeal and two of barley every Monday afternoon up to the cottage brewery on the other side of the hill, where a fast clear stream ran down to the valley bottom. The brewer, Mr Cherry, was a rosy-cheeked, friendly man, and he always gave me a tip for my effort. It was a long and steep lane up which to pull a heavy load, and my arms and back ached afterwards.

That Monday, I was in no hurry to get home and I pulled the empty cart off the lane and left it there under a blackthorn tree whose white flowers had burst into life now that spring had arrived. I followed the stream down towards the floor of the valley, having to duck my head here and there where the branches of the trees hung low over the streambed. A herd of cows had pushed through the trees to drink in the stream, and they looked at me curiously as they lowed and breathed heavily in the warm air, which carried with it the smell of fresh cow dung. I had not followed that stream since I was a small child, when I used to go there with my mother to look for fish. The most we ever came home with in my jar were tadpoles, but I had happy memories of our outings.

The banked bed of the line was up ahead of me now, following the contours of the valley down towards the Gloucestershire border. Below Cobb Hill I was about two miles from Much Purlock, and I had not visited this section of the railway before. Something glinted and gleamed up there on the embankment in the brilliant afternoon light, and I climbed up to see what it was. On top of the ballast, on top of the ladder of beams that was laid across the stony bed stretching away down the curve of the valley, the navvies had already fixed the shining steel rails. The hard matter-of-factness of the metal jarred so loudly with everything else in that valley that I wanted to tear it up with my bare hands. The rails were hot to the touch and bolted into place so firmly that there was no moving them even a hundredth of an inch.

I followed the stream back up the hill, the cattle having moved off in search of fresher pasture, but when I tried to remember our outings with the net and jar, my memories were eclipsed by the thought of the inert hardness of that gleaming steel and all the change that it would mean. My mother would not know what the railway line was if she saw it: it would mean nothing to her, as if a creature had come down from the heavens and left it like an impenetrable cipher on the earth. The railway company had taken something pure, something untouched, and sullied it. It could never go back to how it had been, just as I could never truly go back to the moments of happiness in my childhood.

I retrieved the handcart and made my way back down the other side of Cobb Hill towards home. It was no effort at all now to pull the cart behind me, but rather than feeling free and enjoying the sunshine of the afternoon, my thoughts were overcast by those gleaming rails stretching into the distance. Who exactly were they for? They were for people like my father who saw only opportunity and convenience in the railway. It was time that I gave him another lesson in seeing things differently.

* * *

My father enjoyed a good supper of roast gammon and boiled potatoes, followed by a pudding of stewed apples and cream; he ate in silence, only smacking his lips in delight from time to time and scraping his plate and bowl down to the glaze with his fork and spoon. I had very little appetite, the less so for hearing him eat, and just picked at my plate of meat and potatoes.

After supper, he went into his study and shut the door. He must have been in there for nearly three-quarters of an hour. I could not tell what he was doing, but hoped that whatever it was it included the taking of snuff. Sure enough, when he finally came back into the kitchen he was sniffing vigorously and wiping at his moustache with one of the handkerchiefs that my mother had had embroidered with his initials. The last of the sunlight was streaming through the windows and the trees were all still; there was no breeze that evening, not even the slightest stirring of the air.

He went to sit in his favourite armchair and read the newspaper while I busied myself with clearing the table and washing the dishes. I intended to go out for a walk through the fields and up into the woods before sunset. I could not spend the evening in that house doing nothing but chores or sitting watching my father, whatever the effects of his pep. Perhaps I would even find Sean somewhere out there along the path.

'Very warm in here,' my father said suddenly, mopping at his brow with the powdered handkerchief and tugging at the top button of his shirt.

'Well, it's a sunny evening, Father. I'll open the window if you're hot.'

'No, don't!' he said forcefully, the spittle flecking his lips. 'Don't let the miasmas in!'

'What are you talking about, Father? There's only sunlight and the evening out there.'

'They're swirling about like dust devils,' he said, but would say no more. His eyes were white and staring, like those of a wild beast cornered in a room. I would not have been surprised if I had suddenly seen him grimace and bare his teeth. He was gone into that world where the mushrooms took him; there was no getting through to him now.

Still, I said, 'Father, it's not something out there in the world that's making you like this: it's inside you.'

He did not look at me; it was as if I was not even there. He prowled around the sitting room and kitchen, peering out of the windows into the trees and onto the lane through the half-closed curtains. Then he turned to stare in fear at the rooms in which he found himself, as though the mere act of looking outside risked bringing the world and all of its miasmas in.

Chapter Forty

Hereford Insane Asylum, 1850

Grey Mr Chillingham summoned me into his office this morning. If anything, his room was even more spartan than the last time I was in there. Queen Victoria was still looking down on us, imperious and parsnip-nosed, from high on the wall above his desk. The Warden had both of his shirttails tucked in this time, but it did not look as if he had combed his hair or brushed his whiskers for some days. He smiled at me when I sat down on the chair in front of his desk, but his eyes did not follow suit: they looked down at his desk and all around the room, but they did not once meet mine for the quarter of an hour I was in there.

'Miss Matthews,' he said, 'the wheels have been set in motion and you're to leave here on the twelfth of September for the workhouse over on Commercial Road. I'm told you'll be cleaning hair for wigs and cushions, pounding bones for glue and picking oakum, taking apart old ropes, to earn your keep. You have strong-looking arms and fine fingers, so such work should suit you.'

'And do I have any choice at all in the matter?'

'This is Hereford Insane Asylum, is it not? You have managed to convince us after all this time that you're perfectly sane, so this is no place for you. Your father won't have you, and we can't simply put you out onto the street, so the workhouse is the only option.'

'I won't go,' I said, the anger rising in me again. 'You can't make me, Mr Chillingham. When Mr Osney tries to take me there or they come to fetch me, I shall escape.'

'We shall see about that. It would be much better for you and for everyone concerned if you simply cooperated peacefully and willingly, Miss Matthews. We don't want to have to use the restraints.'

That word *restraints* sent a chill down my spine. I shuddered to think what he meant by it, sitting there on that hard chair with the Queen looking down at me. Was he threatening me with a straitjacket or shackles or simply the muscled arms of Mr Osney and another of the orderlies? I will have to comply, at least to begin with, when I am being taken over there. I will feign complete obedience, a sudden desire to get as far away from this place as I can, and then find a way, by whatever means I can conjure, to escape and disappear.

The clamour of the dinner gong is upon us: I must get myself down to the dining hall near the front of the crowd of women if I want anything more than the scrapings from the bottom of the soup cauldron and the meagre bones of the oxtail stew.

Chapter Forty-One

Much Purlock, 1842

While my father was away in Bath, I had the silent house to myself. There was none of my overhearing of confidences spoken by his patients behind the consulting room door; his shuffling footsteps did not haunt the ground floor hallway or the creaking floorboards upstairs. His endless leafing through medical monographs and his muttered monologues as he looked for the answer, for the Truth, seemed already like a half-forgotten dream. I relished the quiet and my freedom.

The second half of May was blissfully warm, with barely a cloud in the sky and all the birds in the vicinity singing their little hearts out. It was a late spring that promised so much for the long summer ahead: life was burgeoning outwards and upwards everywhere I turned. I went back up to the patch of ground beyond the end of the garden, but there was no sign of any further disturbance of the soil. Whoever it was that buried those black corpses of corvids had not been back again.

The henbane sat in its bag up on the kitchen shelf and the adulterated pep was in the jar in my father's study, waiting for his return. I wanted to add to my apothecary's shelf but knew that the damp earth of autumn, rather than the bone-dry soil of summer, would provide the richest bounties for my pharmacy. I would be patient and wait until the mushrooms came up again deep in the woods. I read the old herbals for suggestions of other plants with which I could dose my father: they had to be exactly the right ones to have an effect, but not the effect of killing him.

* * *

Oh, the long, light evenings of late spring. The last rays of the sun shone low behind the hill until shortly after nine o'clock, and the bats came out just before darkness fell on our valley. In their blind flight they circled the spaces between the trees but never once touched them; there was not even the most fleeting of contact between their wings and the tip of a leaf or branch.

I met Sean under a brilliant sky by the cross in the marketplace on the market day that my father was away. All the stallholders had awnings up to protect them from the heat of the sun, and they fanned themselves to try to keep cool. I was carrying my mother's wicker basket over my arm and had bought provisions for the week: some spring greens and spring onions, potatoes, chard, and a meatloaf. The richness of what Herefordshire had to offer always made me proud. I did not like to imagine what people in Much Purlock would be eating once the outsiders that the railway would bring with it had invaded our world.

'Grace,' Sean said. 'I was just saying that I'd like to visit the church. I've not been into one since I left Sligo.'

'Sorry, Sean. I was miles way. It must be the sunshine; it's making me rather dreamy somehow. We can go over to St. Andrew's if you like. The door's never locked. I go and sit in there sometimes and think about my mother, particularly when the weather's bad and I don't want to be at home but don't want to be out in the wind and rain either.'

'Perhaps we could get out of this heat for half an hour or so. I'd like to light a candle and say a few words for my Pa, my Ma, and my brother Niall.'

'I'll do the same for my mother. I find it hard to think about her without getting sad and angry too somehow. She was still young, and she didn't deserve to die how she did.'

He put his arm round me then, despite us still being in the marketplace with people all around us, and we walked the quarter of a mile over to the church with its square tower that was built by the Normans. St. Andrew's was made of a limestone that was brought by river and then wagon from over the border in Gloucestershire, and its walls shone a bright white in the light of that afternoon. The oak door, banded with wrought iron hinges that ended in a flourish of trefoils, stood ajar, and we went in. My eyes saw nothing at first, going from the bright heat into that cool darkness. There was only the glow of lighted candles near the altar before my eyes adjusted and the shape of the church's interior revealed itself from out of the swirling blackness. There was no-one else in there.

Sean took my hand and led me down the aisle to where two rows of candles on a wooden stand had dripped wax onto the flagstone floor. It was so quiet in the church that I could hear Sean's slow breathing beside me and the guttering of the few candles that were lit.

'It's beautiful in here,' he whispered, 'much simpler than our church back home, but lovely. Look at the light coming down through the stained glass up there.'

'Those windows are probably six hundred years old, and the colours are still so bright. I read somewhere that your Catholic churches in Ireland have a lot more saints and gold and decoration everywhere.'

Sean laughed one of his deep laughs, then looked round to see if he was disturbing anyone. 'It's true,' he whispered again. 'You've none of that here, at least not in this church.'

'Henry VIII has a lot to answer for: stripping all that out, chopping off the saints' heads after chopping off his wives'.'

'I suppose you'd have grown up Catholic without him.'

'I suppose you're right,' I said.

Sean took a new candle from the box near the stand and held its wick to the flame of a lighted candle, then placed it carefully in one of the empty spaces on the stand. I did the same and we knelt down side-by-side on the cushions of a pew, Sean crossing himself, and stayed kneeling there motionless and silent like two marble effigies on a tomb. I tried to focus my mind on my memories of my dear mother and all that she had meant to me and all that I had been without since she had gone, but with Sean's gentle breathing beside me in that silent place and with the excitement of having him so close to me, I found it hard to keep my mind on such painful thoughts. I could feel only joy, not sorrow, with him there and the sunshine outside.

'I want to show you something,' I said after we had been kneeling on the cushion for perhaps ten minutes, our eyes screwed shut. My knees and thighs were beginning to ache. We got to our feet again and I led him by the hand up the aisle to a heavy red velvet curtain at the back of the church, away from the main door. There was still no-one else in the church with us. Behind the curtain was a small door that led to the narrow stairs up the tower.

'Come on. Let's go up and look at the view from the top.'

'Are we allowed to go up? I remember being boxed around the ears once by a priest back home for trying the same thing after a Sunday service years ago,' he said, laughing.

'No-one's ever stopped me before. Come on: I'm going to run up. Catch me if you can!'

I set off up the steep, spiralling stairs as fast as I could, but very quickly slowed down because I was out of breath and the tower seemed somehow taller than I remembered. Sean was some way behind, breathing hard and clattering with his hobnail boots on the wooden steps. He caught up with me as I was about to go out of the low doorway onto the crenelated roof of the tower. He took me in his arms, lifting me over the threshold into the blazing sunshine. It was so startlingly bright that I had to shut my eyes for a moment.

'Nothing but blue sky and green woods and fields beyond the town for miles around,' he said, holding me by the waist, his breath hot on the nape of my neck as I stood by the stone parapet looking out. 'It's beautiful from up here. That must be Gloucestershire over there.'

'I've always loved this view. Whenever I sneaked up here as a child, I used to stare at it for what seemed like hours.'

'Were you ever caught?'

'Never, not even once. I was always away and up here before anyone even noticed that I was missing from the congregation.'

He laughed again and held me tight, and I turned to kiss him. It was such a beautiful day and we had so much life in us. His blue eyes reflected the blue of the sky above us.

'There is something that spoils the view now though, isn't there?' I said, looking up at him. Snaking away to the southwest along the valley bottom beyond Much Purlock, the rails of the line caught the afternoon light. The glinting track curved round the bend into the cutting at Simeon's Pitch and then disappeared from view perhaps two miles from the church tower as the crow flies.

'You mean the railway?' he asked, frowning slightly. 'Perhaps it will bring something good for Much Purlock, whatever you feel about it now.'

'The only thing it'll bring is the destruction of our world and our way of life. The railway company has used you men, it's as plain and simple as that.'

'I needed to earn money and quickly: I had no other way of surviving with the farm the way it was, and I still don't, Grace. It's not work that I enjoy, believe me. I'm a farmer down to my very boots and I miss it. The only good thing to come out of all of this for me is you.'

I pulled him close to me again then and kissed him long and hard. At that very moment, we heard men's voices and the sound of footsteps on the wooden stairs below. We could not stop ourselves from giggling and clamped our hands over our mouths so that whoever was down there would not hear us. The voices and the footsteps grew louder, but the men suddenly stopped climbing, and after a minute or so of silence, the church bells rang out right under our feet. The shock of that great pealing clamour of sound nearly sent us over the edge of the parapet, and the very roof below us shook with the reverberation. On and on it went, the bells going up and down the scales as the ringers practised.

I had heard St. Andrew's bells ringing out countless times, but never like that. Sean and I lay down on that hard roof, holding and kissing each other in the warmth of the light, mother's basket beside me, for more than three-quarters of an hour until the men had had enough, the bells stopped ringing, and the sound of footsteps came again and then faded away as the ringers climbed back down the stairs.

We waited a while longer until we were sure that the men had left, and then got up and made our own way down, as Sean's shift started at three o'clock that day. When we left the church, we were still giggling like schoolchildren caught out after a harmless prank on their schoolmistress and went arm-in-arm back to the marketplace where those stallholders who had already taken down their awnings in preparation for the end of the market were irradiated by the high sun.

Sean and I said goodbye to each other outside the Star Inn, with the promise of meeting there again at midday two Wednesdays from then, when his work shifts next allowed. I went back home to the empty house, glad to be on my own if I could not be with him, but already wishing that I was. I still had the taste of our kisses and the memory of our laughter on my lips.

Chapter Forty-Two

My father returned from Bath on a dogcart with uneven wheels ten days after he had left for that city. The driver, shrouded in a dark cape despite the sunshine, unloaded my father's trunk and deposited it outside the door to the lane before touching his cap and turning his sweating horse around towards Gloucester again.

'Grace, come and help me with this, will you?' my father said, swinging the door open wide and trying to push the trunk over the threshold. He seemed to be in an ebullient mood. I went to the door from the kitchen and pulled while he pushed the trunk and we got it into the hallway.

'What on earth have you got in here, Father?'

'Why, my medical books. My books and some clothes.'

'Perhaps you should have considered doing something other than reading and thinking while you were away, got out into the world more.'

'I did and I've had an epiphany!' he replied, his voice tremulous with excitement as he stood there in the hallway.

'Please do enlighten me, Father.'

'The delightful spa water in Bath and my taking of it gave me the answer. It's a daily swim that I need to restore my vitality and cast off those episodes.'

'Did you see any improvement in your condition while you were away, then?' I already knew the answer, as he had left his pep jar behind in his study.

'I didn't have a single moment of mental aberration all the while that I was away, not one,' he said. 'I've resolved to swim in the Wye each day from now on, come rain or shine, frost or freeze.'

'Well, just so long as you don't give yourself a chill in the winter river.'

'I used to swim there all year round before I went up to Cambridge,' he said. 'Even when there was thick snow on the ground.'

'I didn't know swimming was a cure for mental overstimulation or aberrations of the mind, but if you think it will help …'

'I know it will,' he said. 'It already has!'

For some days after his return, he looked full of the satisfaction of having discovered the cure for his condition, and he went round the house with a smile on his face. He saw to his patients when he had them with good humour and went off with his bathing costume and towel under his arm at noon each day. He ate a hearty luncheon when he came back from the Wye, his hair still damp, leaving his costume outside the back door for me to hang out to dry, and then devoured an even heartier supper. He barely went into his study, however, and he did not once touch his jar of pep. I resolved to make him richer, more sumptuous dishes for supper and to serve him the very best claret we had, in the hope that this stimulation of the palate would lead him to dip into his jar of powders. He was unaware that he was caught up in a game of cat and mouse, and that he was not the cat in this game.

It finally happened on the fifth evening after his return. I had laboured over his favourite dish of game pie, using a fine cut of venison and two pigeons from the market. I made the crust as short as possible without it becoming unstuck, so that he would need to drink more to quench his thirst. He sat down to supper at the kitchen table, humming quietly to himself and seemingly full of his newfound optimism. Although he had not spoken about her for some months, he had mentioned Mrs Samuels in passing once or twice since his return from Bath, and I worried that he might try to win her back, shuddering to think of her moonfaced girls and what any reattachment would mean.

He sipped from his glass of wine between mouthfuls of pie, then asked for a second one. I filled it up almost to the brim again but served myself only a small one. The claret was full-bodied and thick with the taste of blackberries, and I wanted more of it, but my wanting him to have it was stronger still than my liking for its taste and how it made me feel. The pastry had given him quite a thirst, and his second glass of wine was drained even before he had finished his first serving of pie and vegetables. He asked for his third glass with his second helping of the pie, and the colour rose in his cheeks.

'Grace, you make this pie even better than your dear mother made it,' he said, slurring slightly and dabbing at his mouth with his napkin. He had left a clot of piecrust and sauce on his moustache, but I did not say anything.

I had made a rhubarb fool for pudding and served it in our best bowls with thick cream on top. He looked fit to burst after finishing his two helpings of the fool, dabbed at his mouth again with his napkin, supressed a belch, and then pushed his chair back from the table. It seemed for a moment that he would simply go into the sitting room to sink into his armchair and read the newspaper, but to my quiet delight he walked down the hallway into his study and closed the door behind him. Everything was falling perfectly into place. I thought that I heard a sharp sniff or two behind the study door a few minutes later but could not be sure.

He came out a quarter of an hour later, clutching a red Moroccobound book whose title I could not see. I thought then that he had only been reading in there after all, looking perhaps for some reference to the benefits of fresh-water swimming, but as he plumped down into his armchair, I saw him wipe at his moustache with the back of his hand and I knew then that this cat had caught her mouse. He opened the book and stared as if hypnotised at the finely printed text, his spectacles gleaming in the candlelight, and then let the book rest on his lap and seemed to fall into a reverie. He stayed like that for perhaps half an hour, staring into the empty fireplace and then out of the window as the sun slowly sank behind the wood and the dark shapes of birds flitted across the window-space of the sky to roost in the trees.

'Aah!' he said suddenly. 'Aah!' It sounded almost as if he was trying to clear something from his throat.

'Sorry, Father. Is there anything wrong? Would you like a glass of water?'

He did not answer me and carried on staring very intently out of the window at something that seemed to be attracting his attention. I went and looked out, and as I did so he lifted himself up in his chair and craned his neck to try to look round me. All I could see was the sun's orange-pink light on the underside of a low bank of cloud, but it seemed to be this spectral play of the setting sun's rays that was mesmerising him so. There was nothing else there other than the trees and the lane and the coming dark.

'God is here, God is everywhere,' he said, his eyes as wide as saucers.

'Indeed, Father. But what exactly have you seen out there?'

'Immanence,' he said, but would say no more.

After that, he sank back into the armchair and closed his eyes for a while as the sun disappeared behind the hill. When he opened them again, they seemed to be all pupil, as black as the night, as if I could see into his very soul.

I left him sitting there, seemingly half asleep, and went up to bed. Sure enough, a loud snoring came up the stairwell when I was getting into my nightgown, and I shut my bedroom door on him and the night. Sean's carved wooden cross up on my windowsill in the moonlight made me miss him, made me want him beside me all the more as I lay there sleeplessly in that cold and lonely bed.

Chapter Forty-Three

My father retreated into his study and took his pep at least every other night over the second week after his return from Bath. All of his brimming optimism and confidence seemed to slip slowly away, and each morning after one of his episodes of mental aberration he walked around as if stupefied. I asked myself whether he would begin to see a pattern before too long between the nights that he took his pep and those when he did not, but there was no sign of him having noticed any connection yet. Of course, I had the advantage of knowing the cause of his malady; but for him there was still a whole universe of possibilities both inside and outside the corpulent contours of his body that he had to consider before discarding them or investigating them further. It must have been both a torture and a treat for him to think about the sheer myriad of possible causes as he sat dreaming in his armchair or staring out into space in his study.

By early June, he had begun to peer at me suspiciously almost every time I was in the room with him. Sometimes when he thought that I was not looking, he lifted his plate of food up to his nose and sniffed at it before eating and he did the same thing with his glasses of water and wine if I poured them for him. He even took to cooking meals for himself some days and left me a plate of food under a cloth if I was out doing errands for the mill or on a walk somewhere. The weather had become hotter, and it felt as if we were living each day on the brink of a crisis, with the oppressive heat and humidity threatening to break before too long into the fiercest of summer storms.

I missed Sean and wanted to see him but knew I had to be patient for another week before we could meet again in the marketplace, as his work on the line was at its busiest as it came towards its end. Every bolt and sleeper, every section of track and ballast that they had laid over the past fifteen months had to be checked and checked again down to the nearest tenth of an inch under the critical eyes of Mr Menzies before the navvies met the other team coming up their section of line from Gloucester and the railway could be opened. The first locomotive was due to arrive from Gloucester on the Much Purlock branch line on the second Monday in June.

On the first Friday of the month, my father came down red-eyed early in the morning, having told me the night before that all the stones in the walls were moving as if a current was running through them. I said that he had perhaps been swimming too much in the Wye. He was holding a cream-coloured envelope and he thrust it towards me as he drank his first cup of coffee.

'Grace, please take this letter to the Post Office for me this morning,' he said. 'Mr Longbotham's coming in to see me at ten o'clock. Tell him I'm indisposed when he knocks at the door. We'll have to arrange his consultation for another day. I'm going back to bed.'

'No swim for you today then, Father?'

He did not answer me but walked heavily back up the stairs and shut his bedroom door behind him. There was a creak as he sat down on his bed, and I did not hear anything further from him that morning, other than the faint sound of his snoring coming down the stairs from behind his door.

When I was sure that he was fast asleep, I boiled the kettle on the range and held the back of the envelope over the steam. Slowly it unglued itself, and I slid my fingernail under its edge and opened it. My father's letter made for very interesting reading, and I knew at once that I would not be sending it:

Richard Aronowitz

Mrs Josephine Samuels
3, Sydenham Hill
London SE

My dearest Josephine,

    I pray that this finds you well. I know how things looked when you last left here, but I cannot say that I am sorry, as whatever is wrong with me has nothing whatsoever to do with my consumption of alcohol, which is in no way exceptional and only ever moderate.

    I suspect, but have no proof at all at this stage, that Grace has been administering me noxious substances for some reason that I could never understand even if it were true. Perhaps she is mad: I have sometimes wondered about that. There has been something untrammelled, something let loose, about her for as long as I can remember. I write all this because I recently went away to the city of Bath for a week or so and was in rude good health while I was there, yet lo and behold not long after my return here my episodes started again: visions, disassociation, confusion, mild nausea, and never-ending lassitude. I do not know what I have been given or how I have been given it, but whatever it is it is here in this house and not within me nor out in the world.

    I need to get away and to be looked after for a while. Might I come and stay with you? I have no-one else to turn to and, if I was my own patient, I would not advise it prudent to be on my own at the moment. I will wait in devoted anticipation for your answer this week, dearest Josephine.

Yours in love and affection,

William

Having read the letter through twice, I crumpled it up, opened the heavy door of the range and fed my father's supple words and their stiff envelope into the flames. He would be waiting in vain for her reply. It did not surprise me at all that he had now realised that the cause of his malaise was beyond the bounds of his own flesh: he was, after all, a good doctor. What did surprise me, indeed offend me, was that he was pointing the finger of blame so quickly at me, his dutiful daughter, his only child. Well, I would not stop; I would dose him with the henbane again, and then go away with Sean and never come back.

* * *

Oh, the heat that summer: it was delicious, intoxicating. I wanted always to be out in the still air under that blue sky. I left my father snoring and went deep into the woods where the day was still cool. The sky shone down through the canopy where the trees were not growing so closely together, and I went through the denser stands from clearing to clearing looking up at that light from out of the dark. Two red kites were circling up high on the warm air, calling out so mournfully as they rode the currents that had already been heated by the sun at that early hour.

I had no destination in mind: I simply walked, wanting only to get out into the sunshine again somewhere on the far side of the wood, to feel its warmth on my skin and to breathe in the scent of the sunlit meadows. Almost without thinking, I walked over towards the navvies' camp and, when I was above it, I wanted to follow the steep path down the escarpment to see if Sean was around, but through the trees it looked deserted. I knew it was best to leave him to his work. The men were labouring double shifts over the long summer days, and Mr Menzies had banned them from drinking at the Star Inn or anywhere else until their railway was ready to open.

Instead, I took the right-hand path around the hill through a part of the wood that I had rarely visited. There were numerous dips in the ground in the clearings where the Romans had dug for stone, and it was more than I could do to resist running down into them and then up the other side like a small child, scuffing the dry beech leaves as I went. With no-one to see me I ran wild and free, swooping down and up again, arms outstretched, the sunlight catching me where the trees were at their thinnest. For a moment I really did feel like a child again, so full of joy and freedom.

I came out of the woods near Gulliford, my hair sticking to my forehead that was damp with sweat, and followed the chalky path down through an overgrown orchard towards the first of the houses. I had never been into the village before, and it seemed to be somewhere out of another time. The cottages were ancient and crooked, some half-timbered and thatched, and the whole place appeared to be about to topple in on itself. It was tucked behind the far side of the wood out on its own, miles from anywhere, and I imagined that few people who did not live there or have family there ever visited. It had one unmetalled lane winding through it, which led out into the fields one way and back towards Much Purlock the other, where it was more of a track than a lane, skirting around the side of the wood that was furthest from the railway line.

Walking through that age-old place and looking up at the small windows of the cottages, not one of their frames a perfect rectangle, I shuddered to think what changes the hordes of incomers arriving in our valleys on the new line from Gloucester and beyond would bring. Why did the mayor, my father, and now seemingly many of the townspeople see this change as a good thing, when I could only see it leading to disaster?

I wanted to carry on through the village and far out into the fields but went only a little way to where a mill stood on the banks of the Wye, which flowed around a great bend and through the water meadows there. The sun was shining down so strongly, even though it was not yet ten o'clock, that I lay down in its warm embrace in the shadow of an alder tree not far from the mill and dozed off to the rhythm of the waterwheel's ceaseless turning.

When I awoke, I did not know where I was at first, and the hot scent of cattle was all around me. There were perhaps eight of them peering down at me with their soft brown eyes as I lay there, and they licked their pink noses with rough tongues, breathing heavily as they took in my scent, in turn. 'Shoo,' I said. 'Let me up!' They lifted their heads and backed away a little, looking at me curiously with their gentle eyes.

I was still half in this world and half in the world of sleep and went over to the river to scoop up some water and splash it on my face. As I leaned over the bank, there was my reflection in the slow green river. The water had washed away my colour, and I looked like a pale ghost with my hair flowing down over my shoulders. I had left my hat under the alder and went back among the cows to fetch it.

When I got back to the house my father was up but still in his nightgown, yawning and drinking a cup of coffee in the kitchen despite the heat of the day outside.

'Did you tell Mr Longbotham that I was indisposed?' he asked when I came in.

'He must have knocked on the door when I was out at the Post Office, Father.'

'Damn it, he's a peevish man and will no doubt complain at me the next time that I see him.' He frowned and yawned again before adding, 'But thank you for sending the letter for me.'

'Are you hoping to rekindle things with Mrs Samuels then?' I asked innocently.

'Oh, I was just writing to her about one or two incidental matters,' he said, before retreating into his study and shutting the door.

Chapter Forty-Four

Hereford Insane Asylum and environs, 1850

At two o'clock sharp today, a horse and cart came to a stand outside the main doors of the asylum. I was waiting in the hallway staring at the one open oak door with a longing that I can barely describe. Mr Osney was on one side of me and a new orderly called Mr Merryman was on the other. They were not holding my arms but had threatened to do so if I so much as took even one step towards the door without being told to by one of them.

I clutched my canvas bag tightly to my chest as we started on the journey from one side of the city to the other. Mr Osney and Mr Merryman were sitting either side of me on the hard bench seat of the cart, looking about at the townsfolk and the passing streets. For my plan to work, their eyes needed to be kept as busy as dancing bees.

'Look at the light up on the cathedral tower. Isn't it just beautiful, God's own work?' I said.

'Ah, yes,' swarthy Mr Merryman replied. 'Fitting for such a building as that.'

'And look at that gay bunting strung up all along the road up ahead. I wonder what the festivities are for?'

Night Comes Down

On and on I went, and every time I pointed out some landmark or other or something that caught my eye, they both nodded and looked around them. It was like going on an outing with two overeager children. We went north of the cathedral into a part of the city that I had never been to before. The speckled grey pony plodded up in front of us, and the carter with his black-caped back to us said not a single word as we went. The streets became quieter and narrower, and I sensed that the workhouse could not be too far away. I had to make my move before it was too late to act.

A cobbled street that ran alongside a redbrick warehouse made the cart judder and jump and gave me the perfect opportunity: I dropped my hat as if by accident from the bumpiness of the road and bent forwards to pick it up, taking my time to fumble and not find it at first, for it had gone right under my long skirt. Messrs Osney and Merryman did not seem to notice what I was doing and carried on gawping at the passing sights. Quick as a flash, I pulled at their bootlaces and tied the long end of one of the laces on Mr Osney's right boot to the loose end of one of the laces on Mr Merryman's black patent-leather left boot. I put my hat on my head as I came back up and then reached into my bag, uncorking the flask that was nestling inside it. It was still slightly warm to the touch.

'Look over there!' I exclaimed, pointing to a cart that had spilled its load of apples. They both laughed, for the load was a large one and the carter who had been driving it was trying to clear the road while stopping his two horses from eating the fruit.

'He's got his hands full rather!' Mr Osney said and laughed again.

'Have an eyeful of this,' I said, splashing half of the flask of my piss into Mr Merryman's face, then turning to Mr Osney and splashing the rest into his eyes and down his chin. They both gasped when they smelled it and looked horror-struck. As they wiped at their faces with their coat sleeves, I vaulted over Mr Osney's lap and ran off down the street. Before turning the corner into an alleyway,

Richard Aronowitz

I looked back and saw them trying to get down from the cart in pursuit of me and tripping over each other's feet as they did.

Oh, the sweet taste of freedom! I ran like I had never run before, and I was out of the city into open country in less than half an hour. This old barn will give me some shelter until I can find somewhere else: it will certainly keep me dry and warm enough until the autumn turns to winter and the cold creeps back into the land. It does not appear to have been used for some years, although there is enough straw up in the loft for bedding. I will sleep up there so I can keep myself hidden away if the farmer calls by or a cow wanders in. There is a stream for water down in the valley bottom and I have some biscuits that I saved from yesterday's evening meal at the asylum. I will have to forage for food until I can find a way to get it from elsewhere: stealing eggs from coops like a fox in the middle of the night and vegetables from farmers' fields, that kind of thing. But this freedom! I will not give it up again without a fight.

Chapter Forty-Five

Purlock, 1842

The high summer sun shone down on the land and my father spent more and more time sleeping, like an aestivating animal. He came downstairs only to see his patients and for mealtimes and seldom left the house, even moving parts of his library up to his bedroom and reading through his medical books up there when he was not asleep. He no longer mentioned Mrs Samuels and seemed to have given up any hope of receiving a reply to his letter from her.

I ran errands for the mill almost every day during the first two weeks of June, going up and down Channers Lane and out to the inns and the public houses delivering flour, oats, and barley. The heat made pulling the cart laden with its sacks all the harder and the last thing I wanted to do when I got home was to make meals for my father. He barely acknowledged me and mostly ate in silence, chewing at his food and often yawning between mouthfuls. He was taking his pep almost every night (it seemed to be the only reason that he went into his study at all now, with most of his important books being upstairs), and I made sure to replace his pure snuff with my adulterated powders at least twice a week.

His aberrations had not lessened in their intensity when he snorted the dried mushrooms mixed with snuff, but the maelstrom of his emotions during and after an episode seemed to have quietened down; it was his tiredness that was the main consequence the next day, as though he had been wrung out by what he had seen and heard. Still, he did not seem to have made the connection between one thing and the other, and he was eager to get to his pep jar as soon as he ate the last mouthful of food and drank the last sip of wine. The suspicion that he exhibited after his return from Bath seemed to have subsided, although he was still wary of me like an animal that has not been fully tamed.

* * *

I met Sean in the marketplace on the first Wednesday of the month. He was pale with tiredness from the work and his left hand was bandaged where he had cut it tightening a bolt that had then sheared, digging deep into his palm. His smile was still the kindest smile, but he looked careworn and in need of looking after. I could not do that for him, not then, however much I wanted to.

'There are rumours going round that some of us will be moved to a line just north of Birmingham, but nothing's certain yet,' he said when we had walked out of the town and onto the field path. 'I don't know whether I'm going with that team or somewhere else.'

'How soon will they make you leave?' I asked, the sadness like hands around my throat that made it hard to get the words out.

'Days now, I think, but I can't be sure. Mr Jones is coming down on Friday, and we should know more then.'

'I-I can't stand it, Sean. I don't want you to go.' I could not help myself and wept right there in front of him.

'I know, I know,' he said, taking me in his arms and tenderly kissing away my tears. 'I don't want to leave you, but you'll follow as soon as I'm settled somewhere, won't you?'

'I can't wait to get away from here, Sean, however much I love this place.'

How could we be happy with his departure hanging over us like the Sword of Damocles? We walked out towards the Wye but had no real appetite for the river or the land and the sky that day. We held onto each other as if at any moment we would be ripped apart, never to be put back together again. Sean only had a couple of hours to spare before Mr Menzies expected him back on the line, and we knew that every step we took away from the town would, in the end, only take us closer to it and to our parting.

The Wye had the sky in it that day, shining blue and gold in the light. We followed it for a mile or so down the valley, listening to its eddying and gurgling against the high banks. The sound did not soothe me; it made me think only of life rushing endlessly onwards and the danger of being swept away in its current without the time to think or save yourself.

'How will I know when you've heard where you're going?' I asked as we walked back the way we had come along the path towards the town.

'Darling, meet me outside the inn this Sunday at noon,' he said. 'I'm sure to know by then once Mr Jones has visited.'

'If you leave next week or the week after and where you're going isn't too far away, perhaps I could use some of my savings from the mill to hire a carter to take me there.'

'You'll have to give me a little time to find somewhere for us to live first. Just a couple of weeks is all I'll need.'

'I know, I'll be patient,' I said, my throat feeling as if it was being squeezed again. 'On Sunday we can put everything in place.'

He kissed me on the lips and stroked my cheeks before he left me outside the town to take a shortcut up to the woods. I watched him go, striding against the slope of the hill, mopping his forehead with his cap, the back of his neck and hands tanned from working in the heat of the sun. When he had gone into the shadow of the first of the trees, I carried on along the path towards the houses, a tightness in my chest and a heaviness in my limbs for no good reason other than I was afraid that I would not see him again.

***

When I got back to the house my father was upstairs snoring away and I had the kitchen and the rest of the downstairs to myself. I took the bag of henbane down from behind the jars on the top shelf; it still gave off the plant's sickly-sweet scent when I opened it, but the bell-shaped yellow flowers and the long, veined leaves had dried out. I took out about a quarter of what was left and ground up the two or three flowers and leaves in the pestle and mortar, then added in some honey and water to make a paste. All my sadness and worry went into that work. I glazed one side of the gammon that I was roasting for our evening meal with the paste and left the other side untouched. Before I boiled the carrots and potatoes, I uncorked a good bottle of Bordeaux wine and left it to breathe beside my father's glass on the table.

He came down yawning at seven o'clock, the sky outside still a cerulean blue so clear that it felt as if you could see right into heaven when you craned your neck and looked up. The gammon was not yet quite roasted through, so I poured him a glass of the wine, and he took it into his study with a medical book that he had brought down from upstairs. Despite his months, years, of reading, it did not seem to me that he was getting any nearer to the truth of what was causing his aberrations.

'Father, supper is on the table,' I called out at half past seven. A few moments later he came out of his study without his book but holding his empty glass, which I filled again as soon as he had put it down.

'I'm ravenously hungry tonight,' he said. 'Perhaps it's all this fresh air you're letting into the house with the back door open and the kitchen window thrown wide.'

'We might as well enjoy this fine weather while we have it, Father.'

I carved the sizzling gammon on the top of the range with my back to him and put a generous serving of the glazed side of the meat on his plate, piling it high with the boiled vegetables, while I was careful to serve myself only the unglazed meat, giving myself a less generous helping of carrots and potatoes.

'Well, tuck in before it gets cold,' I said, although he needed little encouragement, as he had already picked up his knife and fork before the words had even left my lips.

'It's delicious,' he said. 'Perfectly cooked and flavoured. I like the honey glaze.'

'Why thank you, Father. That's rare praise coming from you.'

'Is there some herb in it?' he asked, looking down at the glazed crackling on his last forkful of meat.

'Oh, only some dried coriander from the garden,' I replied, my heart beating ever so slightly faster, not wanting him to sense even the briefest of hesitations caused by my inventing rather than knowing the answer. He put his fork down with the last piece of gammon still skewered on its tines and untucked his napkin from the collar of his shirt.

'Well, I'm full, stuffed to the gills,' he said. 'I'll finish this glass of wine in my study if I may.'

The adulterated powders were in my father's pep jar that night; I wanted to know whether the henbane would magnify the effects of the ground mushroom or whether there would be no noticeable difference in his aberrations. As I cleared away the dishes, I listened out for the familiar sound of my father snorting his snuff first through one nostril and then the other, but there was only silence punctuated by the sound of him clearing his throat and muttering to himself every few minutes.

He was in his study for almost an hour as I washed the pans, the crockery, and the cutlery and then went into the garden to enjoy the last of the light. The evening was so still, and the sun was beginning to set over the far side of the wood as the swifts darted over the garden and between the trees on either side. The town and the country around it felt under the spell of that golden light, caught in its web as it came slanting down through the trees.

When I went back into the kitchen, I could hardly comprehend what I was seeing at first. My father had stripped down to his cream-coloured drawers and he was dancing bare-chested like an

American Indian down the hallway and around the sitting room, ululating all the while.

'Father, what on earth are you doing? What if the neighbours see you!' I exclaimed, but he ignored me completely and carried on his mad dance, his ululating quieter now but his movements even more exaggerated.

There was no sign of the nausea that had plagued him the last time I had given him henbane, the night before Mrs Samuel's boots had got spoiled, and I could only imagine that he had taken his pep when I was out in the garden, because I had never seen an aberration quite like that one before. My father danced as though some unseen figure was drumming out a rhythm only he could hear, in thrall to something only he could see. Round and round he went with his Saint Vitus dance, like a marionette whose strings were being jerked this way and that, down the hallway and through the kitchen and sitting room, until his head and body were dripping with sweat.

The mania seemed to pass at last and he collapsed, pallid and exhausted, into his armchair. He had his eyes closed and he was breathing hard. He stayed slumped there like that, his breathing gradually becoming slower and more peaceful, for an hour or so, until I had lit the lantern and was getting ready to go up early to bed, as it had been a long day of errands for the mill and chores at home.

'Where am I?' he said suddenly, opening his eyes wide. They were still glazed-looking; he was staring right through me.

'Why, you're sitting in your favourite armchair at home, Father. Where d'you think you've been?'

'I-I don't know,' he said, still looking very disturbed. 'Heaven or hell or somewhere in between.'

'No, only here, Father. You've been having one of your episodes again. I'm going up. You should get some sleep.'

'I'm going to stay sitting here for a while,' he said sighing. 'I hardly have the energy to move.'

Night Comes Down

I gave him a blanket to cover his chest; it was still bare and the night was cooling. Long after I had gone up to bed and was reading by the light of the lantern, I heard the sound of him rummaging around in the kitchen and in the larder, but I thought no more of it and went soundly to sleep.

Chapter Forty-Six

Herefordshire, 1842

We have finished the branch line, but we will not see the first locomotive to run on it. Mr Menzies told us this morning that we are leaving Much Purlock for Bristol later today. Half of the navvies are being moved north-east to Birmingham, but my group of fifteen, Joe and Adam included, will be joining another gang to work on a new line for the Bristol and Gloucester Railway company.

Mr Jones is down from Birmingham again. 'Get these huts cleared out and closed up by one o'clock,' he said to us as we were standing around the embers of the fire. 'Have your belongings packed and ready to go by then. The coaches will be coming to the lane at the bottom of the wood at two o'clock sharp.'

My heart is in my boots: just one more day and I would have seen Grace again. It is my cursed luck to be packing up camp this morning rather than being able to spend an hour or two with her. I cannot let her stand there all alone in the marketplace waiting for me to come tomorrow. Before we go, I must get away from here and walk over to the town to look for her, to tell her that I am leaving.

All this mess that we are leaving behind us here: burnt pots and pans, rotting sacks, piles of bedding and spoiled food. The sun should not be shining down so brightly today. It seems entirely unfitting.

Night Comes Down

It is already a quarter past twelve and I do not have much time. When I have swept around the fireplace and stacked the remaining wood neatly, O'Donnell having done only half a job on both tasks before going off somewhere, I search among the piles of ownerless possessions for an unspoiled piece of paper and find the stub of a pencil in my canvas bag. I do not know what to write in case I cannot find Grace; no words can say what I want, what I *need* to say. Because my hand is so clumsy, I keep my note short and hope she will understand.

Mr Menzies and Mr Jones have gone down to the line with some men from the railway company board, and I can get away for an hour or so without them noticing. I climb up the escarpment into the wood and run along the path over the top of the ridge and straight down towards Much Purlock. The birds are in full song this morning, and the sun coming down through the trees makes the wood alive with light, but I cannot shake this feeling that something is weighing down on my shoulders and pressing in at my temples. It is all I can do to force myself to keep on running, towards Grace and away from her at the same time.

My shirt is wet through when I get to the marketplace, and I use the back of my sleeve to wipe away the sweat from my face. There is no market here on Saturdays, and the town is quiet. It seems mere foolishness of me now to think I would find Grace just like that. I could kick myself for never having asked her exactly where she lives. It is almost one o'clock and I cannot stay standing here for long.

I leave the marketplace and walk up and down the streets and lanes surrounding it, but there is no sign of her. People will begin to wonder what I am doing going round and round this part of the town, apparently aimlessly. I go back to where I was standing outside the Star Inn and wait for another five minutes, but all hope that she will suddenly appear has gone.

John the barman will be my only way of getting my letter to her. I go into the inn and there are only two of the regulars drinking in the saloon bar. He is not behind the bar, but I can hear the rumble of a beer barrel being rolled over the flagstone floor down in the cellar, and he comes up wiping his hands on a cloth a few minutes later. 'The Leominster bitter ran out mid-pull,' he says. 'What'll it be?'

'I can't stay, John. We're moving on to Bristol in under an hour.'

'I'll be sorry to see you and the boys go, Sean.' He sounds sincere.

'I wish I didn't have to leave. I have no choice in the matter, none at all.'

'Well, the best of luck to you for all that lies ahead. Can't I tempt you with just a half pint on the house at least?'

'Go on, then. Thank you, John. I think I need it after running all the way over here.'

'Here you go.' He hands me the glass of bitter, and I drink it down in one go.

'I need to get this note to Grace Matthews.' I take the folded piece of paper out of my pocket and pass it to him across the bar. 'Could you give it to her for me please? She will be waiting for me outside here at midday tomorrow.'

'Of course. Anything to help keep the flame of young love alive.' He smiles kindly at me.

'You promise you'll give it to her tomorrow?'

'You have my absolute word,' he says.

With that, I am off running back across the marketplace and up the lane that leads to the path through the wood. I know that I will not see Much Purlock again, not in this lifetime. The coaches will be coming in three-quarters of an hour, we will be taken across country on rutted roads to begin again.

What am I leaving here with? A purse full of coins of the realm in my sack and all that I have lived through these past fifteen months. And, oh dear God, Grace, Grace! Am I leaving love behind or taking it with me?

Chapter Forty-Seven

Much Purlock, 1842

My father was still upstairs in bed when I left the house soon after dawn. The birds in the wood were all atwitter and a rust-red fox slinked off into the undergrowth when I came near. Nature was wide awake even if most of mankind seemed to be still asleep.

We were going to be seeing each other at midday, but knowing that Sunday was his day of rest I wanted to go over to the camp and surprise Sean, to take him by the hand and lead him off deeper into the woods or out into the fields to who knows where and who knows what. We would not have many more days together in Much Purlock and I wanted to make the most of the sunshine while it lasted.

I was already above the camp at half past six, and I settled myself under a beech tree to watch for the first signs of life below. I had an apple and a piece of bread with me, and I enjoyed just sitting there, listening to the sounds of the wood and watching the morning light slowly brightening. I watched and waited until my legs became stiff from sitting on the hard ground and I had eaten the apple and the last of the bread, but there was still no movement in the camp.

I scrambled down the loose earth and stones of the escarpment, starting carefully but quickly gaining speed and slowing my descent only by grasping at the passing branches and trunks of trees on my way down. Once I reached the camp, there was still no sign of anyone around and the fire had long since gone out. I tried the door of the hut nearest to me but saw it was padlocked shut. The doors to the other huts were also locked. The place seemed utterly abandoned, like no-one had ever lived there, apart from the cold ash in the firepit.

A panic rose in me that I had not felt before: what if Sean had gone away and I would never see him again? The thought of that was so abhorrent that I could not think straight, everything became muddled and confused. I went to the far end of the camp and down towards the railway line in case the men were still working somewhere out that way; but there was only the silence of the morning in that remote place, and the banked rails gleaming in the sunlight as they went round the great curve towards the far end of the valley. All the while it felt as if the very living breath was being squeezed out of me.

I realised soon enough that there was no point at all in my waiting in the camp for the men to return: it was clear they were not coming back there again. My only hope was that they had simply been moved to temporary lodgings somewhere in the town before being sent off to their new place of work the next week. I went back through the woods with a growing sense of foreboding bearing down on me despite the loveliness of the morning. What would I do if Sean did not come? What could I do?

When I got back to the house, I went upstairs to change into my Sunday best, as though that extra effort would somehow summon him. My father was reading aloud to himself in his room, a habit that he had developed during that spring and early summer as he became more and more bound to the house. I put on my white cotton blouse and long black skirt, wrapped my dark-blue shawl around my shoulders and put on my matching satin bonnet, tying its ribbons carefully under my chin. I had not worn those clothes for some years, not since I had last gone to church with my father, but they still fitted me perfectly.

In the hallway mirror downstairs, I saw a beautiful girl done up in her finest, but I did not see a happy one. My brow was creased with worry lines and my eyes had a sadness in them behind the mottled blues of their irises. If only midday had already come and gone, and everything had turned out fine.

I was at the marketplace by a quarter to twelve, and I listened to the stallholders calling out their wares and chatting to one another gaily in the sunshine while I waited for Sean. I felt uncomfortable just standing there, as if all eyes were on me dressed up like that, but I did not want to look around the market, to be certain that he would see me when he came. The clock on the tower of St. Andrew's church struck twelve; my heartbeat quickened with the excitement and anticipation of seeing him, and with the guttural fear of him not coming. At ten past twelve, I moved a few yards from the edge of the market to our usual meeting place right outside the door of the inn. Still there was no sign of him. By twenty past twelve, I had not seen his familiar shape walking towards me across the square between the stalls and the townsfolk and I knew then that he was not coming. My heart ached and I felt like crying.

'Excuse me, Miss Matthews,' a man's voice right behind me said suddenly. I turned round and did not recognise the innkeeper at first.

'Yes?'

'Sean, er Mr McClennan, left this letter for you with me yesterday. He was one of our regulars while he was working here. I promised to give it to you.' He thrust the folded sheet of paper towards me.

'Thank you, thank you,' I said, the ache in my heart receding slightly. 'Didn't you think to tell him where I live?'

'He seemed to be in a great hurry, as if he had no time to get back to the camp. They were about to leave, as far as I understood.' He wiped his hands on his apron.

'He went only yesterday—I missed him by just one day?'

'Yes, yesterday around lunchtime,' he said. 'I'm sorry.'

My tears flowed freely then as I walked away from the marketplace back towards home. Not knowing when I would see him again, not having been able to say goodbye, was the hardest thing. Without him, I only had nature to give me solace, only the woods and the fields to bring me some peace.

I opened the letter when I reached the lane. It was not much of one, only four lines, but it brought some joy and hope to my heart:

My dearest Grace,

    We were told only this morning that we are leaving today. I have no time to find you. As soon as we have reached Bristol and I have had the chance to find some lodging for us, I will write again care of John, the innkeeper at the Star Inn, who I asked to give you this letter. I will write to you again as soon as I can, I promise you that.

I love you—

Sean.

Chapter Forty-Eight

I went to bed that night still dressed in my Sunday best, and by first light on Monday morning I had not taken off my clothes. I had thought and thought about it all night long, tossing and turning there in my bed, unable to sleep: I could not wait for Sean to write to me, I had to follow him to Bristol. I would ask there where the new railway line was being built and find his camp.

I could hear my father walking around downstairs, but I could not tell whether he was in the sitting-room, the dining-room, the kitchen, or the hallway. He seemed to be moving things around again, like his agitated mind would not let things be just the way they were. I was exhausted from the lack of sleep, but I got myself out of bed, pissed in the chamber pot, straightened my clothes, brushed my hair, and went downstairs. I heard the kitchen door being closed as I got to the bottom of the stairs and thought it strange that my father was going out, and at so early an hour.

The mayor's grand opening of Much Purlock Halt and the branch line was taking place at eleven o'clock, and I was going to go along and join the crowd of onlookers. Despite being desperate to get away from my father and to follow Sean, I could not resist seeing for myself just once what all the fuss was about. But much more than that, the railway itself might give me a means of escape, of getting away from Much Purlock as quickly as possible. A year before, I would have made some clamouring protest about the coming of the railway to the town; I would have pointed to the dead birds, the blasted tree trunks and the shattered rock and blamed them, but now all I wanted was Sean.

I made myself some porridge with a spoonful of cream and sugar on top and sat at the kitchen table looking out at the rising of the morning. There was still some time before the opening of the line; it was not quite half past seven. Given my father's newfound mania for moving things around, I thought that, while he was out, I would take the bags of powdered mushroom and dried leaves, flowers, and stems of henbane from behind the jars up on the shelf in the kitchen and hide them under my mattress. I stood up on the stool and reached behind the jars and felt around, but the bags were not there. My heart leaped and lurched, and I tried to suppress the panic that was flowing like a current through my fingers and toes into my limbs and body.

I felt all along the shelf again and then took down every single one of the jars and pots, but the bags were simply not there. My father must have found them since I had last looked at them a day or two before and put them somewhere. My only hope was that he had not looked at them closely, that he had assumed they contained only herbs for cooking, but I feared he had finally made the connection between the effect and its cause.

I searched in all the cupboards and drawers, but there was no sign of the bags, and my fear I had been found out grew. If my father had thought them to be bags of herbs, why had he not left them in the kitchen where the cooking took place? And where had he gone at so early an hour when he rarely left the house?

The only thing I could do was to carry on with my plan. Why change course in any case? If I had been uncovered, it was far better that I got away from Much Purlock as soon as possible. However difficult the journey, I would find a way to get to Bristol and I would not go home again. I had some savings from my errands for the mill and Sean had his work: we would survive even if it was difficult at first. We would have to get married, of course, which would not be easy, given that he was an Irish Catholic and I had been christened into the protestant Church of England.

At half past ten, still in my Sunday best, I left the house and walked to the marketplace and then on towards the new railway halt. Even though I was a daughter of the town, I felt more than ever like an outsider looking in. The good people of Much Purlock were all going about done up in their finest hats and clothes. It was how they usually dressed at Easter or for the Midsummer Fair, but they were heading towards something now the like of which they had never seen before in their lives. A plume of smoke and steam was rising into the clear blue sky about a mile from the town, and it was getting nearer. With it came a rhythmic whooshing sound that echoed off the sides of the valley.

I could not see my father anywhere, but as I got nearer to the halt the stream of townsfolk grew denser and more animated. A hubbub of anticipation was building, and people did not seem to know quite what to do with themselves on so momentous a day. They went around all giddy and laughing, some of the men even throwing their hats up into the air and catching them again with hands outstretched towards the brilliant blue sky. All the while, the sound of the engine was getting louder, and the clouds of steam and smoke were billowing into the air just beyond the town.

There was the mayor in his ridiculous tricorn hat and gold chain of office, parading about with a large pair of scissors in his hand. A solitary bugler stood just outside the stone-arched entrance to the halt. His glinting silver bugle dangling unused by his side gave him a lonely, dejected look quite at odds with the gaiety and celebration that the mayor was obviously hoping to conjure for the occasion.

The crowd were agog as they gathered in front of the red ribbon stretched across the stone facade of the building; roaring and hissing filled that part of the town as the engine crept into the platform from the valley beyond. I could not see the locomotive itself nor the train behind it; the crowd was forty deep, and I could not get anywhere near the front. All those men and women who had protested at the coming of the railway only a year and a half earlier were certainly among that throng of gawpers and gossipers. How easy it is for people to abandon their principles when there is some excitement or entertainment to be had.

As the clock on St. Andrew's church struck eleven, the mayor pushed through to the front of the crowd of three or four hundred people and gave a signal to the bugler, who took up his instrument and put it to his lips. Out came the purest, most beautiful notes that I had ever heard, which were soon drowned out by the clamour of the crowd as the mayor held up his scissors, their steel blades catching the summer sun, and with a flourish cut the ribbon, which fell limply to either side of him.

The crowd surged forward as soon as the mayor had announced that they would be allowed onto the platform without a ticket to look at the locomotive. I stayed back, but when many of them had streamed in and out again—beatific smiles on their faces as if they had just glimpsed the Messiah—I went to the front and made it through the archway onto the platform.

A throng of people still stood there looking at the black engine, which was almost silent now and slumbering. Its funnel was as tall as a chimney, and its huge boiler made a ticking sound as the water heated. Every now and then, great clouds of steam rose out of the funnel and the pistons strained at the wheels, seeming eager to unleash their power again. The driver and his soot-faced fireman were standing by the engine as the boys and girls of the town, alone or with their mothers and fathers, crowded around these heroes of progress. Everyone kept asking questions and touching the engine: I noticed that the driver had a white cloth in his trouser pocket for wiping away their handprints from the gleaming paintwork. Mrs Jenks and her children were there, and I saw Mrs Part the butcher's wife and many of the stallholders, who must have come in from the villages just to be part of the spectacle.

'She's a Firefly class locomotive,' the white-whiskered driver said to someone, smiling proudly and patting her boiler for the umpteenth time. 'And she's a beauty to drive.'

Her nameplate said *Venus* on it, and I had to laugh quietly to myself. Would this goddess of love and desire take me towards Sean, or would I be going nowhere? The mayor was standing beside the train's last carriage at the far end of the platform, surrounded by a group of councillors and aldermen and men from the railway company board. It was doubtless those old men who would be taking the train to Gloucester and back, and I could see no way of slipping into one of the open carriages, the only woman, the only girl, among those bearded, wing-collared bigwigs. My plan would be far from easy if I could not get on the train. I could not go home again, that was for certain. I thought about pleading with the driver and the fireman to allow me to stow away somewhere, but they were still surrounded by children with ribbons pinned to their hats, chaperoned by their longsuffering parents, and time was against me. It was already five to twelve, and the train was leaving at midday.

The mayor laughed loudly, his double chin wobbling and his gold chain flashing in the light as his chest went up and down, and he clapped one of the aldermen on the back. One by one the dozen or so men stepped up onto the last carriage and the one next to it. There were only two carriages that were empty now, but I saw that the mayoress was walking down the platform towards them from the front of the halt with a gaggle of women, matronly types who were no doubt the wives of those men. I would try to attach myself to the group, one woman thinking that I was another's daughter, and so on, and no-one questioning who I was and why I was with them. If they were getting on the train, I would join them. This was my best, my only chance, and I walked back down the platform past the engine and its tender to join the tail of this group. Just then a shout roused the remaining crowd and made the women turn around as one to see where the noise was coming from.

'Grace! Stop!' my father's voice echoed down the platform. 'Stop! Come back here!'

I ducked my head and tried to mingle with the crowd, but he had seen me and I knew that he would not give up. Beyond the platform, the bottom half of the end wall of the building was cut away to allow for the running of the rails and the engine out of the halt into the open air. I could see the bright sunlight out on the valley beyond and I thought of escaping down the rails before the train left the platform.

I turned back towards the front of the halt and saw my father no more than forty feet away, advancing through the crowd with his eyes fixed on me. He was followed by a brutish-looking man in a tall top hat, dressed all in black with a row of brass buttons shining down the front of his tunic. I took him to be a parish constable, although I had never seen one before. I began to panic then and did not know which way to turn, whether to follow the mayoress and the other women onto one of their carriages before the train departed, which would take me back towards my father and the black-clad man, or to run for the opening.

Before I knew it, a whistle sounded announcing the departure of the train, and I had no time to run over to one of the carriages. I ran instead as fast as I could to the back of the building, away from my father and towards the freedom of the sunlight and the valley. As I leaped down onto the rails ahead of the train, whose carriages were now being pushed slowly out of the platform in front of the engine and its tender, there were horrified cries of 'A suicide!' and 'Help us here! Come quick! The girl's gone mad!' Rough hands and arms grabbed at me and pulled me back up onto the platform quite against my will. My satin bonnet was still lying down there on the rails, and I saw it being ground into the dirt by the wheels as the train passed.

'Are you hurt, Miss?' a stranger asked. 'Call a doctor!' another man shouted as the locomotive and its carriages slowly gathered speed and huffed and puffed out of the halt into the sunshine of the valley beyond, the clouds of steam and smoke floating up to the ceiling of the halt all that was left of the train's immense presence there only a moment before.

'I am a doctor: let me through,' my father's voice said, suddenly almost at my shoulder. I knew then that I was quite undone. A local woman who recognised my father said 'Ah, Doctor Matthews, come quickly, this girl has just fallen, jumped, onto the line.'

'She's my daughter,' he replied. 'I'm quite sure it was just an accident. I'll take care of her now.'

'Oh, she's the doctor's daughter!' some of the onlookers exclaimed. Then the penny dropped for those who knew me and my father. 'It's Grace! Grace Matthews!' someone said. 'Poor, poor girl," added another. 'What on earth's come over her?'

My father took me by the hand with a vice-like grip and led me to where the constable was waiting. While we were still in the halt with the people all around us, they walked either side of me with my father gripping my hand, but as soon as we were outside on the road, they seized my elbows and walked me away from there, my feet barely touching the ground. All thoughts of getting to Sean had gone; now I could think only of my own survival.

They dragged me in the brilliant light of that morning to a part of the town I had never been to before. All the way I tried to wrestle free, but they held me so tightly I could not get away. There was no-one out on the streets that far from the halt and the marketplace; there was no point in crying out for help. Who would confront a uniformed constable and a learned doctor with accusations of wrongdoing, of rough treatment, against me, in any case? Once we had reached a weather-beaten building with five stone steps leading up to its front door, my father finally broke his silence.

'It's you who's been doing this to me,' he whispered, his face white with anger. 'It's been you all along hasn't it, you wicked child? You've been putting poison in my food.'

'That's not true! That's a lie, Father!' I cried, my heart pounding. 'It's nothing like that.'

'What are these, then?' he demanded, pulling the three cloth bags out of his coat pocket. He still looked ashen-faced, but he was triumphant now. The constable peered at the bags curiously but said nothing.

'T-they're only herbs, father, nothing more than that.' I was shaking so much that I found it hard to get my words out.

'She's lying, Constable Peters. This brown powder smells like ground-up fungus of some kind and this other plant looks noxious to me. These are certainly not herbs fit for putting in your food.'

The constable took the bags out of my father's hands and looked at them suspiciously, then held them under his long nose to sniff at them one by one. Whatever he saw and smelled, it seemed to leave him none the wiser.

'I swear that I wasn't trying to poison you,' I blurted out, on the verge of tears again.

'So, then you *are* admitting that you gave these substances to your father?' the constable asked, speaking to me for the first time. He had a curiously nasal voice, and it sounded like he had a summer cold.

'I'm admitting nothing,' I proclaimed, still shaking violently and hardly able to see the constable's face, the sunlight to his back. 'They're just remedies, medicines that I use sometimes.'

'Miss Matthews, you can explain all of this to the magistrate in the morning,' he said, making careful notes in his black pocketbook with a propelling pencil.

'Constable Peters, my daughter talks about remedies and medicines, but she's no apothecary and certainly no doctor. She's suffering from some kind of hysteria of the mind, some madness. I have long wondered whether that might be the case. She's a danger to others as well as to herself in this maniacal state.'

'We're going to keep her in here until tomorrow at the very least. She won't be a danger to anyone else down in the cells, let me tell you,' the constable said, putting a reassuring hand on my father's arm.

I can hardly describe the loneliness and despair of that sleepless night down in the cell, although of course much worse was to come. There seemed to be only one cell in the whole building, and I was the only prisoner. At least I was given a hard mattress, some bread and cheese, a jug of water, and a pot to piss in. Even then I set myself to thinking of ways to escape. Given the quietness of the place at night, the warder must have locked the front door and gone home.

The next morning at nine o'clock Constable Peters came to unlock my cell and take me across the road to the magistrates' court.

Night Comes Down

My Sunday best was now crumpled from the two nights that I had slept in it and my hair was unbrushed. When I appeared before the ancient magistrate, I was still shaking and trembling almost uncontrollably. The only other people in the room were my father, the constable, and a clerk wearing halfmoon spectacles.

The magistrate asked my father to give him an account of my alleged crimes, and his face became redder and redder and more and more serious as my father recounted the many months of his terrors of the mind, his attempts at self-diagnosis, his loss of life, love, and livelihood, and his eventual discovery of my secret. I was allowed to speak in my own defence, but I found that I had nothing at all to say.

What else could the magistrate do but find me guilty of the charge of administering noxious substances to a person? My father repeated that I was insane, that I was a hysteric, and he suggested that I be sent to the asylum in Hereford rather than to the prison there. That very afternoon, I found myself being driven in a closed carriage beside the constable and his colleague all the way to Hereford along the most uneven roads that I had ever known. I could have had no idea then just how long it would be before I would find a way to reclaim my freedom again.

Chapter Forty-Nine

County Sligo, 1844

I have walked all the way inland from Sligo with the sun at my back. The scarred face of Binn Ghulbain is shining green and gold up ahead, almost filling the horizon. After the crossing from Liverpool to Belfast and the boat from Belfast skirting round the north coast of Ireland down to Sligo, I still feel like I am onboard ship when I walk, with the rolling rhythm of the sea still in my legs.

These familiar lanes and paths between Sligo and Rose Farm know their twists and turns a little better than I do now after three years away in England, but I have not forgotten them. The April sun is high above me as I follow the last bend in the lane, coming out through the trees into our valley. And then there it is, my beloved Rose Farm Cottage nestled at the top of the valley less than a mile away! The spring wheat looks healthy this year, and the fruit trees are already beginning to come into flower. Oh God, how I have missed this place. I need to get back to ploughing the soil and to the cattle on the pasture fields. Are these fields even still ours?

Ma and Niall are not expecting me home, and it has been months since I last heard from them. What will they say when they see me? What life will I make for myself back here now that I am twenty-two? Niall will always run the farm, but will I always be happy to work for him, to play second fiddle, or will I want a farm of my own around here one day?

Night Comes Down

I will not miss the men or the work in England, that is for sure, but I will miss Grace, always. I could not understand why she had not written back to me, until I had sent her my third letter and John wrote to tell me Grace had left Much Purlock but he did not know where she had gone. He promised me he had given her my first letter, and for a long time afterwards I prayed, really prayed down on my knees, that she would follow me to Bristol and find me, but she never came. She would have made my last year and a half in England a joyously happy time, rather than the lonely labour it was.

We would have made a happy life together, me and Grace. There was so much about her that I never got to know.

Chapter Fifty

Open country, 1850

This evening I left the barn that was my home for three days and nights and followed the setting sun west. On a mild autumn night such as this I can still sleep out under the stars, and I should keep moving in case they decide to come looking for me. I will not be taken somewhere against my will or locked up again. I would rather die than suffer that fate a second time. If I keep walking westwards into Wales, I will reach the Irish Sea one day.

This is empty country with no villages or towns for miles around, only a farmhouse and its barns and outhouses every ten fields or so. The lights in the windows of the farmhouses bewitch me when I pass them, but they are traps. I must carry on walking, keep to myself, and find food where I can. Yesterday I stole two hens' eggs from a coop and ate them raw. Blackberries are everywhere here now, and the crab apples are ripening day by day.

Winter will be much harder out here. Before the weather turns cold, I will have to find myself some shelter again and a way to get food when there is little to forage. If I keep walking westwards into Wales, I will reach the Irish Sea. When I reach the sea, I will find a way to get across to Ireland and look for Sean. The names Sligo and Rose Farm keep going around and around in my head …

Acknowledgements

Writing is mostly a solitary thing, but life usually, and mercifully, is not. I would like to thank all the people who have encouraged me along the way with this book, especially Charlotte Arnold, Mark Fishman, Sharon Galant, Dickon Hall, and Rebecca Lloyd. Writing is also a lesson in persistence and perseverance, things that I want to teach my son, Henry, so that he grows up knowing what can be done if you only try. This book, then, is a gift to him, as well as being my love letter to the English countryside.

Perhaps nowhere was the confrontation between 'modern life' and the 'old ways' more powerfully expressed than in the early Victorian era, when immense changes—technological, socio-political, cultural, colonial, and environmental—saw the world shift on its axis. But even before that, in the mid-eighteenth century, almost three hundred years ago now, the harnessing of the power of steam to the strength of iron and steel had brought with it irreversible change.

I only hope that nature will find a way to survive, indeed outlive, all that we have thrown at her.

About The Author

Richard Aronowitz was born in 1970 and grew up in rural Gloucestershire. He studied at the universities of Durham, Heidelberg, London and Oxford and works in the London art world. He has one son and lives in Oxford. Richard's debut novel, *Five Amber Beads*, was published in 2006 and was followed by two further novels, *It's Just the Beating of my Heart* (2010) and *An American Decade* (2017), and by a book of poetry, *Life Lessons* (2019).

Printed by Imprimerie Gauvin
Gatineau, Québec